The stuff of dreams . . .

If you were a high school quarterback, a *Texas* high school quarterback, this was the moment you imagined for yourself from the first time somebody said you had some arm on you.

This was football now, pure football, the way you drew it up, but not in some playbook.

In your dreams.

And in Texas, usually your dad had dreamt all the best ones first.

Two minutes left, ball in your hands, game in your hands, *season* in your hands. State championship on the line, the new 1AA championship for small schools like yours. One of those small-town, big-dream schools. Like you were the one in the book or the TV show and you were playing for Friday Night Lights High.

Only this was *your* school, the Granger High Cowboys, against Fort Carson, in Boone Stadium, the fancy new stadium at Texas State University.

Fort Carson ahead, 20–16. Cowboys' ball at their own twenty-yard line.

One time-out left.

Even if you were a high school senior, already had a college scholarship in your pocket to the University of Texas, even if you could see yourself in the pros someday, there was no way to know if it would be exactly like this for you ever again—one shot like this with it all on the line.

BOOKS BY MIKE LUPICA

Travel Team

Heat

Miracle on 49th Street

Summer Ball

The Big Field

Million-Dollar Throw

The Batboy

Hero

The Underdogs

QB 1

Fantasy League

THE COMEBACK KIDS SERIES:

Hot Hand

Two-Minute Drill

Long Shot

Safe at Home

Shoot-Out

MIKE LUPICA

QB 1

PUFFIN BOOKS
An Imprint of Penguin Group (USA)

PUFFIN BOOKS
Published by the Penguin Group
Penguin Group (USA) LLC
375 Hudson Street
New York, New York 10014

USA * Canada * UK * Ireland * Australia
New Zealand * India * South Africa * China

penguin.com
A Penguin Random House Company

First published in the United States of America by Philomel Books,
an imprint of Penguin Young Readers Group, 2013
Published by Puffin Books, an imprint of Penguin Young Readers Group, 2014

THE LIBRARY OF CONGRESS HAS CATALOGED THE PHILOMEL BOOKS EDITION AS FOLLOWS:
Lupica, Mike. QB 1 / Mike Lupica. pages cm
Summary: Jake Cullen, fourteen, lives in the shadows of his father and older brother until he becomes the starting quarterback for the high school football team and finally has his chance to shine.
ISBN (hardcover) 978-0-399-25228-0
[1. Football—Fiction. 2. Self-confidence—Fiction. 3. Fathers and sons—Fiction. 4. High schools—Fiction. 5. Schools—Fiction. 6. Family life—Texas—Fiction. 7. Texas—Fiction.]
I. Title. II. Title: QB one.
PZ7.L97914Qb 2013 [Fic]—dc23 2012049557

Puffin Books ISBN 978-0-14-751152-2

Printed in the United States of America

5 7 9 10 8 6

For my wife, Taylor, and our four children,
youngest to oldest this time,
Hannah and Zach and Alex and Christopher:

Sometimes you're asked where you are happiest.
I am happiest with them.

01

IF YOU WERE A HIGH SCHOOL QUARTERBACK, A *TEXAS* HIGH school quarterback, this was the moment you imagined for yourself from the first time somebody said you had some arm on you.

This was football now, pure football, the way you drew it up, but not in some playbook.

In your dreams.

And in Texas, usually your dad had dreamt all the best ones first.

Two minutes left, ball in your hands, game in your hands, *season* in your hands. State championship on the line, the new 1AA championship for small schools like yours. One of those small-town, big-dream schools. Like you were the one in the book or the TV show and you were playing for Friday Night Lights High.

Only this was *your* school, the Granger High Cowboys, against Fort Carson, in Boone Stadium, the fancy new stadium at Texas State University.

Fort Carson ahead, 20–16. Cowboys' ball at their own twenty-yard line.

One time-out left.

Even if you were a high school senior, already had a college scholarship in your pocket to the University of Texas, even if you could see yourself in the pros someday, there was no way to know if it would be exactly like this for you ever again—one shot like this with it all on the line.

Unless you were somebody like Eli Manning, and you got to do it twice, in the Super Bowl, the way Eli had done it twice to the Patriots. Eli: bringing his team from behind in the biggest football game there was, winning both of those Super Bowls in the last minute, something no one—not even Eli's big brother Peyton—had done in the history of the National Football League.

But the quarterback in Boone Stadium now wasn't a Manning. It was Wyatt Cullen. Son of Troy Cullen, who'd been the greatest quarterback to come out of this part of Texas—at least until his son Wyatt came along.

Around here, people lived out *their* dreams through their high school football stars. All the ones who'd grown up in Granger and knew they'd probably die there wanted to know why you'd ever want to be one of those Manning brothers when you could be a Cullen in Granger, Texas.

Now Wyatt: in his senior year, in the last high school game he was ever going to play, his last chance to be a total high school hero and win the state title in the last minute the way his dad had once.

Like Wyatt was born to do it, born for this kind of moment, with what felt like the whole town of Granger in the stands on their side of the field.

Some sportswriter would quote Wyatt later as saying he imagined every pickup in their town was parked outside Boone Stadium, like there had been some kind of caravan of pickups all the way from Granger to here, to the kind of big game that made a small town like Granger feel like the capital of the whole world.

First down pass for him, left side, the kind of deep-out-pattern throw you needed a big arm to make, the throw all the scouts wanted to see and had been seeing from Wyatt since he became Granger's starter as a freshman. This one was to Wyatt's favorite receiver, Calvin Morton, a sophomore with big speed and big hands, tall as a tight end at six five, but skinny as a fence post. Gain of twenty to Calvin right out of the rodeo chute, as Wyatt's dad liked to say.

Ball on the forty, just like that. Room for Wyatt to maneuver now. Room to *breathe*. Clock stopped when Calvin went out of bounds. Minute fifty remaining.

All day.

Everybody standing in Boone Stadium. All those familiar faces on the Granger side, Dad and Mom pretty much in the same spot they had for home games at Granger High, fifty-yard line, maybe ten rows up. All the other Friday nights and Saturday afternoons had built up to this one. Cheerleaders on the field in the big area between the wall of the stands and the Cowboys' bench, not doing much cheering right now, almost like they were frozen in place, all those pretty girls watching along with everybody else to see how the big game would come out.

Sarah Rayburn, the only freshman on the squad, she was *that* pretty, looking so scared and so nervous you were afraid she might be about to cry, even with that cheerleader smile of hers locked in place.

Wyatt went right back to Calvin on the next play. Fort Carson's pass rush made Wyatt work this time, flushing him out of the pocket, same kind of pressure they'd been putting on him all day. But Wyatt bought himself just enough time, scrambling to his right. Wyatt was as accurate on the run with that arm as if he had all day in the pocket and hit Calvin in stride at midfield.

Clock running.

Wyatt hurried everybody up to the new line of scrimmage, going with the second play he'd called in the huddle, a right sideline route to his tight end, Roy Gilley. Another strike, Roy shoved out of bounds by their strong safety.

One minute, one second left.

Next came the play they'd talk about for a long time in Granger, in the ice-cream parlors and barbecue joints where they all grew up, where the only thing they talked about all week in those places, and on the town's lone radio station, was last week's game.

Wyatt Cullen, number 10, in that Cowboy blue that matched the blue of the Dallas Cowboys, surrounded this time, huge pressure now, one of the defensive linemen with a handful of blue jersey, trying to fight off a blocker and pull Wyatt down with his free hand.

The action actually seemed to stop in that moment, everybody saying afterward that they were sure Wyatt was getting sacked, guys on both teams saying they kept waiting for the ref to blow his whistle.

But he didn't.

Because Wyatt wasn't about to go down.

Instead he stumbled as he somehow freed himself of the guy's grasp and left the pocket, pulling free, *getting* free, running for his life to his left.

Half the Fort Carson defense still coming for him.

But Wyatt wasn't looking behind him, he was looking down the field. Having bought himself just enough time to do *that,* Wyatt was able to fling the ball while running, barely taking long enough to plant his right foot, heaving it half-sidearm as far as he could in the direction of Calvin Morton.

Letting it rip even though Calvin was double-covered by a corner and a safety. Wyatt told everybody later that he'd overcooked the sucker on purpose, that's why it looked like an overthrow as it started to fall out of the sky, Wyatt wanting Calvin to be the only one with a chance to go up and get it.

And there was Calvin, going up for that pass like this was the way he'd drawn it up in his dreams.

The safety and the corner could both jump pretty good. Yet not like Calvin Morton, who went up and outfought both of them, bobbling the ball just slightly, somehow pinning it to the front of his right shoulder pad with his huge mitt of a left hand.

Landing hard on his back, helmet going sideways as he did, somehow maintaining control of the ball.

Now there was Wyatt racing down the field, maybe as fast as he'd ever moved on a football field, waving his teammates to run with him. Not wanting to burn that last time-out in his pocket, wanting everybody lined up as soon as the ref started the clock again, having stopped it because of the first down.

He spiked the ball as soon as it was snapped to him.

Twenty-eight seconds left.

Ball on the Fort Carson seventeen.

Wyatt figured he had all the time he needed, even if they didn't make another first down, that he could make four throws to the end zone, easy, if he had to.

But he needed only one.

Needed only one because Calvin made this sweet, tight inside move on the corner, like he was going to run a post, then just flat froze the guy and the safety giving inside help when he made an even better cut, at full speed, toward the left corner of the end zone.

Wyatt's pass, dead spiral, hit those big hands as softly as your head hitting your pillow, and it was 22–20, Granger.

Now it had become the high school moment, in Texas or anywhere else, they had all really dreamed about their whole lives, going ahead in the last seconds of the big game like this.

Couldn't tell it by watching Wyatt Cullen, though. He was the coolest guy in Boone Stadium, pointing up to where his parents and his kid brother were, all of them losing their minds the way everybody around them was.

There was Sarah, the close-up of her face they'd use not only in the TV highlights, but also in the *Granger Dispatch,* looking about as happy as a high school girl ever could, eyes on Wyatt.

There was old Coach John McCoy, his Granger jacket halfway zipped the way it always was, no matter how hot the Texas weather was, showing you the white shirt and the tie he always wore, had worn since he coached Troy Cullen in games like these. Coach getting some love from the TV cameras his own self, as they liked to say in Texas, calmly holding up one finger, not saying the Cowboys were already number one, not getting ahead of himself, just telling his boys to kick the point after.

Clay Smolders's kick was center cut. Now it was 23–20 for Granger.

Fort Carson managed to get off three desperation heaves. When the last one fell harmlessly to the ground at around the Granger forty, it was over.

Then Wyatt Cullen was in the air, above it all, carried around by the bigger guys on his team. Even looking cool up there, above the action now instead of in the middle of it. Smiling when the cameras closed on him, like he was exactly where he was supposed to be, like he knew all along that this was the way his day and his high school career were supposed to end.

His kid brother, Jake, froze the scene right there.

Hit the remote and froze his big brother on TiVo. Right there on the close-up, on Wyatt's smile. Like Wyatt really had known all along, since he first played catch with Troy Cullen in the pasture behind the barn, the first time Dad was the one telling him he had the arm.

Jake pointed the remote at the big screen, sat there in the quiet den, waiting for his buddies to come pick him up and head over to Mickey's Bar-B-Q tonight, wondering all over again what the view was really like up there for Wyatt. What it was like to actually *be* Wyatt Cullen, even though he'd grown up in the same house with him, looked up to him his whole life.

Jake: wondering if he'd ever get anywhere near a moment like that at Granger High.

Or if he'd ever even *be* the first-string quarterback at Granger High, whether he was a Cullen or not.

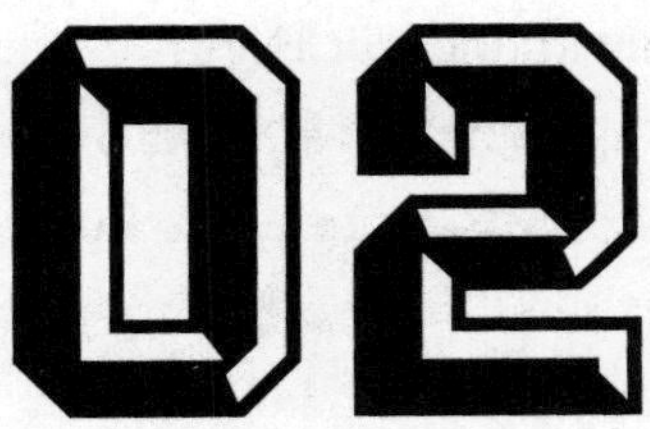

JAKE CULLEN—ONLY HIS MOM STILL CALLED HIM BY HIS BIRTH name, Jacob—had always known he was going to have to get out from two shadows in high school football:

His brother's.

And his dad's.

Most guys in sports only had to get out from under one, if they were good enough, that is. Oh, he knew that Eli Manning, one of his total heroes even if he did play for the hated Giants, had managed to do it, managing to escape the shadow of his dad, Archie, at Ole Miss and *then* his big brother Peyton's in the pros by winning two Super Bowls.

Eli had made himself into the most famous kid brother in the history of football, and maybe all of sports.

Two shadows still seemed like a lot to Jake, who sometimes felt he'd lived his whole life thus far in the shade—not that shade was always such a bad thing in the heat of Granger, Texas.

He had been good enough to start at quarterback in Pop Warner and then for the town football team in the eighth grade. But

Jake knew the deal on *that*: None of his coaches so far were going to be the ones to *not* start a Cullen at quarterback in Granger. Going into his freshman year at Granger High, he knew he'd really done nothing so far to convince anybody that he had the arm or the game or the nerve or the leadership to ever be as good—as *great*—as either his dad or brother had been before him.

Oh, he was a quarterback, all right. No choice for him there. His dad said he didn't want to push him when Jake was old enough to try out for Pop Warner, said Jake could play any position he wanted.

"Your call, son," Troy Cullen had said at the time. "You make your own path in football the way you do in life."

But Jake knew that he didn't really mean it, that it wasn't really his call at all, or his path, that if he didn't play quarterback people were going to wonder what was wrong with him. Granger wasn't much different from any other town in Texas; they loved their football here, it was the thing that held the town together. People in Granger were more likely to miss church on Sunday than a high school football game on a Friday night, under the lights at Cullen Field, built for the town by Jake's grandpa, a cattle rancher who'd never played football himself but came to love it because of his only son.

Troy Cullen ran the family ranch now, having never made it in the NFL, even though he'd been drafted in the first round out of TCU by the Cardinals after nearly winning the Cotton Bowl game his senior year single-handedly. He'd played his fair share in the pros, and even gotten a few starts at the end of his rookie year. But then came three concussions his second year, and another—the bad one—the next year. At that point the doctors finally sat him down and said they weren't really concussions at all, let's call them what they really were, brain wounds.

Told him it was time to walk away, and that was nearly twenty years before they really started to understand about brain wounds people got playing football.

He came home to Granger. A lot of people in town thought that when Troy Cullen had gone off to the NFL, he was never coming back. Instead, he came home and took over the family ranch, not only took it over but tripled it in size over the years, made it competitive with bigger and more famous ranches all over the state.

"Who you are is where you're from," Jake's dad liked to say.

Still, quarterbacking was the family business for the Cullens as much as anything, like it had been passed down the way the ranch had. Wyatt was at the University of Texas now, already the starter at QB as a freshman. For now, Jake was the last one in the line, maybe the last Cullen for a long time and maybe ever to play quarterback for the Granger Cowboys.

Just not this season.

Jake was a third-string freshman, locked into that slot less than a week into preseason practice, still a week before school was supposed to start. Not the starter, not even on a JV team, Granger High being one more Texas school that had lost its JV team because of budget cuts.

Tim Mathers, the senior who'd waited his turn behind Wyatt Cullen, was going to be the starter. Not because he was a great quarterback; he wasn't. He didn't have the arm or the size or the feel for the game. He had the job for now because he had waited his turn, and Coach McCoy, without coming out and saying it, clearly believed he owed Tim his shot.

His backup, and maybe not for long, was a junior transfer from San Antonio named Casey Lindell.

"All's Tim did," Jake's best buddy on the team, Nate Collins, said, "is move up in the line after your big brother got out."

They were stretched out in the grass, taking a water break in the high August heat before the last hour of practice today, drinking as much water as they could hold.

Jake said, "Sometimes that's the way it works in sports, that's the way the line keeps moving."

Nate was a freshman, same as Jake. But last year's center had graduated, and Nate was so big and so good, everybody knew when he was still in eighth grade that he'd be starting this season.

Nate said, "Coach ought to give you a better look, not just see you as a freshman and put you in the back of the line."

"In your dreams, big man."

Nate, who looked like the old Hall-of-Fame player Warren Sapp, everything about him big, starting with his smile, said, "My mama thinks I'm a dreamer, too!"

Nate Collins was six four and two hundred and sixty pounds already. And was still growing, both up and out. By next year, when some of the other guys on the O-line had graduated, Jake was sure they were going to move Nate over to left tackle, the *Blind Side* position on the line, the glamour position, the one where offensive linemen made the biggest money in the pros.

In his spare time, he was also the biggest cheerleader at Granger High.

For Jake, that is.

From the time they'd started playing together when they were in grade school, Nate had always had way more confidence in Jake as a quarterback than Jake had in himself.

It wasn't that Jake didn't think he had talent; he knew he did, had an ability to get the guys around him to play better, a knack for figuring out a way to make a play and win a game. He definitely had the brains for the position, grades in the classroom being the one shadow Jake had no trouble emerging from. He was a straight-A student. And it was his brains that made him a realist. He knew already that he just wasn't going to be the player his dad had been before him, certainly wasn't going to be the player his big brother had been.

He had talent, just not *Cullen* talent, at least not that he'd noticed so far in his young life.

"I know you get tired of hearing this," Nate said. "But you got that magic in you."

"Here we go with the magic," Jake said. "You brag on me like I'm Harry Potter trying to run a spread offense. Except we both know if my last name wasn't Cullen, I'd be lucky to get time on special teams this season."

"You got to show Coach, every time you can, that when you absolutely got to make a play, you do," Nate said. "Even if it isn't always as pretty as, say, Sarah Rayburn."

"Ask you something?" Jake said. "You think you could ever go one whole conversation without mentioning her?"

"Unlikely," Nate said. "It's too much fun for me, the way you're crushin' on her."

"Really? Hadn't noticed."

"You just got to approach this with a better attitude," Nate said.

"Sarah or football?"

"Football, least for now. Can't let you just give up before the season begins, assume there's no way for you to move up this season."

"You've got enough attitude for both of us," Jake said. "I'm just being honest, is all."

"You know what the problem really is?" Nate said. "You're the one needs to be more of a dreamer."

Jake sighed. Different day, same song. Nate was always giving him pep talks like this, on the field and in the locker room, at his house or Jake's. Sounding like Jake's mom sometimes.

But never his dad.

Troy Cullen kept telling his youngest son to just look at this season as a "learning experience."

And Jake would think to himself, *Yeah, learn how to be the Cullen standing next to Coach McCoy while somebody else plays quarterback for good ol' Granger High.* Wyatt had started as a freshman, of course, becoming the first guy to ever be a four-year starter at quarterback for the Granger Cowboys—something even their dad hadn't done. And yet Jake was already bigger than Wyatt, who stopped growing at six two. Jake? He at fourteen was already a skinny six three, on his way to what the doctors said would be six five when he finally stopped growing.

Somehow, though, in all the important ways, Wyatt Cullen was all growed up, as they said in Granger, when *he* was fourteen, as if he had already been an upperclassman when he was a high school freshman.

Jake was different, in so many ways he'd lost count. He had shared the quarterback's job on the eighth grade team until halfway through the season, when he had made enough plays to take his team to the district championship game, where Granger had lost to Lovett.

That and his last name were enough to put his name last on the depth chart at quarterback now.

"You think I'm better than I really am," Jake said to Nate. "Like you think that's part of being my best friend."

Nate leaned closer to Jake, lowering his voice.

"Gonna tell you a little somethin' here," Nate said. "Our senior quarterback ain't getting it done this year. Don't want to sound like a bad teammate, you know I'm not. But he ain't the answer. And the transfer, walks around like he's such a hotshot? He ain't as good as he thinks he is. It's why you got to make every snap count when we scrimmage. Open their eyes and make them see, dude."

"Isn't that what that laser surgery is for?" Jake said.

"Funny how the ball ends up where it's s'posed to and when it's s'posed to," Nate said. "You think your arm's your problem. It's your brain."

"What's wrong with my mind?"

"You want the truth?"

"Yes, please give me the truth, big man, so I don't have to beat it out of you in front of the whole team."

"You just haven't figured out you're the Eli Manning of your family."

"Eli's a freak."

"Well then," Nate said, sitting up, hearing the same whistle from Coach McCoy they all did, "time to get your freak on, boy."

"You're an idiot, you know that, right?"

"Nah," Nate said, "but I do snap the ball to one sometimes."

The two of them stood up, put their helmets back on, started walking back toward the newly painted white lines and brand-new turf of Cullen Field.

"I'm telling you straight up," Nate said. "It's up to you to make them *see* what you got."

Jake thought to himself, and not for the first time:

How do I do that when I still don't see it in myself?

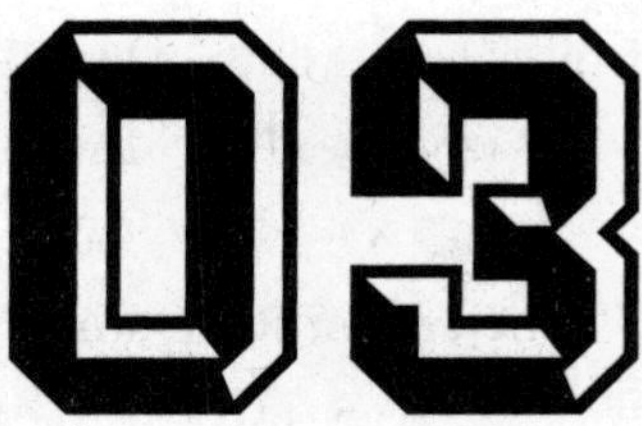

EACH OF GRANGER'S THREE QUARTERBACKS WOULD GET ONE series today, one crack each at the first-string defense, a chance to start at the twenty and see if they could take the ball all the way down the field.

Soon as they didn't make a first down, or turned it over, it was next man up.

Tim Mathers went first and was shaky at the start, nerves already an issue with him even though he'd practically been handed the job. Jake had seen it when they'd started scrimmaging at the end of last week.

Jake watched Tim, thinking this poor guy wasn't the only one worried about the reach of Wyatt Cullen's long shadow.

But Tim settled down after a couple of bad throws, moved the offense past midfield, looked like he might go all the way until he telegraphed a deep sideline throw to Calvin, eyes locked on him the entire time, the ball intercepted by the Cowboys' best corner—maybe best in the state this season—Ollie Gray, who had already committed to LSU for next year. Ollie had run with Calvin step for step all the way, turned back for the ball at exactly the right moment, caught it in stride inside the ten-yard line, as if he was the one who'd been Tim Mathers's intended receiver all along.

Casey Lindell's turn.

Casey looked old enough to be in college already, same height as Jake and easily weighing twenty more pounds. He had a rocket for an arm, had even started for his high school team in San Antonio since he was a freshman. But his parents had gotten divorced and his mom, who was from Granger, had moved back to her hometown with her three kids. Casey didn't seem too worried about the move, or about Tim Mathers being the starter, at least for now. He was a cocky kid, not coming out and saying it but clearly thinking he was the one who'd be starting before too long.

He was good and he knew it.

One of those guys.

One more quarterback Jake wanted to be like.

And if he *was* as good as he thought he was, and did get the starting job, it meant Jake would be playing behind him for the next two years.

It was just a week into practice, but Coach was only sending in about every other play, letting his quarterbacks decide what to call sometimes, wanting to find out about their decision-making as much as he wanted to find out about their arms. Wanting to see how much they'd been studying his playbook. And every time Casey got to make the call, he called Calvin's number, four straight times, completing all four throws. It helped him move the ball, all right. But Jake, even as a freshman third-string quarterback, knew that was a mistake for a quarterback at any level.

When you locked in on one guy the way Casey had, the defense was going to figure you out sooner or later, even if it hadn't happened yet today.

Calvin? He was fine with it, because as much swagger as he had on and off the field, Jake knew something about Calvin that Wyatt had told him:

Behind the swag, Calvin was insecure, totally, worried that without Wyatt this season, he wouldn't be the same kind of star he'd been last season when it was Wyatt Cullen throwing him the ball. And that was the thing about wide receivers, even the famous ones. It all went back to the immortal words of Keyshawn Johnson when he was still playing and not working for ESPN: They all needed somebody to throw them the damn ball. Today, Casey was keeping Calvin happy.

It was funny, Jake thought, watching the two of them chest-bump when Calvin came back to the huddle—even as they acted like they'd become instant best friends, it was like they were using each other.

Casey called Calvin's number again from the defense's fifteen-yard line even though it wasn't his turn to call the play. Showing some rope, changing the screen pass Coach had sent in for Spence Tolar, calling an audible at the line of scrimmage. The new guy doing that, in *training camp.* Even with the screen set up to the left, Casey faked in, turned, and threw a perfect high fade to Calvin in the corner of the end zone for the score.

The same play that Wyatt had called to win the state championship.

Casey ran down to Calvin, the two of them celebrating as

though they'd just won the BCS championship game, starting with a flying chest-bump, finishing with some complicated handshakes, like they'd been practicing together.

But when Casey came back up the field, Coach McCoy said, "You changed the play we sent in."

Casey showed even more rope, impressed Jake by not backing down.

"Safety read the screen perfectly, was moving over to that side as I was calling signals," Casey said. "I knew that left Calvin single-covered."

Calvin was there, too, now, heard Casey say, "And Coach, I don't think even Darrelle Revis can handle Calvin straight up."

Calvin smiled and pointed at Casey.

"Lucky," Coach said to Casey.

"Sir . . . ," Casey said, but Coach held up a hand before he walked away and said, "Lucky you were right."

Jake's turn.

When he got to the huddle, Nate said, "You got this."

"Long as I got you blocking for me, big man."

"Just pretend we're playin' at your house like when we were kids."

But Jake floated his first pass to his fullback, Spence Tolar, and nearly got picked off when the ball soared five yards over Spence's head. On second down, he pulled back from center too soon, dropped Nate's snap, and fell on the ball for a two-yard loss.

Third-and-twelve, just like that.

Jake knew he had to make a play now, find a way to swallow his nerves so the day wouldn't be a total loss. He stood tall in the pocket, stepped up, hit Roy Gilley over the middle, Roy breaking a tackle and running all the way to the forty-five.

Nate gave Jake a high five, said, "What I'm talkin' about."

Now Coach had Jake throw the same pass to Spence he'd missed on first down, and this time Jake led him perfectly and Spence ran all the way to the defense's thirty-eight before Ollie caught him from behind.

They ran Spence off-tackle for four yards, followed by a short pass to Roy that got them to the defense's thirty. Then came a quick slant to Calvin on third-and-two, Jake wobbling the throw—if you were looking for spirals every time, Jake Cullen wasn't your guy—but still putting it right on the 1 on Calvin's chest.

First down at the twenty.

But Jake and Spence messed up on a handoff, Spence falling on the ball in the backfield for a five-yard loss. Then Jake threw behind Roy on second down. Third-and-fifteen. A sideline throw to Calvin gained ten.

Taking them all to fourth-and-five.

And at the end of practice, just for the fun of it—because Coach McCoy had always wanted football to be fun—he called the same pass for Jake that Casey had just called on his own.

Wanting to see if Jake could deliver the goods on it the way Casey Lindell had.

Jake took the snap cleanly, dropped back, plenty of time, Nate taking out Luke Kelly, their big-as-a-barn nose tackle, with a block that knocked Luke back before it just flat knocked him down.

Having been given the extra time, Jake told himself not to rush the play, to let it happen, waited as Calvin faked out even the great

Ollie Gray, broke into the clear the same way he had against Fort Carson, turned and waited for Jake Cullen to get it to him the way Wyatt and Casey had.

Not even close.

Jake tried to put too much on it just to make sure he didn't miss somebody as wide open as Calvin was, not give Ollie a chance to recover and get back into the play. He knew the ball had sailed on him—big-time—as soon as it came out of his hand. He threw it over Ollie and over Calvin and nearly threw it to the cheerleaders, having their own preseason practice behind the end zone at Cullen Field.

Calvin put his head back and made a big show of watching the ball fly over his head like he was watching a plane take off.

Jake didn't move, stayed right where he was in the pocket when he'd released the ball, thinking that the only thing anybody was going to remember from practice today was the last thing they saw, a god-awful, piss-poor throw like that.

Nate was next to Jake, of course.

"Got away from you, is all," he said.

"You *think*?" Jake said.

Then Calvin was there, like he was as fast getting back to Jake now as he usually was running his pass patterns.

"Dude, you sure you and Wyatt are related?" he said.

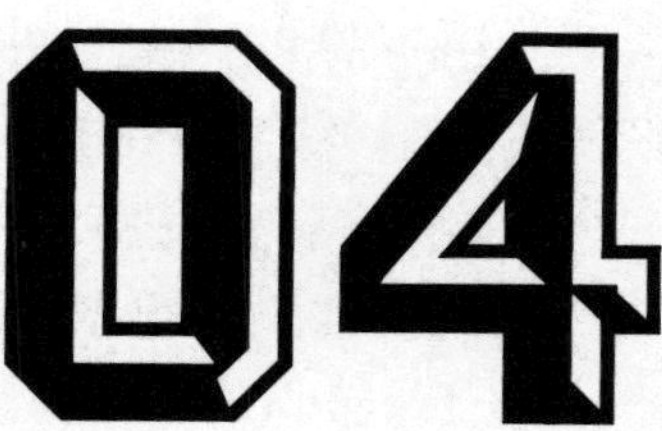

JAKE DIDN'T KNOW WHAT TO SAY TO THAT, JUST WATCHED Calvin walk away, shaking his head.

Coach blew his whistle and said he'd see everybody tomorrow, bright and early. Jake didn't even stop for a drink, just headed for the parking lot. Tim Mathers had said he'd give Jake and Nate a ride home.

Jake felt a hand on his shoulder, was about to turn and tell Nate he didn't need any more pep talks, not today. But then he saw it was Ray Jessup, the team's new offensive coordinator, a former Granger wide receiver, not even thirty years old yet, but already having gone into coaching. And you could see two things about Coach J already, in just a week. One was how much Coach McCoy trusted him to call plays.

The other was how enthusiastic he was.

Jake said, "Coach, I stopped watching after a while. My throw come down yet?"

Ray Jessup smiled. "I think you might have taken out one of

the cheerleaders doing the pyramid." Shrugged like it was no big deal, said, "You tried to make it too perfect, is all."

"Ended up doing the opposite."

"But you made two third-down plays when you had to, that's what I took away from today." Giving Jake a little fist-pump.

"You, maybe. Not me."

"You're gonna get better," Coach said.

"Yeah," Jake said. "One of these years."

"No, I mean you're gonna get better *today,*" Coach said. "Stick around after the other guys are gone."

"I was gonna catch a ride with Tim."

"Let's you and me have a little game of catch," Coach said. "I'll give you a ride home. Not like I don't know the way; I used to work summers at the ranch for your grandpa."

"Coach, I'm a whupped dog."

"You just think you are." Smiled and said, "C'mon, dog. You gotta love it!"

Some days, Jake wasn't so sure.

How much he really loved it.

Jake was too tired to still be on the field after all his buddies were gone. The day was too hot even for Granger, a town Jake had always thought of as the brown-grass capital of Texas, which meant it was probably the brown-grass capital of the world. Plus they'd spent the first hour and a half of practice today doing conditioning drills in full pads, Coach telling them that the heat wasn't going anywhere even when the season started up for real.

And he still was kicking himself for missing Calvin the way he had, by a country mile.

But somehow, to Jake's surprise, Coach Jessup made their one-on-one workout fun, doing play-by-play even as he was running his pass routes, his voice booming in Cullen Field, telling Jake at one point he was ready to go all day and all night, put the lights on if he had to.

Coach J seemed to be having so much fun that Jake started to think that maybe the only reason they were still out here was because Coach needed someone to throw him the ball.

They had been going for about half an hour, Coach running his outs and slants and deep posts nonstop, when he finally announced they were stopping for a water break. Jake wondered why he was dying and Coach barely seemed to be out of breath.

Jake was gulping down his second bottle of water when Coach said, "You're not your brother."

That got Jake's attention. Coach didn't say it in a mean way, just came out with it, like he was saying to Jake that it sure was a hot one today.

"Kind of figured that out for myself, Coach," Jake said. "Like, practically since birth."

"Oh, hell," Coach Jessup said, the word sounding like "hale," the way it usually did around here. "I *know* you know that. What I'm saying to you is that you're not your brother, so stop trying to *be* him."

Jake waited.

"Man, you got to stop trying to throw the ball like him," Coach said. "It's like you're trying to copy that straight-over-the-top motion of his." Coach himself straightened up now, as if throwing an imaginary ball, mimicking Wyatt's form perfectly. "That might work for him, but off what I've seen already, it sure ain't you."

"It's the only way I've ever known," Jake said, "from the time my dad first showed me where to put my fingers on the laces."

"And I'm not telling you he was wrong, don't get me wrong. He pretty much used to chuck it the same way. But you're longer than Wyatt, and got way longer arms, and it looks to me like there are just too many moving parts before you're ready to lock and load. It's why you're as wild as you are sometimes. Little like Tebow, you ask me." Coach drank some water, spit, and said, "I know what a man of faith he is, but I don't even think the Lord Himself ever thought much of that motion of his."

Jake couldn't help it. He laughed. "You're saying I throw like Tim *Te*bow? That's it, I'm quitting football."

"In your family, you're more likely to quit breathing first," Coach said. "C'mon, let's get back to work, I'll show you what I mean. If you're ever gonna be the quarterback *you* need to be, you got to quicken up your release and stop worrying about setting the ball so high. Your brother has to, he doesn't have your height. Only time I see you releasing the ball the way I want you to is when you're on the run and not overthinking it."

At first it felt to Jake as if he were almost throwing the ball sidearm, even as Coach J assured him he wasn't. And even as he got more comfortable, he started to think he wasn't going to throw another spiral today even if they did practice into the night.

Finally he said, "Coach, my arm's about to fall off."

"Gimme five good minutes," Coach said, "and then we'll call it a day."

And somehow, as tired as Jake was, he did give him five good minutes, stopped thinking about what he was doing and just let it happen, throwing instead of aiming, the ball starting to come out of his hand more cleanly. Jake even managed some spirals.

He was already wondering what his dad was going to say the first time he saw him throwing the ball like this.

"Jake?" he heard Coach Jessup saying.

"Yes, sir."

"Where'd you go?"

"Mind started to wander," Jake said. "Been a long day."

"Well," Coach said, "let's end it with that pass you missed to ol' Calvin about an hour ago. Take your three-step drop, and then let 'er go. Like my golf coach tells me, don't think about anything except where you want the sucker to land."

Coach J gave him a mild head-slap to the side of his helmet and said, "And remember something else about sports: Ever'body gets nervous. The trick is not letting 'em *see* you nervous."

Ray Jessup, who'd been a decent wide receiver at Baylor after he'd left Granger High, ran an inside route, then broke toward the corner. This time Jake didn't airmail his receiver. Didn't try to be perfect. Or Wyatt. Just put the ball on the money, Coach J hauling it in three strides before he ran out of bounds, letting out a holler before doing about the mutt-ugliest touchdown dance Jake believed he'd ever seen in his life.

"Coach," Jake called out to him, "is that your end-zone strut, or are you just having some sort of heatstroke?"

"You looked like a quarterback on that one," Coach yelled back at him, "not somebody impersonating one."

At last they were done. Coach said he had to go get some stuff in the locker room, make a quick phone call to his wife. Told Jake he'd meet him in the parking lot next to his F-150. Jake thought, *Maybe someday I'll live in a world where half the people I know don't drive some kind of truck.*

Just not in Granger, where you heard a lot that the roads led everywhere except out of town.

Jake was too tired to even go get himself one more bottle of water. He just walked through the tunnel, feeling like he'd walked into an air-conditioned room just getting out from beneath the sun, helmet in one hand, towel in the other.

Then he was out Gate B and into the parking lot. Glad that Coach had made him stay. Had taken enough of an interest in him to *make* him stay. Feeling a little better about himself than if he'd left with everybody else when practice had ended.

"Hey, Jake. Hey, Jake Cullen, wait up."

He didn't even have to turn around. He felt his heart turn over at least one time, knowing that the voice belonged to Sarah Rayburn.

Still the prettiest girl at Granger High.

Wanting to talk to him.

Jake stood there and waited for her, wishing he did have a bottle of water with him. His mouth felt as dry as dirt, Sarah's long legs eating up the distance between them in the parking lot. She must have showered since the end of cheerleading practice, and changed; Jake could see right away this was a different T-shirt and shorts than she'd been wearing before. Jake spent a lot of time stealing looks at her across the field every chance he got.

Before, she'd had her brown hair pulled back into a ponytail. Now it was hanging soft to her shoulders.

"Hi," he said when she got to him.

"Hi yourself."

They had seen each other before and after Wyatt's games last season. Their parents knew each other, and Jake would see Sarah in town sometimes, at Spooner's Ice Cream or Mac's Diner or Mickey's, or at the old-fashioned movie theater whose marquee still dominated Granger's main street. But Jake hadn't officially started yet at high school, having spent eighth grade at Granger Middle.

So even though he and Sarah technically knew each other, they really didn't, had never really had a conversation that went past where they were now, both of them saying hi.

Now or never.

"I got kept after practice by Coach Jessup," Jake said. "What's your excuse for still being here?"

Telling himself that sounded fine, he hadn't sounded like he was trying too hard to start a conversation, even though Sarah was the one who'd called out to him. Jake heard Coach J's words inside his head, telling himself not to let Sarah see him nervous.

Telling himself not to sound like some kind of moron.

"Was just hanging around with some of the other girls on our team," she said, "and waiting for my mom, who's late, as usual."

Jake gave a quick look over his shoulder, hoping Coach J was still inside talking to his wife, wasn't on his way to the truck. He was relieved to see he wasn't anywhere in sight.

He looked back at Sarah, and Jake thought she looked a little nervous herself.

"So," she said, "how we looking?"

"*Our* team?"

"Only one that matters around here."

"Coach'll figure it out," Jake said. "Always has before."

Sarah put one arm in the air, then the other, smiled, and said, "Go team!" And they both laughed, knowing the cheerleader girl was having some fun with herself.

Then came an awkward silence that didn't end until Jake said, "So what's up?"

"Well," she said, like she was screwing up her courage, "I just wanted to ask you . . . how's Wyatt doing at college?"

And Jake felt like he'd been hit.

That blind-side hit in the pocket you didn't know was coming, all the wind coming out of him at once, hoping that Sarah couldn't see the disappointment he felt in that moment, knowing that she only wanted to talk to him about his brother.

"Doing fine," Jake said. Forced up a smile and said, "He's Wyatt, after all."

"I check him out on Facebook all the time," Sarah said, "but it's not like you get a whole lot of intel there."

"He's threatening to go on Twitter," Jake said, "though knowing my brother, how careful he is, I'll believe that when I see it."

"I'm on Twitter now!" Sarah said. "You gotta tell me if Wyatt does go on."

"Absolutely," Jake said.

Looked back over his shoulder again. Now he saw Coach Jessup making his way from Gate B, looking like one of the Cowboys players himself in the distance, T-shirt and shorts and sandals and a backpack.

Now Jake was happy to see him coming.

"Well," Sarah said, "if you talk to the big college man, tell him Sarah said hi. Okay?"

"Will do."

"Promise?" she said.

"Hey," Jake said, faking his way through one more smile. "What's a brother for?"

They heard the brief sound of a car horn, saw Sarah's mom's SUV pulling into the lot.

"Gotta go," she said.

"Go team," Jake said in a quiet voice.

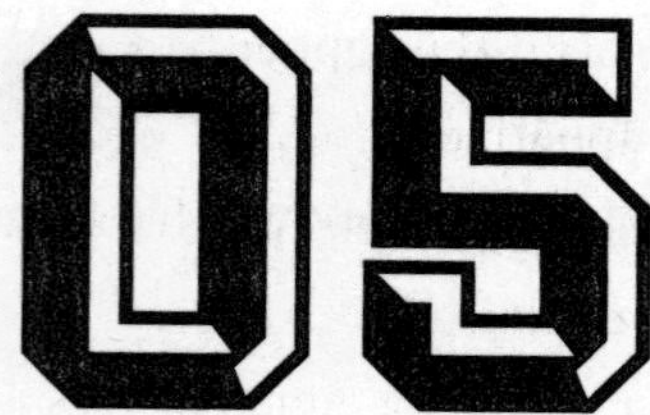

BARRETT "BEAR" LOGAN, ANOTHER FRIEND AND TEAMMATE with a driver's license, slow in football pads but always prompt, came by about seven to pick up Jake. They swung by Nate's house to pick him up, then headed to Stone's Throw, the most popular restaurant and hangout in Granger. Best steaks, best burgers, best dessert.

Biggest TV screen.

Bobby Ray Stone had been a blocking back for Troy Cullen in high school. But in the league championship game their senior year against Morrow, in what Jake's dad said was still the worst rain he ever played in, somehow Bobby Ray Stone completed an option pass for a touchdown in a game the Cowboys won 6–0.

"Stone's Throw" was the front-page headline in the paper the next day, and later that became the name of Bobby Ray's restaurant and bar and gathering place, even if everybody by now just called it Stone's.

The way Jake looked at it, Bobby Ray Stone was another

ex-player who'd not only never left Granger, it was as if he'd never left the team.

Jake was only going for dessert, but he knew Barrett and Nate well enough to know they would be having a second dinner, something they did a lot after practice, as if the supper they had at home was just some kind of big-boy appetizer.

"It's all about replacing the body weight you left out there on the field," was the way Barrett liked to explain it.

"Imagine it like this," Nate said, "like you were emptying out a glass of water and then filling the sucker back up."

"Yeah," Jake said, "with ribs and baked potatoes and onion rings."

Barrett, a sophomore linebacker, wasn't as big as Nate, or nearly as good a football player. Mostly he was just a big, amiable, good old Granger boy whose father was a wrangler for the quarter horses on the Cullen ranch the way *his* father had been a wrangler for Jake's grandpa.

Barrett liked to say all the time that he'd been born in Granger and was going to die there, too; it's what men in his family had always done. Liked to tell Jake, when it was just the two of them, that when he thought about his world, in his mind's eye, it always fit inside the Granger city limits like a glove.

But as much as Barrett loved Granger, he loved Granger football more, loved the fact that he was a part of it now, a part of this team, even if it looked like he'd be lucky to do more than play on special teams this season. It would be enough for Barrett.

More than anything, his vision of his world had always been built around wearing Granger blue someday.

He loved football the way Nate did, and the way Jake *wanted* to. He had played on Granger's last JV team the season before. Now all he talked about, even though he wasn't much of a talker, certainly not when Nate was around, was what it was going to be like for him the first time he ran out of the tunnel at Cullen Field with his teammates as an honest-to-God Granger Cowboy.

His dad had always been a real cowboy, not a football player. So Barrett, his firstborn, was the first in the family to make the team. Sometimes Jake was more excited about Barrett making that run out of the tunnel and through the line of cheerleaders than he was about making the run for the first time himself.

If you were a Cullen, just wearing the blue, being on that field, wasn't enough.

Barrett was back to talking about the opener, against Shelby High, as they pulled into the crowded parking lot at Stone's, the three of them squeezed into the front seat of Barrett's daddy's pickup, an old F-250 with an extended cab, one that had been navy blue once, or so Barrett said, but was now the color of the Texas sky. Even though Barrett was just a sophomore, he'd been held back once in grade school, so he was closer to seventeen now than sixteen, and had had his license long enough that he could legally have his friends in a vehicle he was driving.

Barrett said, "Tell the truth: you guys think I talk about the start of the season too much, don't you?"

"Nah," Nate said. "But I have noticed that when you start goin' on, like you do, it does make me hungry."

"A wind out of the east makes you hungry," Jake said.

Barrett said, "You're the only guy I know who starts to feel hungry while he's still workin' on the meal he's workin' on."

"Lookee at who's talking," Nate said. "Guess it musta been some *other* Barrett Logan won the rib-eating contest at the Sparksville rodeo last year. Ended up looking like he'd swam himself through barbecue sauce to get to the ribbon."

Their waitress was a girl from school that Jake and Nate both knew Barrett liked, a junior named Emma Jean Duhon. It was why lately anytime they were kicking around places to eat—not that there were all that many in Granger—Barrett would immediately vote for Stone's, as great as the barbecue was at Mickey's. But only on nights when Emma Jean happened to be working.

Even though she was a grade higher than him in school, the way Sarah was with Jake, Barrett and Emma Jean were the same age, which would have been helpful to Barrett as a way of doing something about his feelings for her if he was able to form sentences in her presence.

This would have been a lot more amusing to Jake, Barrett rumbling and stumbling the way he did when he got around Emma Jean, if it didn't remind Jake so much of the way he acted when he got around Sarah.

Sarah.

There she was, back inside his brain. He was trying not to dwell on what had happened with her after practice, wanted to just kick it with his guys tonight, have some pie and ice cream, sit around Stone's the way they did a lot, the way so many other guys on the team did, the restaurant sometimes feeling like part of their locker room.

Before Jake could stop Emma Jean, she was taking them to a booth she must have assumed Jake wanted, one surrounded by so many pictures of Jake's dad and Wyatt, it was like the two of them had showed up and joined the damn party.

Wyatt posing with last year's state championship trophy. Troy Cullen, the first Cullen ever to wear number 10, helmet in hand, with Libby, back when Libby was still captain of the cheerleaders, the two of them posing under the goalposts in black-and-white, after some big game out of the past. A replica of Wyatt's road-blue number 10, mounted under glass. A team picture of Troy Cullen's state championship team right next to Wyatt's team.

And a blown-up picture from the newspaper, big brother getting carried off the field after the Fort Carson game.

To Jake it was like sitting in the middle of a family scrapbook.

Nate looked around as he sat down in the booth, taking up what looked like half of it, and said, "Every time we sit here, I feel like I should be ordering something for your brother and your daddy."

"So you can eat their helpings, too?"

"Look at what I eat another way," Nate said. "Like it's fuel for a big old train."

Barrett said, "You mean one car? Or, like, the *whole* train?"

"Don't look to me like you're missin' many meals, there, Bear."

"Hey," Jake said. "Let's not forget why we're really here: to see if Bear can get somewhere with Emma Jean."

"Just get a smile out of her," Nate said.

"Both of you be quiet, I'm beggin' you," Barrett said.

Nate smiled. "That would be my advice for you with Emma, now that I think of it."

"Really, be quiet, here she comes!" Barrett said in a whisper, like he'd been caught doing something bad. Then Emma Jean was handing them their menus, and Nate was opening his like he was opening a birthday present, saying, "I want everything!"

Barrett managed to say to Emma Jean, "He's been fasting since, like, six o'clock."

"Poor baby," Emma Jean said.

Barrett and Nate did order second dinners, ribs for both of them, baked potatoes, and onion rings, as Jake had predicted. He went for apple pie and vanilla ice cream.

As Emma Jean headed back to the kitchen, they all heard Calvin Morton before they saw him. It usually happened that way. As talented as he was, as much as his amazing skills on a football field drew attention, somehow that wasn't enough for him. He acted like he wanted a spotlight on himself every time he walked into a room.

Melvin Braxton, his cousin, was with him. Melvin was a defensive back and kick returner who was more like a brother to Calvin than either a bud or a teammate, as quiet and nice as Calvin was loud.

The third member of the group—no shocker there, the way the two of them had been buddying up at practice—was Casey Lindell. Why not? Calvin had already made it clear, just one week into practice, just by some of the comments Jake had overheard, that Calvin thought Casey was the best quarterback on the team.

To Calvin, that just meant the quarterback with the best chance to get him the ball as often as possible, make him look as good as he possibly could to college recruiters.

Didn't mean Calvin didn't want to win. He did. Jake knew that he hated to lose as much as he hated it when the ball wasn't coming to him. But Calvin believed that Granger High was just the beginning of the process for him, that he was going from here to be a big star in college football and then the pros after that. A big, fast guy going places. Mostly out of Granger the first chance he got. The opposite of Barrett that way.

And now that Wyatt Cullen was gone, he was the star of the team, at last.

Long as somebody could get him the ball the way Wyatt had.

"Look out!" they heard Calvin say now, looked over and saw him point at their table with both hands. "Cullen in the house."

He waved at Jake now, who gave him a quick wave back, trying not to do anything that would encourage him to come over. Jake liked Calvin, he did, thought he was a show. Just didn't want to be part of the show tonight. So he turned away, asked Barrett about a cutting horse his dad had been working, trying to act as if he were a lot more interested in that. Not ignoring Calvin—that was pretty much impossible—but making sure he did nothing to engage.

Too late.

Calvin was as fast getting across Stone's as he was in the open field, turned out.

"Man, look at you, the last Cullen in Cullenville," he said, "sitting here like y'all are in the middle of a family photograph."

"Yeah," Jake said, "they like my dad and my brother here. I keep waiting for them to put their pictures on the menu."

"I been askin' Mr. Stone," Calvin said, "when he's gonna clear a wall for me."

Nate grinned. "You sure one wall will be enough?"

Calvin seemed to notice Nate for the first time. "How you goin', big man?" Calvin said. "See Jake's got his number one with him."

"We all know you're the only number one around here, C," Jake said, trying to keep it light.

"Only way I stay that way is when I got somebody throwin' the ball *to* me," Calvin said, "not *over* me."

"That last throw was crap, no doubt," Jake said. "But I think I found something on my mechanics after practice."

"Yeah," Calvin said, putting on a big smile. "I saw you out there, acting like teacher's pet with Coach Jessup."

"Whoa," Jake said. Honestly surprised. "*He* asked *me* to hang around."

"Course he did, dude; like I said, you're the last Cullen in Cullenville."

Nate said, "You seemed to do all right with a Cullen throwing to you last season."

"Was a different Cullen."

In a quiet voice, Barrett said, "You think Wyatt looked like an All-Pro after his first week of practice, back when he was a freshman? Maybe you could cut Jake a little slack."

Barrett had no use for Calvin, didn't think he was a show, just a show-*off*. Oh, Barrett liked him fine as a teammate, knew Calvin would do as much as anybody to help Granger win games this season as the Cowboys tried to defend their title. But he stayed out of his way at practice, and rarely spoke to him.

There was no rule book for the way you were supposed to act when you were part of a team. But somehow everybody knew his role. Knew his *rank,* like they were in some kind of army.

"I'm sorry," Calvin said, still smiling, "was I talkin' to you, Bear?"

Barrett stared at Calvin, not saying anything, keeping whatever he did want to say inside. Like he'd remembered his rank.

It was Nate who spoke next. "Now, you be nice to my boys, Calvin, you hear?" Nate was smiling, too, but there was something in his voice telling Calvin to stand down now, not asking.

Calvin must have heard it, too:

"C'mon, I was just playin'," he said.

"Yeah," Nate said. "Me too."

"You know I love you, big man," Calvin said. To Jake he said, "You keep workin' on those mechanics, case I need you 'fore this season is over."

"I'm third string," Jake said.

"Right," Calvin said, then turned and walked back across the room, Jake watching him go, wondering what all this had really been about, why Calvin had come over in the first place.

"Does he really think I *wanted* to stay out there on that field today one minute longer than the rest of y'all?" Jake said.

Nate was busy mixing up what looked like the whole butter plate and sour cream into one of his baked potatoes.

"You may not think you got a chance to play, but you sure seem to be on Calvin's radar," Nate said.

"But I'm third string!"

When they had finally finished eating, Jake signaled for the check. Emma Jean came over and said to him, "On the house. Compliments of Bobby."

Meaning Bobby Ray, the owner.

"Emma Jean," Jake said, "he doesn't have to do that. I don't *want* him to do that."

Emma Jean looked over to where Bobby was standing near the hostess stand, smiling and waving at him. "Yeah, Jake, but Bobby wants to. So please don't make a big deal of this, okay?"

"Okay," he said.

They all got up, started walking over to thank Bobby for the food. Jake acted as if he'd forgotten something at the table, went back there and slid a ten-dollar bill, what he'd brought with him for dessert, underneath the saltshaker as a tip. Then he went over and shook Bobby's hand himself, Bobby saying, "Make sure you say hi to Wyatt, you talk to him."

"Sure will."

When they were in the parking lot, Nate and Barrett were talking about their free meal like they'd won some kind of lottery.

"Maybe there's no such thing as a third-string Cullen in Cullenville," Barrett said.

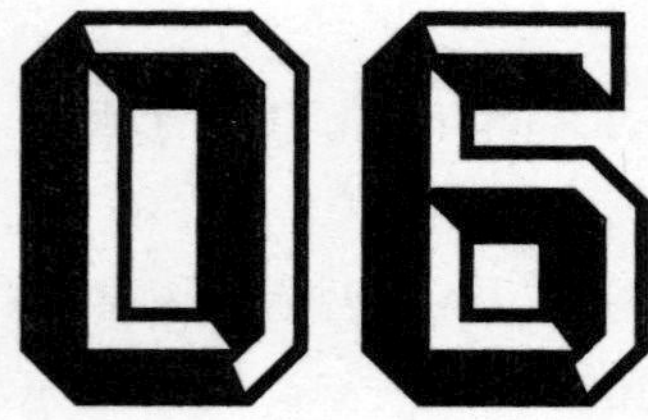

THEY DROPPED OFF NATE FIRST, AT HIS SMALL TWO-STORY house on the outskirts of town, almost to the border of Ashton. Nate's dad drove for UPS and his mom worked as a teller at the same bank, Granger National, that Libby Cullen's dad had once run.

On the way back to the Cullens' spread, all hundred acres of it, a working ranch that raised Black Angus cattle and horses, Barrett was still talking about Calvin.

"You know what bothers me the most?"

"None of it should bother either one of us," Jake said. "That was just Calvin being Calvin. He's fine."

"If he's already made up his mind that Casey's gonna be our starter, what's he stressed out about you for?"

"Maybe it's just another way of him looking up the field," Jake said. "Maybe he's worried that if Casey can push Tim out of a job, I can do the same to Casey."

"Well, maybe he's right about *something* then," Barrett said. "Like a blind squirrel finding an acorn."

"Except I'm not as good as Casey," Jake said. "So Calvin doesn't need to go hunting more acorns. Casey seems to be feeding him just fine."

"My daddy says that if you think of yourself as a backup, that's all you're ever gonna be," Barrett said.

They had made it to the other side of town now, the west side, were on the bumpy back road that felt like dirt, getting close now to the ranch. It was one of those Texas summer nights, under what they called the big sky, when you felt like you didn't even need headlights. All the light you needed came from the stars and the big moon hanging in the sky.

"Bear," Jake said, "I only think of myself as a backup because I *am* a backup."

"Sounds more like a backup *plan* to me," Barrett said.

"More like a basic truth. There's nothing wrong with being a backup."

Barrett took a deep breath, blew it out so hard it put a circle of fog on the windshield.

"No, there's nothing wrong with it. Unless you tell yourself you're not good enough to start, in which case maybe you don't *have* to be good enough." He paused, like he was deciding whether or not to keep going. Then he did. "And if you've spent your whole life believing your daddy didn't think you were good enough, then maybe you can't let him down."

Jake turned his head and looked at Barrett, his eyes on the road, lit by the dashboard and the sky. He was never a big talker, even when Nate wasn't around. So this was the same as a long speech for him.

"I never said anything about not wanting to let my dad down," Jake said.

"So maybe I'm saying it for you," Barrett said. "You got him. You got your brother. Everybody in this town acts like y'all are some kind of football royalty, like y'all just fell into it like a pig in slop. But they don't take time to think what it must be like to be you. Have to walk in their football shoes. I don't know a whole lot about the Mannings. But I know their dad Archie *never* favored one son over the other. Wish I could say the same for *your* daddy."

Not even Jake's mom had ever come out and put it straight to him like this, the truth that Jake carried around inside himself. You heard people all the time, grown-ups mostly, telling you to speak from the heart. Only now Barrett wasn't just speaking from his heart.

He's speaking from mine, Jake thought.

They passed through the main gate to the ranch. Barrett pulled over and stopped the truck next to a fence that Jake had painted last summer to earn extra money. No cattle around now, no horses, just open fields on both sides of the gravel drive where Jake and Wyatt used to come down and throw the ball around, sometimes their dad with them.

"C'mon," Bear said to Jake, "let's see that fancy new throwing motion of yours." Like he was reading Jake's mind.

Jake said, "Even if I did want to throw, where would I find anybody this time of night good enough to *catch*?"

"Ha-ha," Bear said.

Jake got out, and the two of them climbed over the fence, the way they'd been climbing this fence to play football since they were kids. And after just a few minutes, Jake knew, just by feel, that he was already more comfortable throwing the way Coach Jessup had shown him at Cullen Field.

Barrett had trained his headlights on the field they were on now, and with that and the light from the sky, they could follow the flight of the ball just fine. It was late, and neither one of them cared, acted like they didn't have a care in the world, laughing and woofing on each other, Barrett not only looking like a guy who could be a decent tight end, but doing some funny imitations of the little shimmy Calvin would do after he caught a touchdown pass.

"Need two favors," Jake called out to him at one point.

"You got 'em."

"Don't ever shake your hips like that in front of anybody except me," Jake said. "And don't ever dance fast with Emma Jean."

"Later it gets," Barrett said, "funnier you get."

They weren't under the lights of Cullen Field on a Friday night of Texas high school football. But it was all right, Jake thought. More than all right. Out here with his friend, under the lights they had, Jake was happy.

Tonight he loved it.

THE NEXT SUNDAY, THE DAY BEFORE SCHOOL BEGAN, WYATT surprised his family by showing up at about three in the afternoon, no advance warning, just walking through the front door.

His coach had given the Longhorns the day off, and one of Wyatt's freshman teammates lived two towns over. So Wyatt had hitched a ride and here he was, his hair shorter than when he'd left for Austin a few weeks ago, a little soul patch of hair under his lower lip, something his mother noticed immediately.

"You must be a college man now," she said, pulling back from hugging her oldest son. "Seems to me you still couldn't grow facial hair when you left."

"I *could,*" Wyatt said. "I just chose not to."

"I think it's cool," Jake said. "Coach McCoy said no facial hair for us, that the times might change but he won't."

The brothers didn't hug each other, just did lean-in shoulder-bumps.

"Maybe someday if you're starting," Wyatt said, "you can be the one to get him to change some of his ways. I never could."

Troy Cullen, just in from a ride on his favorite cutting horse out to check some broken fence at the far end of the property, said, "You know in my day—"

Far as he got before Wyatt, grinning at Jake, said, "In *his* day."

"The only day that really mattered," Jake said.

"Couple of comedians I raised," Troy Cullen said, taking off his black Resistol cowboy hat and banging the dust off it. "But in my day, we'd *want* to shave first thing after the game, when the girls would start to come around."

Libby Cullen smiled. "And, Lordy, weren't they always around you like bees around honey?"

He put his arms around his wife, his sweetheart since Granger High, and said, "Who can explain the power Cullen men have over women?"

"It's almost like a scent you give off, dear," their mom said, waving her hand in front of her nose. "Unless that's just the smell of horses."

Then she said for the Cullen men to go sit down and get reacquainted in the den while she made up a batch of iced tea for them.

Jake wondered why they needed to get reacquainted, leastways his dad and Wyatt. Wyatt had only been gone a day under three weeks, and Troy Cullen had been in Austin more than half that time watching the Longhorns get ready for their season. The last time he'd been over there had been on Thursday, watching a nighttime practice.

Now he wanted to know if the left side of the offensive line had gotten any better, and if Wyatt was on the same page finally with his senior tight end, and whether or not they'd put in more play-action.

Wyatt said, "Yes, yes, and yes," then was telling them both—but really telling his dad—how they'd strapped on their helmets the last couple of days and practiced for real, Wyatt scrambling yesterday and taking such a hard lick from an outside linebacker, he thought it would take till the middle of this week to catch his breath.

"Hits'll get even harder when you're wearing the orange for real," his dad said.

"Tell me about it," Wyatt said.

"Hey!" Troy Cullen said, turning to Jake. "Why don't you go ask Mom to fix us up some guacamole and chips to go with that iced tea?"

Jake nodded, got up, and left the two of them there, Wyatt telling their dad now that he was throwing the ball as well as he ever had in his life, didn't matter who he was throwing to these days. And saying he felt that more and more the coaches were tailoring the offense around him even though he was just a freshman.

From the hall he heard his dad's big voice telling Wyatt, "Everyone's got to stop thinking of you as a freshman and understand you were a college QB when I dropped you off there."

When Jake got to the kitchen, he grabbed a dish towel and put it over his arm like he was a waiter and gave his mom the order.

"I think your sense of humor was one more thing you got from me," she said.

"I think Dad was afraid I might interrupt while he and Wyatt were game-planning for Washington," Jake said.

"Oh, you know your father and Texas football," she said. "He's never gotten over that the Longhorns didn't want him when he was coming out of Granger High."

Jake grinned. "You think Wyatt's coaches are gonna mind when dad starts trying to explain football to them?"

Libby Cullen turned around at the counter and smiled now. He'd see it sometimes when his dad was going on about something or other, being an expert on something new because he was an expert on everything, usually in a voice you could hear all over the property. It was a smile that loved her husband, understood him, *and* made fun of him all at the same time.

"He's an involved football parent," she said.

"Well," Jake said, the words out of his mouth before he could stop them, "at least with the other quarterback in the family."

The smile disappeared off her face, wiped clean, as she said, "Jacob Cullen, your father loves both his sons, and you know it."

Do I? Jake wondered, thinking about what Bear had said the other night.

But that was a thought that stayed inside him, the way it always did. He dropped it, just like that. Jake understood something about himself: He'd always hated tension, his whole life. Had always gone out of his way to try to make things right with the people around him, even when he knew they were wrong. Even when they were a part of his own family. "My pleaser" his mom had always called him, always letting him know that she thought that was a good thing.

But the truth was, Jake didn't know how much his father loved him. Just knew he didn't love him the way he wanted him to.

The way he loved Wyatt.

He carried the guacamole and a bowl of chips back to the den. His mom carried a tray with the pitcher of iced tea on it, glasses, cut-up lemon and lime and even oranges, because she knew Wyatt loved orange in his iced tea. Libby Cullen, Jake knew by now, never did anything halfway, not even a snack, where her family was concerned. Jake had always thought she was the one who really did know everything, in her quiet way, that quiet way she said Jake got from her.

She sat with them for a few minutes, listening to Wyatt's report from preseason practice, the one she had been getting practically on a daily basis from her husband, who had been living the whole thing right along with Wyatt.

"Game's starting to slow down now, that's what I see happening," Wyatt was saying.

"Wish I'd see it happening for me," Jake said.

"Yeah, little brother," Wyatt said, still calling Jake that even though Jake was taller now. "I forgot to ask, how you goin' so far with the blue and white?"

Jake walked over to pour himself some iced tea, saying over his shoulder, "Gettin' there, I guess. Coach Jessup's been working with me a bit after practice, and that's helped. Can't get a read on Coach McCoy, though, except when I mess up and get that hundred-yard stare of his."

When Jake turned back around, waiting for a response, he saw Wyatt staring down at his cell phone, sitting there next to him on the couch. Giving it that quick look down you gave your phone when you had it out like that, seeing if a new text had come in the last five seconds or so.

Wyatt held up the phone now to Jake. “Calvin,” Wyatt said. “Wants to meet up in town later, hear all about UT.”

Then: “You were saying something about Coach McCoy?”

“Nothing important.”

With that, Wyatt stood up and said, “Might as well head in to town now, meet up with some of my guys.”

Meaning his old teammates at Granger. Like he was still captain of the team. Didn’t ask Jake if he wanted to come along; Jake didn’t expect him to. Jake never took it as mean or took offense, just saw it as Wyatt being Wyatt.

Libby Cullen said, “You just make sure you’re home in time for dinner, college man.”

“Wouldn’t miss it, Mama, been thinking about your home cooking since I woke up this morning.”

Wyatt gave Jake a pat on the head as he went by him, said he’d text him later when he knew where he was going to be, probably at the new Amy’s Ice Cream that had opened in Granger during the summer, trying to give Spooner’s a run for its money.

“Have Dad show you this pass I threw when he was watching us Thursday night. Coach said it was the best deep sideline he’d seen, no lie, since your boy Eli hit Mario Manningham the Super Bowl before last.”

Then he was gone.

Troy Cullen was already pointing his remote at the big screen, saying, "Man, did he ever get 'er done with that throw. Just gimme a second till I find the right place on the DVD I burned."

Jake said, "Love to."

He felt his dad looking at him then, turned and saw the funny look on his face. Jake realized as soon as he spoke that Troy Cullen hadn't heard him right.

"Well, hell, son, I love you, too," he said.

Jake had to sit there and watch more than just the throw Wyatt was talking about, had to watch and listen—mostly listen—as his dad broke down the last twenty or so plays of practice like he really was one of Wyatt's coaches.

"Good for you to see what it all looks like at the next level," his dad said, staring intently at the screen, like he was going to pick up on something he'd missed the other times he'd watched these same plays.

Jake thought to himself, *I can't handle the level I'm* at, *and he's already talking about the next one.*

"You *see,*" Troy Cullen said now, freezing the picture, showing him where all the downfield receivers were, all covered, then hitting Play again as Wyatt checked down to his tight end for a ten-yard gain. "See the feel your brother has for this game at nineteen, 'fore he ever takes a for-real snap in college football?"

"He's really something," Jake said.

When the film session was finally over, Jake went up to his room, got on his computer for a while before he got a text from Barrett telling him that he and Nate were on their way over. They wanted to go into town and just hang out.

Barrett arrived about fifteen minutes later, and the three of them were on their way into Granger, Jake telling his buds that Wyatt was home.

"Whoa," Barrett said. "Wyatt *Cullen*? You get to, like, talk to him?"

Barrett had never been Wyatt's biggest fan; neither had Nate. Neither one of them went too far making a thing out of it, mostly keeping it light, sarcastic comments about Wyatt being Mr. Perfect, in Jake's family and in Granger.

Jake said, "Let's not start in on my brother."

Barrett said, "Who thinks you're just one more person in this town's supposed to kiss the ground he walks on."

"C'mon, Bear," Jake said. "You grew up in our house almost as much as you did your own. You know Wyatt's not really like that. He's just got his own deal goin', is all."

"Whatever." Dropping it like he'd taken it as far as he wanted to. Or as far as Jake did.

When they got into town, Barrett parked the truck in front of RadioShack, saying he needed a new phone charger. Then the three of them walked around a bit. Most of the stores were closed on Sunday afternoon. They ended up walking past the hardware store and the feed store and Jake's Deli and Mo's Coffee Stop and Artie's Mobil Mart gas station and convenience store, which was always open, even on Thanksgiving and Christmas. They walked the four blocks of Granger's main downtown area and then crossed the street and came back, none of them in any hurry or needing to be anyplace, enjoying their day off from practice, nobody mentioning that school would be starting in the morning, the official end of summer, even though their summer had really ended the day practice had started.

"How's Wyatt doing with the 'Horns?" Nate said.

"You can ask him yourself, you want; he just texted me he's at Amy's already."

"Man, now that *is* good news from your brother. I've been thinking about Amy's since we got to town," Barrett said. "Tryin' to decide whether to get me a shake or a banana split."

"Why's it got to be either-or?" Nate asked.

As soon as they walked into the front room, they could see the big crowd in back, past the counter, bunch of tables pulled together, Wyatt right in the middle of it all, his back against the wall, holding court the way he used to at Stone's after another big win for Granger High.

A bunch of players were there, Jake saw, Calvin and Melvin and Casey Lindell and some guys from the defense. Wyatt was doing all of the talking, everybody laughing now at something he'd just said. Almost like high school still hadn't ended for Jake's big brother.

Or might never end, at least in all the good ways.

Barrett said, "You sure you want to do this?"

"You feel like we'll be joining the crowd," Nate said, "or the audience?"

"We'll just order our stuff and pull up a table of our own," Jake said. "We don't have to stay long."

Just as he said that, he took a better look at the table that had been pulled up to Wyatt's left, saw Sarah sitting there with two other cheerleaders, Sarah's hair pulled back into a ponytail.

Sarah looking at Wyatt the way Jake wanted her to look at him, just once.

She didn't see Jake at the counter because she wasn't seeing anything at Amy's except Jake's brother.

Jake turned around and started heading toward the door, saying, "You're right, Bear. Let's get out of here."

Nate said, "But we haven't even ordered yet."

Barrett said, "We can order when we get out to Spooner's." Then he leaned close to Jake and said, "I saw her, too."

Before the door closed behind them, they all heard one more burst of laughter from the back room, everybody happy as they could be that Wyatt was back in town, if only for a day.

Nobody looking happier about it than Sarah Rayburn.

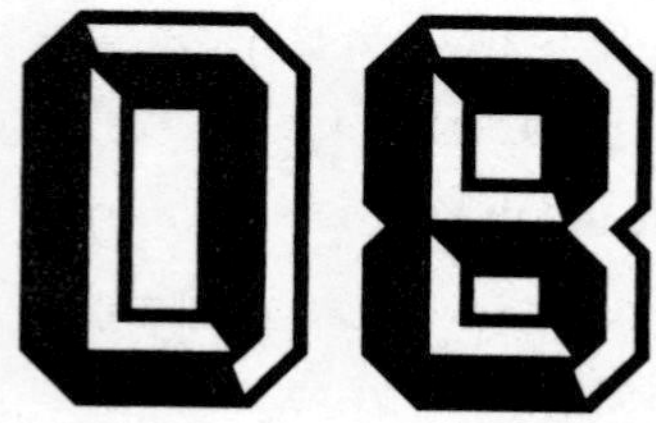

JAKE TRIED EVERY WAY HE COULD THINK OF TO GET HIS MOM to go to Austin with his dad for Texas's opener. But once she made up her mind, you had a better chance of turning around the Pecos River. So that was that, her decision final: She'd go to the Granger game at one at Cullen Field, and Troy Cullen would be in Austin watching Wyatt at three thirty, the big national TV game on ABC.

"Mom, you're not being logical, and you're usually the most logical person I know," Jake said the last time he went at her. "Wyatt is starting for the *Longhorns*. As a *freshman*. You don't want to miss his first college game."

"You make it sound like I'm missing Sunday services, Jacob."

It was Friday, just the two of them at breakfast, Troy Cullen not due back until that night from quarter-horse sales run by one of the most famous ranches in Texas, the 6666, known to everyone as the Four Sixes. Buying and selling horses for him was just another form of competition, one more thing he used to fill up the hole in his life that once held playing football.

"Mom," Jake said. "It would be one thing if I were going to play tomorrow. But I'm not."

"You don't know that."

"I've got a better chance of being hit by lightning," he said. "Go to Austin with Dad in the morning."

She smiled, what somebody else might have seen as a sweet mom smile, across the breakfast table. But Jake knew better, knew it was a game-ender.

"I can't imagine why we're still even talking about this," she said. "Now finish up your eggs before Barrett gets here."

"Did I ever have a chance?"

"Better chance of being hit by lightning, dear," she said, and started reading one of the morning newspapers on her iPad.

Friday's practice was just a walk-through, no pads, the way Coach John McCoy had always done it the day before a game, whether it was being played on Friday night or Saturday afternoon, this decade or the ones before it.

When they were finished, Coach Jessup came jogging over to Jake, told him to stick around for a few more minutes, there was some this-and-that he thought they could work on.

"Coach," Jake said, "you know I appreciate all the extra work y'all have been doing with me . . . but it's Friday night."

"Not yet, it's not," Coach said.

Jake realized he wasn't changing anybody's mind about anything today.

Every time Jake stayed after, it was something different. They'd moved on from Jake's throwing mechanics, which Coach J thought were getting better, looking more natural all the time.

Sometimes they wouldn't even work on the field, they'd go inside Coach J's tiny office, and he'd start drawing up plays on an old-timey black chalkboard. But then he'd stop about halfway through the play, have Jake go up to the board and finish it, showing what his progression was supposed to be if his primary guys were covered.

Coach J's big thing was that a quarterback's brain was as important as his arm.

"It's all about reactions," he'd said the day before. "Sometimes you got no choice, you got to react to what the defense is showin' you. But more often than that, you got to make them react to *you*." He'd nodded and said, "You know what the difference is between a win and a loss sometimes? Just freezing a 'backer or safety for one beat of their heart. Or yours."

Jake actually knew what he'd meant.

"I read somewhere where one of Peyton Manning's old coaches said the only language Peyton wanted to speak was *quarterback*. Like a musician thinking in theory or something."

Coach Jessup had slapped him on his back and said, "That's gonna be you, boy. You just don't know it yet." Grinned and said, "One of the many things you ain't figured out yet, and not just about football."

Today Coach promised they wouldn't be out here long. But he still had Jake help him bring out some of the super-sized orange traffic cones they'd use, ones that Coach J had written numbers on in Magic Markers, one through five—the usual number of available receivers Jake might have on a given play in Coach McCoy's spread offense.

Once they started, Coach J would have Jake turn his back, then he'd move the cones around to different points in the red zone. Jake would walk up to an imaginary line of scrimmage, call out a play, roll to his left or right, like he'd been flushed from the pocket, then Coach would yell out a number, his way of telling Jake to find a secondary receiver. Jake would do his best to find the cone and hit it with the ball, knowing Coach would blow his whistle if he took more than a second or two.

Now, Coach yelled, "Roy's covered . . . locate number one!"

Even here, with cones, number 1 was Calvin.

Jake rolled to his left, stopped, and threw a perfect spiral, clipping the tip of the cone in the right corner of the end zone.

"Look at you, Cullen! You're better with cones than with humans."

Not Coach J. It came from Calvin himself, standing there with Casey Lindell.

Coach Jessup heard him, too. Couldn't help it.

"Hey, Coach J?" Casey said. "How come I never get any tutoring?"

"On account of your already knowin' everything," Coach J said, grinning at him. "Or so you say."

"You bustin' on me?" Casey said.

"Never," Coach J said. "Care to join us?" When Casey didn't move, Coach J smiled and said to Jake, "Last one."

Coach J moved the cones around one last time, then Calvin and Casey watched as Jake dropped back, rolled to his left again, kept rolling, waiting for Coach Jessup to call out a number. Finally he yelled "One!" again, and Jake didn't hesitate, didn't come to a complete stop, didn't even square his shoulders, just flung the ball across his body to where the cone he wanted was, still in the right corner. Hit it square, knocking it over.

This time Calvin didn't say anything, just looked at Jake and nodded and pointed. Was still nodding as he and Casey walked off the field and into the tunnel.

Like maybe Jake had finally showed him what Nate Collins liked to call a little somethin'-somethin'.

Coach John McCoy, who never said much, didn't say much in the locker room before the opener against Shelby the next day.

"Just remember," he said, "you're lining up against the Shelby Mustangs today, not last year's Granger Cowboys."

They all nodded, some standing, some sitting on benches, Coach in the middle of them.

"So you boys go out there and make some memories for your own selves today," he said, then turned and walked out the door. Then this season's Granger Cowboys followed him, the way Cowboys players had been following John McCoy for the past thirty-five years.

They followed him out of the tunnel and into the sun, into the sound and force of high school football in their small Texas town, like the New Year in Granger, Texas, didn't start until they came out of that tunnel for their first game.

They were yelling as they came into the sun, but you couldn't hear them above the shouting from the stands, the first loud roar of the season for Cowboys football, as they ran past the cheerleaders—Jake saw Sarah at the end, on the left—and across the field.

The PA announcer's booming voice rose above the roar, welcoming "*your* Granger High School . . . *Cowboys*!"

Taking the last part of *Cowboys* and making it sound as if he was running all the way down the field with it.

Jake knew, from growing up in this town, from being related to the two greatest quarterbacks in Granger history, that this was the time of the year when the town was most alive. All the waiting for the opener, the waiting for football to be back on this field, was over.

So was all the wondering, at Stone's and Amy's and the filling stations and coffee shops and street corners, all the talk on the one radio station Granger had, about what this year's team would be like, how the 'Boys were gonna do this time. Whether they had a chance to get 'er done the way last year's team had.

They would start finding out today how the 'Boys would do without Wyatt Cullen standing back there in the pocket flinging the ball around, with Tim Mathers being the one throwing it to Calvin, with Nate anchoring the offensive line. All that, in what people had been speculating might be the great Coach John McCoy's final season.

Liza George, the girl with the prettiest voice in the church choir, sang the national anthem. Then the mayor officially presented Coach McCoy with the league championship trophy that would go in the case in the front hall of the school with all the others John McCoy had won.

Granger won the coin toss, elected to receive, and the ball was kicked off. It *was* football season again in Granger, the one played on the field from September through November, not the one talked about the rest of the year, as if the main business in town wasn't ranching or horses or cows, it was high school football.

Casey Lindell took his place next to Coach McCoy, and Jake was next to Coach Jessup, the coaches wanting both their quarterbacks right there, hearing what they were saying, understanding why they were sending in this play or that, even why they'd be making their substitutions.

So that was where Jake was standing when he saw Tim Mathers scramble to his right on the Cowboys' fourth play from scrimmage, saw him try to plant and make a cut when some field opened up past the linebacker right in front of him, saw Tim's cleats catch in the grass, saw the terrible angle of his left leg.

Saw him go down without being touched, grabbing his left knee with his free hand, and start screaming in pain in the sudden quiet of Cullen Field.

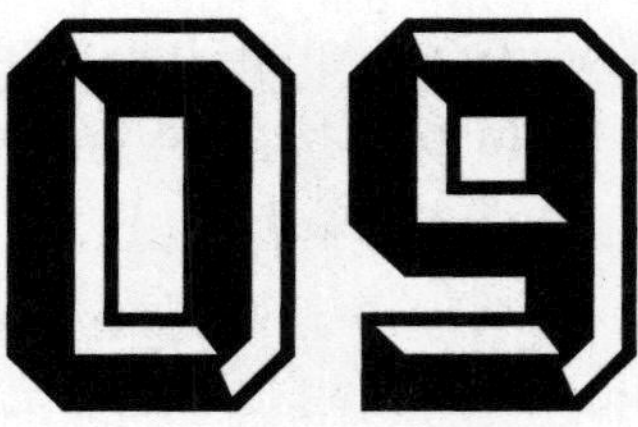

JAKE DIDN'T KNOW THEN THAT TIM'S ACL HAD EXPLODED ON him, nobody did. But he did know was that it was always real bad in sports when it wasn't a hit that put you down like that, put you in that kind of pain.

Dr. Mallozzi wasn't out there too long before he signaled for a stretcher. But Jake could see Tim shaking his head, saw Tim reach up to the teammates in a half circle around him for a little help, saw Nate pull Tim up all by himself. Then Tim put one arm around Nate's shoulders and his other around Dana Padgett, who played right guard next to Nate.

Slowly they made their way off the field. When they got to the sideline, Jake and Barrett took over for Nate and Dana, who had to get back into the game. The three of them began the long, slow, careful walk to the locker room as the fans at Cullen Field, even the fans who'd come over from Shelby, stood and applauded.

Casey Lindell was behind the bench, quickly taking some

warm-up throws, before Jake and Barrett and Tim Mathers were halfway to the tunnel.

Jake had asked Tim if he wanted to take off his helmet, but Tim said he'd keep his hat on till he was inside; it was the last time he was going to wear it at Granger High.

Tim said, "Shortest season on record."

"You'll be back."

"No," Tim said, "I won't." And Jake knew the hurt he was hearing, from the kid who'd played behind Wyatt Cullen and waited his turn, waited for this day, was about more than whatever he was feeling in his left knee.

Then Tim said to Jake, "You better hustle back once you get me inside."

"Why?"

"'Cause you just moved up in the line, that's why."

Jake knew what he meant. They both knew Jake was the backup quarterback now. But all Jake said was, "C'mon, man, I'm not thinking about me."

They were out of the sun and into the tunnel, the noise of the crowd in the distance now, like somebody had turned the sound on the day way down. Dr. Mallozzi was up ahead, waiting for them outside the locker room door, Doc having already told Tim they were going straight to the hospital so he could have machines take a look at the knee.

What had just happened back on field was just sports. It had happened fast, all right, because sports did that, too, everything changing with one bad cut. Sometimes that's all it took.

Just sports. Coach McCoy had told them to go out and start

making memories for themselves this afternoon. Just not a memory like this. But Tim's season had ended and the Cowboys' season had changed, all in less than ten minutes after it had begun.

Jake Cullen, like it or not, ready or not, wanting to talk about it or not, *had* just moved up in line.

It was already 7–0, Shelby, by the time Jake and Barrett were back on the Cowboys' sideline, Shelby lining up to kick the ball off, the Granger offense ready to go back on the field.

"I was only gone five minutes," Jake said to Nate. "What the heck happened?"

"Pick six is what happened," Nate said. "First pass was to Calvin, and the new guy never looked at anybody *'cept* Calvin, and that there was all she wrote."

Casey was standing next to Coach McCoy, shifting his weight from one leg to the other, like he couldn't wait to get back out there.

"It's early," Jake said. "We still got this."

"You sure about that?" Nate said. "Our backup quarterback seems to have lost some of his swag now that it's a real game on this field. Now that he's doing more than woofin' about who should be the starter."

Casey started to move the ball on the next series, hit Justice Blackmon with a nice throw over the middle for fifteen yards. But then on first down from just past midfield, Casey looking to his right at Calvin, Shelby blitzed an outside linebacker from his blind side. Jake wanted to yell out, warn him somehow, knowing Casey never saw the guy coming, but there was nothing to do except watch him get buried and cough up the ball, which the linebacker who'd just hit him recovered.

Three plays later, the Mustangs' halfback took a pitch, got to the outside so fast it was like he'd been shot over there, and ran all the way down the sideline for a score. The kick made it 14–0, Shelby. With six minutes left in the first quarter.

First game of the season.

As the Cowboys lined up to receive the kickoff, Jake saw Casey seated now, end of the bench, head down.

Jake went over to him.

"Plenty of game left," he said, crouching down next to Casey. "I don't think you've even taken six snaps yet."

Casey turned his head, looked at Jake. "I'm *good,*" he said, as if he suddenly needed to convince Jake of that. "You've seen me. You know I'm good. Only now the whole town, first time it gets to see me play, thinks I'm a choke artist."

"Nah," Jake said. He stood up and pulled Casey up. "It's like my grandpa says: They're all just sittin' there waitin' for the good parts."

"I don't need much time," Casey said. "But I need more than this."

"Hang in there," Jake said, trying to be a good teammate. "They'll give you more time, and you'll get to show off that gun you got."

But the problem with Casey, Jake was discovering, *was* that gun. Jake didn't know what it was like to be able to bring that kind of heat, believe you could throw the ball into any kind of coverage and get away with it. Casey managed to complete a couple on the next series, including one throw to Calvin into double-coverage, that reminded Jake of Casey's hero, Brett Favre.

But then, the very next play, Casey tried to force another one, and this time Calvin had to turn himself into a defensive back when the safety stepped in front of him. Calvin knocked the ball from the safety's hands or it would have been another pick six and 21–0 against Granger before the first quarter of the first game was over.

That's what the score was at halftime, though, the Cowboys down three scores because, in the last minute of the half, Shelby's version of Calvin—a kid almost as big and almost as fast as Calvin, named Michael Gilmore—beat Ollie Gray on a deep sideline route and ran away for what turned out to be an eighty-yard catch-and-run touchdown play.

As the Cowboys ran off the field after Casey's last pass of the half fell incomplete, Nate said to Jake, "We waited all summer for this, and now we come out and it's like we stepped in something."

"We'll play better in the second half," Jake said, knowing he was talking just to talk, not really believing what he was saying. He looked for Sarah in that moment, finally spotting her at the end of the line right before the tunnel, last cheerleader on the right.

Jake wondered if she even knew what his number was. Even if it was the number 10 that the sons of Troy Cullen were born to wear at Granger High.

"Can't get worse than this," Nate said.

"No way," Jake said.

They were both wrong. It was 28–0, Shelby, before the Cowboys—who hadn't lost a regular-season game since Wyatt Cullen's junior year—got on the board, set up when Melvin Braxton returned a punt all the way to the Shelby twenty. Casey followed with a bullet to Roy Gilley on first down to the ten. Then he threw one even harder to Calvin on a slant, Calvin getting popped good at the two, but managing to hold on to the ball. Spence Tolar ran it in from there, and the Granger Cowboys were on the board at last.

The Cowboys started moving the ball after that with some consistency. Casey aired it out on nearly every down, making a throw or two every series that you had to see to believe. But then he would turn around and make decisions you absolutely *couldn't* believe, the way Favre used to even in the best of times, flinging the ball around in a boneheaded way as if he thought his arm could beat any defender and any defense. He finally threw another interception when it looked like the Cowboys were driving for their second score of the game. His eyes locked on Justice this time, not even seeing an outside linebacker who drifted back into coverage. The kid picked the ball off and returned it all the way to the Shelby forty-eight.

But the Cowboys' defense held the Mustangs, keeping the score where it was, and forcing a punt. Melvin fair-caught the ball at his own twelve.

Two things happened then, one right after the other.

First, Jake saw Coach McCoy put a hand on Casey's arm as Casey started to run back on the field with the rest of the offense, saw Coach talking to him, saw Casey say something back, saw Coach shaking his head no, patting him on the back and walking away.

That was when Jake felt a hand on his own shoulder, turned around, and saw Coach Ray Jessup grinning at him.

"Okay," he said. "Let's see what you got."

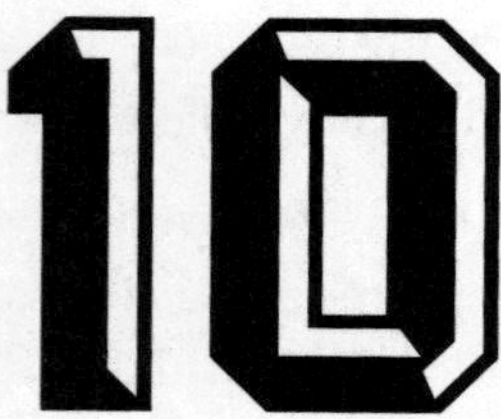

"BEFORE YOU DO," COACH JESSUP SAID, "YOU MIGHT WANT TO fasten your helmet strap."

Jake did.

"Hand it to Spence on first down, then go with a tight end slant to Roy on second. Then throw that little thing we call a step-back screen to Calvin after that." Coach shrugged. "We'll worry about what comes next if it's still our ball at that point. We good?"

"Gonna try," Jake said.

"I know you got the head for this," Coach J said. "Now go show me you got the game. 'Cause once you get out there, you're not a freshman. Just a QB."

Jake nodded and ran out on the field as the quarterback of the Granger Cowboys, if only for these few mop-up minutes at the end of a blowout game. But somehow the day had brought him here, like some crazy ride on a horse one of their wranglers was trying to break.

And Jake couldn't help it as he ran out there: He gave a quick look over his shoulder, like he was giving one last look to the sideline for instructions. But really looking past his coaches and teammates to where he knew his mom was, knowing the seat next to her, the one that always belonged to his dad, was empty this afternoon.

He found her easily enough. Everybody around her was sitting down, no reason to stand and cheer for the Cowboys right now. His mom, though, she was standing, staring right at him, nodding her head. Like she was telling him, from up there in the stands, that he could do this.

Now Jake was glad she had come, glad she was here to see this, not knowing how long this would last, not knowing if he'd be out here again anytime soon.

Glad that she was here, but wishing in that moment that his dad was with her.

Act like you belong.

If there was one thing his dad had drummed into his two boys' heads from the time they'd understood the things he was saying to them about life and football—and ranching and horses and bulls and just about everything else under the sun—it was *Act like you belong.* Like it was the Eleventh Commandment.

Even if you weren't sure you belonged somewhere, act like you did.

He got into the huddle, everybody looking at him, Jake trying not to look scared. He told his teammates the three plays he'd brought with him from Coach J, clapped his hands, and told them all the snap count. Wanting to get on with it. Grabbed Nate on the way to the line and said, "Don't let me drop the snap."

"Better chance of me droppin' my pants in front of everybody," Nate said.

Jake managed to handle Nate's snap cleanly, but then nearly made a mess of the handoff to Spence, rushing it, wanting to get on with that, too, putting too much air between them. Spence saved him, though, collected the ball, gained four, running right behind Nate Collins's big ol' butt.

They lined up quickly. Jake straightened up, saw Roy Gilley open on a slant route, but threw the ball behind him, incomplete. Third-and-six. Calvin and Justice were switching sides. As Calvin ran past Jake he said, "Get me the rock, I'll do the rest."

They went to a quick count this time, Jake took a one-step drop, ready to gun it over to Calvin in the left flat. Keep it simple. But the same cornerback who'd been giving Casey fits all day, who'd been reading him like he'd been in the huddle with Casey and the rest of the Cowboys, was just sitting there, ready to step in on Calvin the way he'd been doing all game long.

Jake managed to pull the ball down at the last second, making it look like the showiest pump fake anybody'd ever seen at Cullen Field. Then he just took off, the way those hotshot young quarterbacks in the pros did all the time now. Colin Kaepernick. Russell Wilson. RG III. Took off the way Johnny Football Manziel did on his way to winning the Heisman trophy as a freshman over at Texas A&M, ran down the sideline to the thirty-yard line. Even tightroped the last few yards the way Johnny Football did sometimes. Finally got bounced out of bounds.

First down.

Yee boy, Jake thought. He was in the game. Not with any chance to win it. Just trying to show he belonged. David Stevens, their other halfback, came running in to replace Spence, told Jake the next three plays, the first a curl route to Roy Gilley.

But Jake overthrew Roy, the ball nearly sailing all the way into the arms of a safety. He then missed Calvin on second down, the ball too low, Calvin giving Jake a look on his way back to the huddle.

Third-and-ten.

This one was a crossing pattern with Calvin and Justice, Justice being the primary receiver. Jake led him perfectly, Justice gathered the ball in, and ran all the way to midfield before getting knocked out of bounds again, stopping the clock.

Jake was aware of the crowd then, louder than it had been since the first few minutes of the game, before everything had started to go wrong, starting with Tim Mathers's knee.

The crowd was cheering the completion to Justice.

But cheering Jake, too.

From there the Cowboys moved to the Shelby nineteen, finally out of time-outs. First down, twenty seconds left. Maybe three plays left if they were lucky. A chance to get one score and at least walk away from this game feeling like they had done *some*thing today besides just show up.

The coaches sent in a play for Calvin, a quick inside move and then a fade route to the right corner. Jake dropped back, surprised in this moment how calm he was, how comfortable he felt, ball in his hands.

Not trying to win a state title, maybe just some respect. Or maybe just trying to prove something to himself.

The line gave Jake plenty of time, the way they had been, but Calvin Morton was smothered. There was a cornerback in front of him and a safety behind him. Jake could try to force it, let Calvin go up and try to make one of his hero catches. But if he missed, short or long, and Calvin couldn't save him, then the day was going to end with one more interception from another Granger quarterback trying to squeeze one in to Calvin.

Jake saw Roy Gilley in the middle of the end zone. But he was covered, too, by the middle linebacker. So Jake just threw the ball over his head and through the goalposts, not wanting to risk a scramble, knowing if he didn't make the sideline, the game was over. At least this way, the team lived to see another play.

Ten seconds left.

In the huddle, Calvin said, "You did right, throwing it away."

"Thanks."

"You want to thank me?" Calvin said. "Throw me the rock on this one."

But the coaches had seen what Jake and everybody else had seen, that Shelby was going to double-cover Calvin all the way to the locker room. When Spence brought in the second-down play, it wasn't for Jake to throw Calvin the rock; it was what they called tight cross, Roy running for the left corner, Justice coming in behind him, running into the area in front of the goalposts that Roy had just cleared out.

That was the way it was supposed to work, anyway.

As they broke the huddle, Nate said, "I feel like we're tryin' to win the game."

"Way we're supposed to feel, big man," Jake said. "We play all sixty around here."

But Shelby was playing all sixty, too. So the Mustangs came with an all-out blitz now, both outside linebackers, the strong safety, blowing through the Cowboys' offensive line, on Jake almost as soon as he had the ball.

He felt the pocket—what there was of a pocket, anyway—collapsing on him, felt somebody with a fistful of his jersey pulling him down. But the defenseman was finding out now that, as skinny as he was, Jake Cullen was a hard man to bring down, the "tough out" Coach Jessup was always telling him he was.

He stumbled slightly before escaping the pocket, like he'd somehow found a side door to get himself free. Knowing this was the last play of the game now, score or not. Saw Justice breaking his pattern, running toward the corner where Roy was, waving his arms.

Too much traffic over there now.

Jake kept running to his left, starting to run out of field.

But the quarterback in him—or maybe the Cullen in him—realized in that moment that if there was all that traffic in front of Roy and Justice, *and* all those guys blitzing him, Calvin Morton was somewhere to his right. With only one guy on him.

Like one of Coach J's orange cones waiting to be hit.

Jake, still being chased, almost to the sideline, had time to give one look over there, saw a white uniform that could only be number 1. He didn't even have time to plant his foot, didn't need to, before throwing on the dead run. He flung the ball across his body in Calvin's direction, right before getting buried by the Shelby defense.

Jake's helmet would end up sideways on his head; that was the picture that would be in the paper the next day, a big chunk of grass sticking out of his face mask.

His right shoulder pad was outside his jersey when he finally got up. By then the noise inside Cullen Field told him it was a touchdown. A lot had changed in this place since last fall, starting with the final score. But at least this was an ending people could understand and take away with them so they didn't think the day was a total loss.

Cullen to Morton for a touchdown.

11

CALVIN HAD THE GOOD SENSE NOT TO CELEBRATE AND TURN the end zone into a dance floor, not at the end of a beatdown like this.

What he did instead was ran over to where Jake was still kneeling, extend a hand and help him up. "Maybe you got more rope to you than I thought." Then walked away before Jake could say anything.

The players on both teams were milling around on the field now, even the big guys like Nate who'd been banging one another around all day hugging it out, some laughing, like they'd turned back into high school boys now that the game was over, no matter how much they looked like men. It was all a part of it, what happened on these fields, something you all had shared.

The Shelby quarterback, Cody Bretton, came over to Jake and said, "We're lucky they didn't put you in sooner."

"You guys were better," Jake said.

"You really Wyatt Cullen's brother?" Cody asked, making it

sound like he wanted to know if Jake was related to the Lord himself. "Like Eli following Peyton?"

"I *wish*," Jake said.

Finally it was time to leave the field, get back to the locker room, listen to what Coach McCoy had to say about the game, find out if there was any news about Tim's knee, then hustle back home with Bear and Nate to watch the Texas game that had already begun in Austin, watch the star freshman quarterback in the family do it up big in front of the whole country.

Jake looked around for Bear and Nate, saw them up ahead of him, nearly to the tunnel, at the front of a long parade of Granger Cowboys, a lot of them with their heads down, everything so much quieter now than it had been when they ran out of that tunnel a couple of hours before.

Some of them had their helmets in their hands, what Coach McCoy called their hats. Same hats that had just been handed to them, big-time, by the Shelby Mustangs.

It was then that Jake saw Casey Lindell, helmet in his own right hand, walking underneath the goalposts with Sarah.

The two of them walking close, Casey casually reaching around with his left hand and putting it around her shoulder.

Wyatt struggled for Texas in the first half, looked more nervous than Jake had ever seen him, throwing two early picks. One play he just flat missed a perfect snap when he was standing back in the shotgun. By halftime he had completed only five of his first seventeen passes, none for scores, Texas down 17–7 to Washington, the announcers talking about the high school hero from Granger acting his age.

It was 24–14 for Washington going into the fourth quarter. And that was when Wyatt Cullen turned into, well, Wyatt Cullen, starting the Longhorns comeback by going six-for-six on the eighty-yard drive that got his team back to 24–21.

The drive that won it started at the Texas forty with four minutes and change left and ended with ninety seconds left, Wyatt throwing a dead-solid perfect strike to his tight end over the middle, putting the 'Horns up 28–24. That's the way it ended after what looked like the whole defensive backfield knocked down the Hail Mary pass the Washington quarterback managed to launch into the end zone on the last play of the game.

A TV reporter interviewed Wyatt on the field when it was over, Wyatt as cool and calm as if he'd been practicing up for this moment the way he'd been practicing up to be a college quarterback.

When the great-looking reporter—not much older than Wyatt himself—asked what it felt like to take the Longhorns down the field like that, bring them from behind to win his first college game, Wyatt grinned at her and said, "My daddy told me before the game he wanted to see if the boy could become the man today." He gave her that aw-shucks look of his and added, "Guess I took that first step."

The sideline girl looked in that moment like she wanted to kiss Jake's brother right there on TV.

It was just Jake and his mom watching now, Bear and Nate having left.

"Well," Libby Cullen said, "quite a day for both my boys."

"Mom, are you *serious*?" Jake said. "You, like, *get* what Wyatt just did, right, winning his first game like that? On national TV?"

"You won something today, too, Jacob."

"And what would that be?"

"The respect of your teammates. Making them see you belonged out there in a varsity game."

"That game was over by the time I got in there."

"If it was already over, why was Shelby still blitzing you?" she said, winking at him, letting him know she had been paying attention, delivering the knockout punch again.

She said she was going upstairs, saying she'd try to stay awake until Jake's dad got home from Austin.

Jake was watching the end of the Saturday night game on ESPN, LSU against Auburn, when his dad came through the front door. The trip from Austin, Jake knew, took three hours for a normal driver, which Troy Cullen was not. He liked to brag to his sons that he could make it in two if Jesus was willing and enough state troopers knew the plates on his Lincoln Navigator by now.

Jake thought that most troopers in this part of the state had a pretty solid chance of recognizing those plates, since they read "CULLENQB-1".

It was the way Troy still thought of himself. As a dad, sure, went without saying. Husband. Rancher. Son.

But a QB most of all.

"Jake, where you at, boy?"

Filling the front hall and maybe the whole house with his big voice.

Jake came out of his dad's den, their game-watching room, a screen in there so huge that Troy Cullen joked that it belonged hanging from the roof in Cowboys Stadium. He gave his dad a hug, his dad already getting right to it, even before he had his arms around his youngest son.

"Did your big brother make the family proud today or what?" Troy Cullen said.

"Always does," Jake said.

"All he did was take the damn Texas Longhorns down that field at the end like he was beatin' on a bunch of pissant *high school* boys."

"Wyatt bein' Wyatt," Jake said.

"Some boys get small as jockeys when the lights get turned up. Your brother, he plays bigger."

"Must get that from his daddy," Libby Cullen said on her way down the stairs.

"Oh, sweetie, did I wake you?"

"Me and Oklahoma and parts of Louisiana," she said, getting to the bottom of the stairs, getting up on tiptoes to kiss her husband on the cheek. "By the way? Your other son had a pretty good day himself for Granger High."

"And I want to hear all about it. But for now I got to get my boots off and start begging my beautiful wife to get me some of her special iced tea."

She headed off to the kitchen, and Jake and his dad went into the den, Jake grabbing the remote and muting LSU-Auburn, seeing how full of Wyatt's day his dad was, like the game had just ended, knowing he was going to want to go over it, big play by big play, hoping he wasn't going to ask Jake to crank it up on TiVo.

He was about halfway through the winning drive when Libby Cullen came in with a pitcher of iced tea and the sandwiches she knew her husband wanted without his having to ask.

"Jacob ended his game with a touchdown pass," she said. "Did he tell you that? Threw one to Calvin."

"That so? What was the final score?" Troy said.

Jake told him, and Troy Cullen grinned and said, "You know what ol' Ricky Bobby says in *Talladega Nights,* right?"

Jake knew this one the way he knew the way to school. "If you're not first, you're last."

"Least you got on the field," Jake's dad said.

"It was pretty cool, not gonna lie."

Troy Cullen drank some iced tea, smacked his lips, and said, "You know what was *really* cool? That scramble your brother made before the touchdown pass won it for the 'Horns, starin' fourth down square in the eye if he doesn't get the first down, findin' a way to get to the sticks."

What Jake wanted to say:

How 'bout breaking free somehow after somebody has a whole fistful of your jersey, not going down when most quarterbacks—maybe even Wyatt—would have, getting loose, then throwing one across your body that felt like it traveled halfway 'cross the ranch and somehow hitting Calvin for a score?

How about that?

But he didn't.

Because he knew his place on the Cullen family depth chart the way he did at Granger High.

"All about making plays," Jake said. "Like you always tell us."

Libby Cullen said, "Tell your dad about the one you made," and gave her husband a look as she did that told him to hush now and listen.

Jake took him through it, fast as he could, feeling like he was reciting something in front of the class, saying he knew Calvin had to have single coverage somewhere over there, letting it go, getting his helmet knocked sideways on him, hearing from the crowd that he'd completed it.

"How about that. Ain't nothing better than hearing it from the crowd. Speaking of which, you haven't *heard* a crowd till you hear it roar in Austin. Your brother had the whole stadium shaking today."

Jake heard his mom sigh even though he knew his dad didn't, and grinned at his mom as he said, "I'm sure Wyatt's got 'em all eating out of the palm of his hand."

Libby Cullen left them to football then, saying she'd had her share today.

"Yee boy!" his father said, slapping his forehead. "Speaking of which, guess what your brother's already gone and did at *the* U of T."

"What's he gone and did?"

"Gone and got hisself fixed up with the prettiest cheerleader on the squad, is all," Troy Cullen said. "And an *older* cheerleader at that. Last thing I saw before I went to the parking lot was Wyatt and Miss Mindy walkin' hand in hand away from the stadium."

Troy Cullen nodded, smiling at the image, talking as much to himself as Jake as he said, "Wasn't a cheerleader born yet who doesn't want to date the quarterback of the football team."

A few minutes later, he was snoring.

Jake left him there, left the television on, went upstairs to his room, thinking nobody on Shelby had hit him harder than his own dad just had.

12

"THIS IS AN OLD-FASHIONED QUARTERBACK CONTROVERSY, IS what it is," Bear said on the way to school Monday. "Plain and simple. If you can't see that, you just don't want to."

"Really," Jake said.

"Just callin' it out for what it is," Bear said.

"An old-fashioned quarterback controversy," Jake said, making his voice announcer-deep. "You sound like you're practicing to sit around on one of those pregame shows where they all crack each other up."

"I wouldn't last on those shows, I don't laugh at everything," Bear said. "And you can treat this like it's funny all you want, but you didn't play like a backup when you got out there on Saturday."

"Doesn't change the fact that I *am* a backup," Jake said. "And that Casey, no matter how much you don't like his attitude sometimes, has the arm to back up his swag."

"Yeah, he does. Takes more than swag to be a quarterback, though," Bear said.

"I could work out with Coach J from now till the end of time and never have an arm like Casey's," Jake said.

"Joe Montana didn't have the world's greatest arm," Bear said. Bear knew his football and his football history. "Even Tom Brady doesn't have the arm a guy like Casey's hero, Brett Favre, did. But last time I checked, Brady had three Super Bowls and Favre had retired with but one. And even you know that Brady started out as a backup his rookie year with the Patriots, 'fore he ended up winning the Super Bowl."

"Now I'm Tom Brady?" Jake said. "From one touchdown?"

"Didn't say that," Bear said. "I just keep tellin' you: You didn't look like no backup to me."

Coach McCoy didn't treat Jake like one at Monday's practice.

And he sure didn't treat Casey Lindell as his number one. What he did was divide the first-team snaps evenly between Casey and Jake. No announcement beforehand.

Halfway through practice, it was clear that he didn't *need* to say anything, about an official quarterback competition with the Granger Cowboys or anything else. There it was on the practice field, for all of them to see. He was treating his two quarterbacks like they were equals. They knew it, everybody on the team knew it.

During a water break, Jake kneeling with Bear and Nate, Bear said to him, "Yeah, you were right on the way to school, you're still a backup."

As they were walking back to the field, Coach Jessup, acting casual, walked alongside Jake and said, "I'm just gonna say this to you one time, son. It ain't against the law for you to want this."

Jake said in a low voice, "I just don't want this to work itself into something where it divides up our team."

"Not your concern," Coach Jessup said. "You either want to compete or you don't. And by the way, though I might be out of line for saying this, this ain't your family."

"I don't know what you mean by that."

"I *mean,*" Coach J said, "you don't have to take a backseat on account of that's where you think you're supposed to be sitting."

He left it at that, walked away, blew his whistle, told the first-team offense they were about to work in the red zone.

"Casey'll get the first set of snaps," Coach J said, "then Jake. Like we've been doing."

While Coach McCoy was setting his defense, Casey Lindell got next to Jake and said, "I don't know what's going on here today. But I'm not giving up this job."

Loud enough for only Jake to hear.

Jake said, "I'm just doing what Coach tells me, is all."

Jake started to walk away then, not wanting this to turn into something real stupid, real fast, in front of the whole team.

But Casey reached out, grabbed his arm. "I just want you to know where I'm coming from," he said. "I wouldn't have been a backup if we hadn't moved, and I'm not gonna back up a freshman here."

Maybe it was seeing him with Sarah, maybe it was Casey's tone of voice. Whatever it was, Jake decided in that moment he'd heard enough. He tipped back his helmet, looked Casey square in the eyes, and said, "It's yours if you earn it. Same as it's mine if *I* earn it."

Jake made sure to smile, in case anybody was watching them. But before he tipped his helmet back down, he said, "And Casey? Don't ever put your hand on me again."

Showing him some rope right there, surprising himself, almost as if the words had come out of somebody else's mouth.

Jake didn't wait for a response, just walked away for real this time, feeling good about himself, wondering if maybe this was some new Jake Cullen, one who didn't just automatically take a backseat, certainly not to this guy.

A Jake Cullen who did want the starting job.

Bad.

It wasn't a game of one-on-one Jake and Casey played the rest of practice. This wasn't basketball. It was football, Granger High football, Casey showing what he could do with the first team, then Jake getting his chance to do the same.

There were no numbers on the scoreboard, but Jake knew everybody on this field, players and coaches, was keeping score.

It was on now between Jake and Casey, all the players on the field knowing that this quarterback competition wasn't happening if Coach John McCoy, the man, the legend, didn't want it to happen.

Wasn't *making* it happen.

Jake had always heard, starting when he heard it from his own daddy, that in football if you had two number one quarterbacks, you had no number two quarterback. Jake had heard it from Troy Cullen all over again when the Jets went and traded for Tim

Tebow and said they were guaranteeing him a bunch of snaps every single game, way before that idea blew up on the Jets.

"You know why that won't work?" Troy Cullen said to Jake and Wyatt at the time. "Because it ain't *never* worked, that's why."

Jake wasn't sure why it was playing out this way. And it wasn't like he expected Coach McCoy to explain himself, because he hardly ever did, on the play he wanted you to run or the defense he wanted to be in or anything else. Bottom line, as far as Jake was concerned? If this was Coach McCoy's last season, if this was it for him after all he'd done and all he'd won at Granger High, he wasn't declaring the quarterback job wide open because he thought it was going to *hurt* his football team.

And for this one practice, it actually seemed to help everybody on the field, starting with Jake and Casey, who managed to raise their own games, along with everybody else's. Sometimes Coach McCoy or Coach Jessup would even call the exact same string of plays for both of them. Like this was a game of H-O-R-S-E on a football field.

Jake wasn't sure how many passes he completed compared to Casey. At the end of practice, he figured they'd both put the ball in the end zone the same number of times. And both had looked real good.

Two number ones, at least on this day.

As they were walking toward the tunnel, Jake saw Casey jog to catch up with Calvin and Justice and Roy, the three best receivers on the team, high-fiving each one of them, saying in a loud voice, "Was that fun today or what?"

Like he wasn't just competing for the job, like he was running for it, the way you did for class president.

Like he was ready to compete with Jake off the field as well as on it.

Jake just let him go, waiting until he was inside the locker room. Then instead of going to the locker room himself, he went looking for Coach Jessup, knowing he'd be in his small office next to the equipment room.

"You can't possibly want to go back out there today," Coach J said when he looked up and saw Jake standing in his doorway, still in uniform, helmet in his hand.

"Nope," Jake said. "I want to stay right here."

"And do what?"

"Look at film," he said.

"Of what?"

"Of Benton."

Their next opponent.

"You haven't even showered yet," Coach J said. "You're tellin' me you want to look at game film *now*?"

"What I want to do," Jake said, "is *learn*."

13

AS BAD AS IT HAD BEEN SEEING CASEY AND SARAH WALK OFF Cullen Field together, it was worse seeing them hang around at school. Every day now in the cafeteria at lunch. Walking away from practice together.

You didn't have to be some kind of rocket scientist to figure it out, even if Casey hadn't been in town all that long. He was a year older than she was, he was a quarterback, she was the prettiest girl in school. Why wouldn't they want to hang out together?

Jake would have lost respect for the guy if he *wasn't* trying to be with Sarah Rayburn.

"I've got a better chance to beat him out at quarterback than beat him out with Sarah," Jake was saying Friday at lunch.

"Didn't Wyatt always end up with the pretty girls?" Nate said.

"He was Wyatt," Jake said. "I'm me."

"Wasn't he a freshman once?" Bear said.

Jake smiled. "No, I don't think he ever actually was."

"Don't worry," Nate said. "Sarah's too smart not to see through this guy."

"And way too cool," Bear said.

Casey and Sarah were three tables away, Sarah with two of her cheerleader friends on her side of the table, Casey with Dicky Grider, the team's left guard, and Roy Gilley on the other side. Every few minutes, Casey would laugh at something so loudly that nobody in the room could miss where he was sitting, who he was sitting with.

"What she's not, though," Nate said, "is that funny."

Bear said, "Nobody is."

"Maybe," Jake said, "she just likes him. That ever occur to you two geniuses?"

They both looked at him, slowly shook their heads no.

Coach McCoy finally shared his thoughts about his quarterback situation with Jake before the start of Friday's practice, the day before they'd make the short bus ride to Benton for the second game of their season.

"I'm gonna tell you what I told Casey just a few minutes ago," Coach said. "He's gonna start tomorrow, but I'm gonna get you out there in the first half, too. Then we'll just take it from there."

"Yes, sir," Jake said.

"You both have shown me enough, in different ways," Coach said. "Now I want to see more. The rest is pretty much up to the two of you."

Jake, heart beating pretty good, walked over to get himself a drink of water. He turned around and saw Calvin walking toward him.

"It true what Casey just told me?" Calvin said. "I got both of you throwin' me the ball in Benton?"

"Seems like."

He tried to keep his voice low, hoping Calvin would take the hint and do the same.

"I know Coach thinks he'll be the one decides which one of you gets the job eventually," Calvin said. "But if you think about it logically, it'll probably be me. Coach deciding which one of you can keep *me* happy."

Jake felt the smile coming, he couldn't help it; he just got a kick out of Calvin. He annoyed him sometimes, no lie, and you had to get through that act of his, and sometimes that was *real* hard. But Jake tried to take people as he got them, and what he got from Calvin was somebody who wanted to do well. Didn't always care whether you liked him or not, but in the end Calvin was all about winning the game.

Far as Jake could tell, nobody on their team wanted to win more.

"Calvin," Jake said, "you know I'm not the one decides to call your number, right, that Coach McCoy and Coach J call the plays?"

Now Calvin smiled.

"Just make sure you do right when they *do* call my number tomorrow, cowboy."

He started a slow, cool run toward where their teammates were collecting at midfield, then stopped and came back, the way he came back for an underthrown ball sometimes.

"Funny how stuff works out, though. Casey thinks he's the one ought to be the next Wyatt Cullen in Granger, not Wyatt's little brother."

14

COACH MCCOY SENT JAKE INTO THE BENTON GAME TWO minutes into the second quarter, the score 7–7.

The Benton Panthers had scored on the first drive of the game, taking the opening kickoff and going seventy yards, mostly running the ball. But Casey and the Cowboys' offense had answered right back, a fast four-play drive of their own, all passes, the last for thirty yards, Casey to Justice for the score.

Casey ran as fast as Jake had ever seen him getting to the end zone to celebrate with Justice, even banging helmets with him.

"That's gotta hurt," Jake had said to Bear on the sideline.

"I know everybody's worried about concussions and all in football these days," Bear said, "but I'm thinkin' Casey's head is too daggone hard for him to have to worry."

Both offenses came to a dead stop after that, though, neither one coming close to scoring. Casey had overthrown his receivers a few times and taken a sack that seemed to leave him rattled. He yelled at his offensive line to hold their blocks better and then forced a throw to Calvin into double coverage that was intercepted by the opposing team's safety. After watching Casey rip off his helmet in disgust, Coach McCoy said something to Coach J, who turned to Jake. "Start loosening up. You're going in next series."

By the time Jake's arm was ready, the Panthers were lined up to punt the ball. Coach J grabbed him before he ran out with the offense and said, "You always hear the one about 'let the game come to you.' I was never one for that. Go out there and take it."

"Gonna try," Jake said.

When Jake got to the huddle, Nate tipped back his helmet and said, "Let's get this party started."

Jake told them the first play, a quick out to Justice. He thought he'd be more nervous, but he wasn't, maybe because he'd played last week, maybe because he had that good week of practice under his belt and had been told he was going to play.

Or maybe this *was* the Cullen in him, not being afraid once somebody turned up the lights, like his dad said. His dad who was here today, up in the stands with Jake's mom, the Texas Longhorns having the week off.

Jake dropped back, remembered to look to his left at Calvin, knowing that was a way to lure the safety over there, turned back to his right, and hit Justice one stride before he reached the sideline.

First down.

Jake heard a cheer from the Granger side of the field at Benton High, and while he waited for Spence Tolar to bring in the next play, Jake couldn't help himself from thinking that his dad had just seen him complete a varsity pass.

Jake didn't know how many other games Troy Cullen would see him play this season, knew Wyatt would win out every time there was a conflict. Obviously. But his dad was here today, watching Jake today, and that felt good.

The rest of the Cowboys seemed to be feeling good all of a sudden, too. After back-to-back runs produced a first down, Jake ran a play-action pass, faking the handoff to Spence before threading a dead spiral to Calvin, who sprinted for a twenty-two-yard gain.

Jake then scrambled for twelve more yards, a run that included him putting a stiff-arm on one of the Benton linebackers, putting the guy down, shocking him.

The Panthers defense suddenly looked off-balance, not knowing what to expect, and the Cowboys quickly took advantage. They ran a crossing pattern that left Calvin wide open. Jake slid from the pocket and hit Calvin in stride. Touchdown. It might not have been the prettiest spiral ever, but the ball was going where Jake wanted it to.

Jake waited for Calvin, not acting like a cheerleader the way Casey had after throwing for his score, just putting out his hand so Calvin could shake it.

Calvin said, "You're my favorite."

"For now," Jake said.

"Duh," Calvin said.

When Jake got to the sideline, Bear said, "We havin' any fun yet?"

Coach Jessup was there, too.

"Next time we run that play, remember that you coulda had Justice, too. The defense'll be shading on Calvin all day," he said.

"I know," Jake said.

He got two more series before halftime. The first one, the Cowboys made three first downs and got to the Panthers' forty before even Calvin Morton, with those big hands, couldn't handle the dead spiral Jake threw him over the middle, a third-down pass that would have gotten them a first. The Cowboys punted instead, pinning the Panthers inside their ten.

The next time, Jake moved them down the field in a hurry-up offense, trying to beat the clock, the Cowboys out of time-outs. He worked the sideline with short passes, taking his team all the way to the Benton twenty-one with three seconds left. Jake wanted to take a shot at the end zone, but Coach McCoy sent out the field goal team instead. Bobby Torres, one of their backup tight ends, a big boy with a big leg on him, pushed a thirty-eight-yarder wide right. They went to the small visitors' locker room, not even half the size of their own at Cullen Field, still ahead 14–7, Jake feeling they'd left way too many points out there.

"Coach has to leave you in," Nate said, the two of them squeezed on a bench, Nate's voice no more than a whisper. "You moved the ball every time."

"Hush," Jake said.

"This *is* hushing," Nate said.

Jake took his own voice way down, said to Nate, "Casey moved us pretty good that first drive, if you care to recall."

Coach McCoy came into the room then, told them about the defensive adjustments they were going to make, Jake thinking that Coach used so few words, just about everything he said could stay under the 140 characters for tweets on Twitter.

As if using too many words with him was like the penalty you got for too many players on the field.

At the end he said, "On offense we start the same eleven started the game."

Walked out. The Cowboys followed. As they crossed the running track around the perimeter of the field, Bear said to Jake, "You okay with this?"

"Do I have a choice?" Jake said. "Or do you want me to hold my breath till Coach puts me back in?"

The Cowboys would end up with three possessions in the third quarter, scoring twice, Jake watching them do it from the sideline, seeing what everybody in the place could see, plain as day: how much talent Casey Lindell had for football. And how the only thing that seemed to get in his way sometimes, more than the defense, was his ego.

He'd never just throw the ball away, no matter how good the coverage was. And if he even felt like a sack was coming, saw a pocket about to swallow him up, he'd put the ball up for grabs, throwing it as far as he could sometimes, just hoping Calvin or Justice would find a way to run under it.

But the boy did have an arm on him, no doubt, and was using it today. He made some throws that Jake just *wished* he could make. One of those throws finished off the first scoring drive of the second half, an amazing pass to Roy Gilley, Casey about to go down, somehow seeing Roy behind a linebacker and hitting him with a dead spiral off his back foot. The ball traveled thirty yards in the air, and Roy caught it in stride at the ten and ran in from there.

He finished off the second scoring drive with a post route to

Calvin, who Jake figured had ten catches already. Casey threw the ball so hard, Jake was surprised it didn't make a sound like some police siren.

That second score made it 28–21, Granger. The Panthers had made some halftime adjustments, as well, and had scored a couple of touchdowns of their own, including an eighty-yarder when Melvin flat fell down in coverage.

What had felt at halftime as a defensive contest had turned into a scoring fest.

On the sideline, Nate said to Jake, "I'm starting to feel like I'm watching a flag football game."

"You joking?" Jake said. "They D up way more than this in flag."

The Panthers finally D'ed themselves up good at the start of the fourth quarter, Casey still in there. He tried to stuff a throw into Calvin even though they were doubling Calvin on every play now. The throw was too hard and too high, and the ball went off Calvin's hands and into the hands of one of the Benton safeties.

It turned into a disaster after that. Calvin missed the tackle, the kid picked up a couple of blocks, got to the sideline, and was gone. Just like that the game was tied.

Coach left Casey in there for one more series, a three-and-out. Three incompletions, the last a bullet that bounced off a surprised linebacker's hands before falling harmlessly to the ground. After the punting team left the field, Coach McCoy walked down the sideline to Jake. "Cullen, you go back in next series."

He turned and started to walk back to where he'd been standing. Stopped, like he'd remembered something. Came back to Jake.

"I hate turnovers," he said.

When Coach was gone, Bear came back, stood next to Jake, slapped him on the back, and said, "Tie game? Fourth quarter? Stop it, son. Where else you want to be right now, home fixin' some fence?"

Nine minutes left when the Cowboys got the ball back on their own twenty-three. Jake knew Bear was right: He was exactly where he wanted to be. It was like his dad always talked about, the good parts in sports, the ones you played for, the ones you played through the hurt for, the ones that got you through the grunt work of practice and memorizing playbooks, the ones that kept you going when it was a hundred Texas degrees and you wanted to stop.

Only Jake didn't just want to be good with Troy Cullen up there in the stands watching today.

He wanted to be great.

Like his brother.

15

NOTHING PRETTY ABOUT THE FIRST DRIVE.

But then Jake was used to that by now. There had always been a part of him, even when he could barely see over the center, feeling like he was making things up as he went along, even as he tried to run the plays sent in from the sideline.

Even as he really wanted to run those plays just the way they'd been drawn up.

But he knew that wasn't football. It wasn't just Jake that Coach J had worked with; he'd hear him talking to Casey, too, at practice, telling him that it was all right to throw the ball away sometimes, even knowing that Casey Lindell only did that as some kind of last resort. He'd tell Jake the same thing, that firing the ball over everybody when you were in trouble wasn't against the law, that sometimes that was a better option than taking a sack or forcing a throw into coverage.

"There's all sorts of ways to be a quarterback," Coach J would say. "And one of them is knowing when to fold."

Bottom line? Jake ended up scrambling three times on the

drive, twice on third downs, pulling the ball down when Calvin and Justice and every other available receiver were covered, under big pressure from the Benton pass rush. But he managed to get first downs all three times, taking a good lick as he got the last one, the safety popping him hard before Jake could get out of bounds.

"You're gonna end up like Tim, you don't watch yourself," Nate said when he got back to the huddle, fixing the right shoulder pad that had come out of Jake's jersey.

"Well, let's see if we can get into the end zone before they cart me off," Jake said.

They were at the Benton fifteen by then. Jake rolled to his right, throwing the sprint-out pass to Justice he'd called in the huddle. He thought he'd thrown high, but Justice went up and brought it down for a touchdown. Bobby Torres kicked the point after, and it was 35–28 Cowboys with four minutes left.

Benton came right back—no shocker, it was that kind of game. It wasn't that the defenses, both of them, weren't trying to lay it down. But they were tiring, and the offenses were just better today.

This time the Benton quarterback, Will, went for it all on third-and-one, ball-faked like a champ to his fullback, straightened up and found his tight end behind one of the Cowboys safeties, nothing but green ahead of the kid. Touchdown. Their kick made it 35-all, just under two minutes left.

Jake could see Coach McCoy and Coach J talking, wondered if they might put Casey back in. Let him finish the game the way he'd started it. Jake was smart enough to know that they'd both played well so far today, maybe the only thing separating them, really, being the ball Casey had sailed to Calvin, one the safety had turned into a touchdown for Benton.

They'd both moved the ball. They'd both made plays, Casey more with his arms, Jake with his legs.

Not much to choose from.

He waited, the way he could see Casey waiting on the other side of the coaches, to see which Granger quarterback would get the chance to get the Cowboys their first win of the season.

Coach J nodded, walked down to Jake, and said, "We're stickin' with you."

Jake nodded.

They started at their thirty, Melvin nearly busting the kick return for more, getting tripped up from behind. So Jake had seventy yards in front of him, one time-out in his pocket, feeling like he always had in big moments, though never one as big as this.

Excited.

But not scared.

Busted play on first down, Spence Tolar looking for a pitch when Jake had called a handoff play. Jake had no choice but to keep the ball, lost five yards as the Benton nose tackle just flat crushed him, knocking the breath out of him. Jake stayed down, not wanting anybody to see him hurt or trying to breathe normally.

When he was able to do that, he sat up. Nate was standing over him.

"You okay?"

"Who are you?"

"Funny."

"Not feeling *all* that funny, truth be told."

Nate helped him up and they went back to the huddle. Jake shook off the hit and led Calvin down the left sideline with a perfect pass. By the time the safety knocked him out of bounds, Calvin had reached the Cowboys' forty-five-yard line.

A minute ten left.

Jake faked a quick out to Justice to hold the linebackers, then rolled right and found Calvin again. Calvin brushed off the corner covering him like a horsefly, passed up the chance to run out of bounds, and gained an extra five yards before getting sandwiched by two Panther defenders.

Cowboys' ball at the Benton twenty-two, thirty-eight seconds left, Coach McCoy running out at the ref closest to him to call their last time-out.

Bobby Torres had a nice, sure leg for extra points. But if they had to kick from here, it would be a thirty-nine-yard field goal. Out of his range. They had to get the ball a lot closer, or they had to put up six.

Jake jogged over to the sideline, tipped back his helmet, took a swig from the water bottle Bear handed him.

"Son, one thing you can't do is take a sack," Coach McCoy said, it coming out as *cain't*. "Even if you could get our boys back to the line, by the time you spiked it, we'd probably have time for just one throw to the end zone."

Jake said, "Yes, sir."

"They're gonna be looking at Calvin, which is why I want you to look at him your own self and then turn and throw it to Justice on the other side."

"Yes, sir."

"That all you can say? 'Yes, sir'?"

For some reason it made Jake laugh.

Coach McCoy said, "You think this is funny?"

Jake said, "*No,* sir."

Coach John McCoy might have smiled then. *Might* have.

Jake went back to the huddle, told the guys the play. No chatter now. Nobody in the huddle thinking anything was funny. Lot of guys in the huddle getting after it, a moment like this, for the first time as varsity football players. Jake included. He came up to the line, checked the defense, saw the safety shading over to help the corner on Calvin. But when he looked to the other side, to his right, he saw the outside linebacker do that with Justice at the same time.

So they were doubling Justice, same as they were Calvin. And dropping one of their safeties back to the five-yard line, like he was playing center field for them, defending the end zone.

But opening up the middle of the field. Betting that a short pass couldn't beat them here, knowing the Cowboys were out of time-outs. Daring them to risk one of the last plays they had left, and a lot of spent clock, on a catch-and-run.

Jake changed the play.

Betting on Calvin.

Called a quick post to him, a one-step drop for Jake. Get Calvin the ball and see if Benton could stop him from winning the game.

Three seconds on the play clock.

Two.

Nate snapped Jake the ball, Jake took a step back, saw the nose tackle rise up and stick his big paw up in the air. Jake slide-stepped to his left, only about five yards separating him and Calvin, Jake throwing that five-yarder as hard as he'd ever thrown a short pass in his life. Could have sworn he heard the air come out of Calvin Morton this time as the ball hit him in the gut, like he'd been gut-*punched*.

But Calvin caught it. As he did, the cornerback hit him. Calvin held on, stayed up. The corner went down and Calvin took off. Jake followed right behind. When one of the Panther linebackers came racing across the field, lining up the angle on Calvin perfectly, Jake launched himself at him, getting just enough of a block to give Calvin the room he needed to create. He faked a run outside, getting two Panthers to bite, then spun and raced to the other side, slicing past three more defenders before launching himself into the air as the last Panther tried to get in his way.

Calvin landed on his side when he hit, rolling over, never stopping. He handed the ball to the closest ref, whose arms were still raised, signaling a touchdown.

Ball game.

Jake stood at the ten-yard line, arms up in the air like the ref's.

Suddenly Nate was there, pounding Jake on his back, yelling. "Son, you just done graduated."

"To what?"

"Unclear," Nate Collins said. "But you sure ain't no freshman anymore."

Troy Cullen hugged his boy at midfield, hugged him after Libby Cullen had done the same, his mom who kept smiling and saying "Jacob" over and over again.

Troy Cullen said, "Well, hell's bells, was that really my baby boy?" Telling Jake that his skinny butt was going to end up in a sling if he didn't stop running with the ball so much.

It wasn't until Jake and his parents started walking toward the parking lot, them to their car and Jake to the bus, that his dad asked him about his new throwing motion.

"When'd you start throwing it different?" his dad said.

Jake hoped he wasn't going to make a thing of it, so he just said, "Aw, I just tweaked her a little."

"Didn't look like tweaks to me," Troy Cullen said. "All of a sudden I see you flingin' in three-quarters the way Romo does. And send up a flare when *he* wins something."

Libby Cullen said, "It was Jacob who won something today, I'm almost positive." Poking her husband with an elbow to let him think she was joshing him, even though Jake was pretty sure she wasn't.

"Not saying he wasn't, Libby. I'm just trying to understand what I've been missin'."

A lot, Jake thought.

Like most of my life.

What he said: "It's no big deal, Dad. Coach J and I were just messin' around at practice one day, and he told me to try releasing it a little lower, as a way of getting it away quicker. He thought I might be taking a little too much time to lock and load. And it started working for me, is all."

"Letting it go the way I taught you seemed to work pretty well for your brother."

"I'm not Wyatt," Jake said in a quiet voice.

"Didn't think Ray Jessup was your quarterback coach," Jake's dad said. "Was under the impression I was."

Jake nearly told him that if he was, it sure was a part-time job, but all he did was swallow his words—and maybe his pride—again, something he did a lot in front of his father.

"You are, Dad," he said. "You know that. Heck, everybody does."

"Maybe after I ride tomorrow, we'll do some work, you and me, on your mechanics."

"His mechanics looked just fine to me," Jake's mom said, some snap in her voice that Jake knew was never good for his dad. "I expect they looked pretty good to the Benton Panthers, as well."

Troy Cullen said, "Now, hon, I know you know your football—"

"Hon?" Libby Cullen said.

"Hold on, Libby," Jake's dad said. "You know I didn't mean nothin' by that."

"No," she said, "now you've piqued my interest; go ahead and finish your thought. Because what I heard was that I know my football . . . but. But *what*?"

Jake knew he should get to the locker room and let them sort it out, like they always did. But he wanted to see this, hear it.

"I just want to help the boy get better," Troy Cullen said. "He showed some potential today."

"Potential? Really?" Then Libby Cullen began walking away from the field.

"See you at home," Jake's dad said to him, slapped him on the back, and said, "You did good today."

But it was too late. Sounded to Jake like some kind of afterthought, like he was throwing Jake a bone.

Like somehow, even though Jake *had* won the game today, he still hadn't measured up.

16

IT WAS ALL SET UP TO BE A BIG SATURDAY NIGHT AT STONE'S, the way it always was after a win for the Granger Cowboys, everything half-price when the team won, even the most expensive steaks on the menu, what Bobby Ray Stone called his big 'uns.

Maybe it wasn't the whole squad in the back room by the time Jake and Nate and Bear arrived, but it sure seemed to be close enough, players everywhere, in booths and round tables and the long table against one of the walls.

And soon as they walked in, knowing they were on their way to the corner booth that Bobby Ray always saved for any member of the Cullen family, Jake spotted Sarah with three of her friends from cheerleading: Beth Ayers, Amanda Starling, and Monica Moroni. All of the others cute, but none as cute as Sarah, not even close.

"Well, now, how's this gonna go?" Nate said, all of them standing just inside the door to the back room.

He could see Sarah, too.

"I'm the one who's gonna go—home—if you start in on me," Jake said.

"Chill, my brother," Nate said. "Just be as cool as you were playin' ball today, not getting that cold rush of you-know-what because of some girl."

That was Nate's definition of choking in sports: a cold rush of you-know-what to the heart.

"Who couldn't relax after a fine pep talk like that?" Jake said.

Bear just stood there grinning, taking it all in.

"Here's what we're gonna do, 'cause we can't just stand here all night," Nate said. "We're just gonna pause at the girls' table and you're gonna say hello, the way we all are, and then keep moving. Just on one condition."

Jake said, "Who said you get to make conditions about anything?"

"The condition," Nate said, "is that you *do* say hidy to Miss Sarah."

"And if I don't?"

"Then I'll do all the talking," Nate said.

Bear said, "No one wants that."

Jake said, "And maybe I'll start chattin' up Emma Jean, when she comes to take our order."

"No need to lash out at me," Bear said. "I'm just trying to help."

"Sure you are."

But Jake did exactly as Nate asked, stopped when he got to Sarah's table, knowing he wasn't just doing it because of Nate, that he wanted to talk to her on a night like this, after a game like the one he'd played. Nate was right: If he could take the team down the field against Benton, he could surely do *that*.

He could talk to a girl, even if it was *this* girl.

Nate and Bear led the way, both of them smiling at the girls and saying "Hey," moving on to their booth. Jake stopped and said, "Hi, Sarah," said hi to the other girls, too, calling them by their names, his mom's voice inside his head telling him that there was no fault in being polite to a fault.

"Hi, Jake!" Sarah, smiling at him, actually seeming happy to see him.

Before Jake could think of something else to say, she said, "*Great* game today!"

"Wasn't just me," he said. "Everybody did pretty good there at the end."

"But you were the one making all those plays and all those throws," she said. "Somebody said you looked as cool out there as Wyatt."

"Hey, even Wyatt Cullen knew it's hard *not* to look cool throwing it to Calvin."

Casey.

Jake turned and said, "Man, you got that right."

Casey must have come in right behind Jake and his boys. Casey was with his own boys, Dicky Grider and Roy Gilley. Jake noticed Calvin and Justice behind them, but they seemed to be on their way to Melvin's table.

Jake knew Casey was just announcing himself, a little louder than he needed to, the way Calvin sometimes did.

It was Sarah who spoke next, saying, "Well, all us Cowboys

fans hope he stays lucky *and* good." Smiling as she added, "You *both* looked good out there."

Casey grinned and said, "Miss Sarah, you haven't seen *nothin'* yet, trust me."

Jake knew he was talking about himself, but let it go. Nobody said anything now, both Jake and Casey standing there in front of Sarah's table, Jake knowing he felt awkward even if Casey didn't. Maybe the guy never felt awkward; he always thought he was right where he was supposed to be.

"Well, I gotta go sit," Jake said to Sarah now. "You know how ornery Nate gets when he's hungry."

"Thanks for stopping by," Sarah said. "And again: *awesome* game."

Jake walked across the room, not looking back, sat down with Nate and Bear, still not looking back at Sarah's table. "Tell me Casey didn't sit down with them," he said.

Nate said, "He did not."

"How'd all that go?" Bear said. "We could only hear Casey."

"Went fine," Jake said.

"Figured as much," Nate said, "since your face is the color of ketchup right now."

"Is not."

"Nate speaks the truth," Bear said as they all watched Casey and Dicky and Roy head off to their own table, Jake not caring if they sat on Jupiter or Mars as long as Casey wasn't with Sarah.

It was a good night—even with Casey in the room—to be a high school football player, good to be a Granger Cowboy, good to be at Stone's with what felt like most of the team and half the town crammed into the place. Everybody moving around to everybody else's tables, like it was a party more than a night out on the town. Bear flirted with Emma Jean in his own bumbling way—*like I'm anybody to talk,* Jake thought—and Nate acted like the mayor of the back room, at least between courses.

Calvin worked the room, too, sitting with Jake and the boys for a few minutes, then going right across the room and sitting with Casey and *his* boys. Like he was trying to remain neutral on which quarterback he liked best, not wanting to declare after just one win for the Cowboys.

And why should he, when you really thought about it? They'd won today—always the most important thing to Calvin—and he'd gotten all the touches he wanted. Far as Calvin was concerned, life was good.

And life *was* good. One of those nights when you wondered how anything in your life was ever going to be better than high school, especially this high school on a Saturday night during football season.

Until Casey Lindell came over to their table, right after they'd finished up with dessert.

"Everybody here havin' a good time?" he said.

"Just had pie," Nate said. "Never been a bad time for me that included pie."

But Casey wasn't there to talk to Nate about what he'd ordered.

"How about you, Cullen?" he said, voice not loud enough to be heard over all the chirp and chatter in the room. "Everything good with you?"

Cullen.

"Tonight it is," Jake said.

"Come on, man. You can't be happy with this deal we got going, you against me?"

"The only ones I'm *against,*" Jake said, "are the guys we're *playing* against."

Casey said, "You know better than that."

Nate shifted slightly in his seat. "Come on, man," Nate said. "Let's not do this now."

Casey ignored him. To Jake he said, "You know this can't work in the long run. You get that, right?"

"Last time I checked, we won the game today," Jake said, his voice sounding like a whisper compared to Casey's, wondering if the people starting to turn their way could even hear him.

Hoping that might stop Casey, wherever he was going with all this. Such a good day up to now, a good night.

"You're telling me you're really good with this," Casey said. "I play, then you play?"

"Doesn't matter if I'm good with it as long as Coach is," Jake said. "He's the one makes the substitutions."

The room had gotten quiet, way too quiet, Jake feeling as if everybody was looking their way now.

Casey said, "You know I didn't come here to back up a freshman, even if his name is Cullen."

"Casey, you *got* to move on," Nate said.

"Wasn't talking to you, Nate."

"Well, if you're so on fire to have this talk with Jake, have it in private sometime. And someplace that ain't here."

Again Casey acted as if he hadn't heard. Even Jake had to admit

Casey Lindell had some brass to him, ignoring Nate Collins when he had to know Nate could pick him up like a baby if he wanted.

"You know guys in this room are already choosing up sides, me against you," Casey said. "Right?"

Jake said, "Coach must think it'll work itself out, sooner rather than later."

"Funny how freshman QBs don't have to wait their turn in Granger as long as they have the right last name," Casey said.

Now his voice was the only one you could hear at Stone's Throw. Like he really was talking to the whole town.

Casey said, "We both know this isn't as much about what I can do, much as it is about who you are."

"We won," Jake said again.

"It's gonna tear this team apart," Casey said.

"Not if we don't let it," Jake said.

Almost saying, *Not if* you *don't let it*.

He was at the end of the booth, closest to Casey, and stood up now, knowing he was the only one who could end this.

But also knowing in that moment he was probably making things worse, because when he slid out of the booth, there was hardly any air between them, Casey with that cocky look that seemed frozen on his face, maybe thinking Jake wanted to go, right here, right now.

"You want to do this here or outside?" Casey said.

"I don't want to *do* anything," Jake said, "'cept leave."

Somehow he got past Casey without touching him, looking back long enough to say, "See you at the truck," to Nate and Bear, walking across the middle of the room, past Sarah's table, past where Calvin sat with his cousin Melvin and Justice, past everybody, feeling like he was walking by himself down Main Street, all of Granger watching him, walking through the back room and the front room and out of Stone's.

Trying to tell himself he was doing the right thing for his team.

But feeling humiliated anyway.

Feeling more like a little brother than he ever had in his life.

17

WHAT HAD JUST HAPPENED?

Jake leaned against the driver's side of Bear's pickup, replaying it in his mind like he was watching film with Coach J, thinking of it like a play that had broken down, wondering if there'd been a better option for him. Coach J, he always talked about Jake's decision-making, how you either had it or you didn't, blah blah. But Jake didn't need Coach telling him; it was one of the things he'd always taken a quiet pride in, knowing the right play to make.

But had he done that just now with Casey?

Or had he just looked plain old weak, no matter how good his intentions were, no matter how much of a team man he was trying to be? Had he looked weak when quarterbacks—especially Granger quarterbacks, especially *Cullens*—were supposed to look strong? When they were supposed to look like leaders?

In the moment when he had to decide, under the gun, how far to take it with Casey, Jake had decided that the worst thing for the team was a fight, right there in front of everybody, between the two guys fighting it out to be quarterback of the team.

He wasn't afraid of Casey; heck, Jake hadn't ever been afraid of Wyatt when the two of them would get into it, even when Wyatt was still a lot bigger and stronger. What *was* he afraid of, then? That people would think he was as cocky as Casey Lindell?

"One of the things I love the most about you, Jacob, is that you've always known who you are," his mom once said. "Even before the rest of us knew."

Inside Stone's, Jake had known who he *wasn't,* even though everybody who'd watched him walk out had to think that Casey had backed him down.

He'd taken the high road and then found out how much the high road could suck.

"Hey."

He looked up, and there standing in front of him, having come up on him so quietly it was like she'd just appeared somehow, was Sarah Rayburn.

Nobody with her.

Just her and Jake.

"Hey," he said.

"Nate and Bear were on their way out," she said. "I asked them to give us a minute. I just wanted to tell you something."

He waited.

"I just wanted to tell you I thought you did the right thing back there."

"Really?" Jake said.

"Really. Everybody thought it was about to get out of hand, but you didn't let it."

"Thanks for saying that," Jake said. "But I feel like I must've looked pretty weak in front of the team, in front of you. In front of everybody."

"You're wrong," she said.

"Well, thank you," Jake said. "I guess."

"You're welcome, I guess," she said, smiling.

Past her, he could see Nate and Bear at the front door to Stone's, underneath the Stone's Throw sign, watching them, waiting.

Right now, though, there was just Sarah, just a few feet separating them, just air between them, Jake not sure what to say or do, just knowing he liked breathing that air.

But before he had to think of something to say, Sarah turned and ran back toward Stone's, waving at Nate and Bear as she went back through the front door, taking all that air with her.

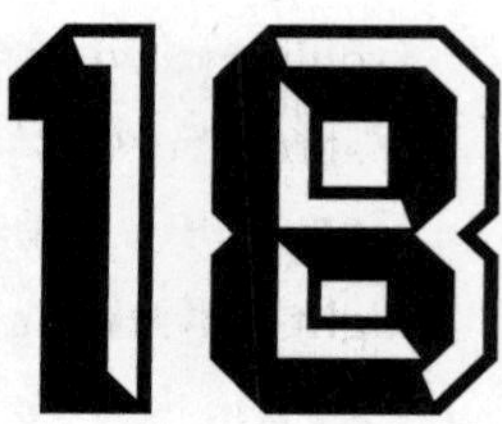

WHEN THEY WERE ALL IN THE TRUCK, JAKE WANTED TO KNOW what had happened in the back room after he'd walked out.

Nate said, "Well, I got up."

"Never good."

"Nah, not what you're thinkin'," Nate said. "Oh, I thought about gettin' up on Casey and askin' him, did he have anything he wanted to say to *me*? But I didn't."

"Would've looked like you were fighting a fight I didn't want to have with him," Jake said.

"Anybody who thought you were afraid of him is too dumb to play football," Bear said.

"Anyways," Nate said, "all I said was that we're all on the same team and everybody *on* the team should keep that in mind or they would have to be dealing with me, in what I described as a permanent-type manner."

"So you basically said what I should've said," Jake said.

"No," Bear said. "You did right. That guy didn't care what you had to say, all he cared about was making you look bad, whether you tried to reason with his dumb self or not. No kidding, how does he even remember the plays, being as dumb as he is?"

Jake felt better, hearing it from his boys like this. He knew what Sarah had just told him, how she'd tried to pump him up. But she was a Granger cheerleader, not a Granger Cowboy.

They all sat in silence now, riding through the two-lane Texas night, on their way to the Cullen ranch, Bear finally saying, "Are we allowed to ask about Sarah?"

"Yes."

"So how'd it go?"

Jake waited. Then he finally said, "Oh, you expected an answer, too?"

Bear said to Nate, "Boy must be starting to feel better. Thinks he's funny again."

"It went amazing," Jake said.

"Care to be more specific?" Nate said.

"I do not."

"Didn't think you would."

There was another silence now that took them through the gate to the ranch, up the long road to the house. As Jake walked toward the front door, he said he'd hit them up in the morning, they'd come up with a plan for what to do on Sunday.

Through his open window, Nate said, "Do me a favor? When you get inside, remember the way you played, not what happened at Stone's?"

Jake said he'd try.

His plan was to head straight upstairs, get himself some quiet and calm, try to sort out the whole long day and night. Try to figure out whether he'd come out ahead on the day or not. Already telling himself that he had, that not even Casey Lindell or his dad could ruin a day that had started with a big win and ended with Sarah Rayburn.

But before he made it to the stairs, he heard his dad's booming voice coming from his study.

"Jake Cullen," he said, "get yourself in here and explain what all just happened at Stone's."

Troy Cullen was on his long leather couch, one of the Saturday night TV games on a flat screen that seemed to take up most of the far wall, Texas Tech against Kansas State, 24-all in the third quarter, Tech in those black jerseys of theirs, driving.

Troy Cullen: big iced tea in his hand, boots off, gesturing with his glass at the game, saying, "Tech's gonna be trouble for us when we play 'em, wait and see. They got more speed on the corners than those sprint cars."

Now he looked at Jake, pointed to the easy chair to his right, Jake's game-watching chair when his dad was around, and said, "Sit."

Jake did.

"I already heard Bobby Ray's version," he said. "Now I'd like to hear yours."

"Mr. Stone *called* you?" Jake said. "You're kidding."

"Actually, I called him, wanting to make sure he didn't give away my table next Saturday night, your mom and me and the

Leylands are going," Troy Cullen said. "I know Bobby Ray'd throw people out of his place for us, but I always feel better having my name on the list, less people think I'm getting special treatment."

Jake smiled at what they both knew was a harmless lie. Truth was, his dad lived to get special treatment; it was part of the fun of being Troy Cullen in Granger, a way for him to feel like the football star he used to be.

His dad put his drink down, careful to make sure it was on a coaster and not the antique coffee table, like Jake's mom was in the room with them even though she wasn't.

Jake wished she was.

His dad said, "Bobby Ray said the other boy gave you some pretty good lip in front of half the town, and that you just took it from him."

Jake thought, *He said he was calling me in to hear my side, but maybe he just wants me to hear* his.

"I did what I thought was best for the team," Jake said. "Didn't think it was the right time or place to make a scene."

"Think you *didn't* make a scene?"

Jake waited, until his dad said, "It's been my experience that sometimes you don't get to pick the time or place if somebody calls you out."

"Dad, it wasn't like one of your old westerns, the two of us drawing on each other in the middle of the street."

"Maybe it was more like that than you think."

"He was just blowin' off steam, is all."

"Blowin' off steam at *you*. In front of your teammates."

"At the situation," Jake said. "At us sharing time. That's what's really making him hot, not me."

"And I'm not hot at you, son, I'm not, just trying to understand how you could just walk away like Bobby Ray said you did."

"It's what I'm trying to explain to you, even though I don't seem to be doing much of a job at that," Jake said. "It was about me not making a bad situation worse."

"See, right there, that's what I'm worried about: that whatever your intention was, you made things worse for your*self*."

"By not fighting him?"

"There wasn't a way to handle it without fighting?"

"There wasn't a way to handle it without me acting as dumb as he was," Jake said.

His dad started to say something, and Jake surprised himself—kind of the way he had been surprising himself, one way or another, all day—by putting up a hand and stopping him. Knowing that the only person who got away with interrupting him in this house was his mom.

"I'm just a freshman, Dad," he said, "but I've been on teams my whole life, and I know how easy it is to rip one apart, even in Pop Warner. Casey and me had a chance to do that tonight. But if he *was* going to do that, I sure wasn't going to help him."

"So you don't think you looked like somebody just takin' his ball and goin' home?"

Jake said, "Anybody thinks that doesn't know me."

Wanting to add: *Do you?*

He saw his dad staring at him now in the glow from the flat screen, this curious look on his face, even though his dad was always sure about everything.

Jake kept going. "It was you who always told me and Wyatt that being the real leader of your team meant making tough calls only you could make. Well, I reckon I made one tonight."

His father stood up now, groaning like he did when he'd been sitting for a long time, pointing the remote at the TV set, now the only light in the room but for a slash of it coming through the half-open door from the front hall.

His dad looked down at Jake, and suddenly he smiled.

"Well, you found out something for sure, and for your own self tonight," Troy Cullen said. "Being the quarterback of the Granger Cowboys isn't a job that ends when the game does."

"No, sir," Jake said. "It does not."

"Ask you something before we drop this and I drag myself up the stairs?"

Jake nodded.

"What do you think your brother would have done, he found himself in the same situation?"

Always back there, to Wyatt.

"I honestly believe he would've done what I did."

"You know something?" his dad said, that curious look still on his face, right eyebrow raised a little, still smiling at Jake. "I believe you might be right."

Then he walked slowly toward the door, saying he felt one of his headaches coming on, what he called one of his Blue Ribbon Specials, saying he needed aspirin and sleep, in that order.

But over his shoulder he said, "You done good."

Jake wasn't sure now whether his dad was talking about the game or about Stone's. Wasn't sure in that moment if he really cared. Just feeling as if he'd won a small victory in this room, even if he wasn't quite sure who he'd beaten.

Or what.

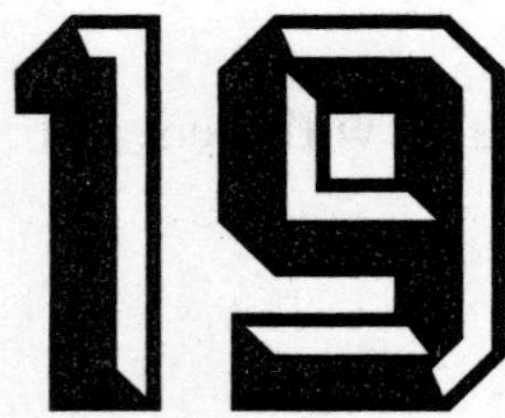

BY MONDAY, PEOPLE WERE CALLING THE RADIO STATION, morning host J. D. Frederick's show, J. D. having announced he was going to conduct a weeklong poll on which quarterback the listeners wanted to be the starter.

The town choosing up sides, even in a place where there was usually only one side: behind the Granger Cowboys.

On the way to school Friday morning, in Bear's truck, windows down, the air clean for a change, not like some kind of furnace, Bear had J. D.'s show on as people were calling to cast their votes.

"You think I could call in, if I gave a fake name?" Bear said.

"You're enjoying this, aren't you?"

"Enjoying it?" Bear said. "Dude, I love it!"

"They're not talking about *you* like you're a horse at an auction."

"J. D., that old boy, hasn't given out the vote count all week," Bear said. "Said he's going to announce the winner at the end of today's show, right before ten o'clock, but we'll be in class."

"Shame."

"But I got a strong feeling you're gonna be the people's choice."

"You *think*?" Jake said. "I'm Wyatt Cullen's brother; I'm Big Troy's son. Like some of those boys say: I'm a Cullen in Cullenville. You act like it'll be some kind of upset."

"You don't think it might have anything to do with people in town thinkin' you're the better football player?"

They listened as a caller, who said his name was LeRoy, started out by saying, "Now, I'm not here to tell you little Cullen is the player his brother was, or his daddy, but just off what I seen so far, he does seem to have some of that Cullen DN-of-A workin' for him when he finds himself in a big spot . . ."

Jake reached over, shut off the radio.

Bear said, "Hey, it was just gettin' good. I thought that guy was gonna talk about what kind of blood type you are."

"More likely, people are trying to turn this into one of those blood feuds out of the Old West," Jake said. "Over high school football."

"You know what they say," Bear said. "You've got your football, and then you've got your *Granger* football."

"I feel like it's all people are talking about."

"It's all people *ever* talk about," Bear said.

Friday's practice was like all the others this week, which meant Jake and Casey didn't speak. Neither one of them made a big show out of that, and the fact was there were a lot of guys on the team Jake could go days without speaking to; that was just football.

And when it was football coached by John McCoy, it wasn't like you had a lot of chances to chat, anyway.

Jake still felt like the other players could sense the tension between them. You always heard about healthy competition in sports, from the time you first started competing. Only this didn't feel all that healthy to Jake.

Every day at practice, every single one, seemed to produce the same kind of pressure games did. Only that was good pressure, if you really loved to compete. That was fun.

Nothing fun about this.

And the thing that Jake didn't want to happen, the thing that made him walk away at Stone's—guys choosing up sides—was happening anyway. You could just tell which ones were Jake guys and which ones were Casey guys.

Like the players on the team were just more callers to ol' J. D.'s radio show.

"You think Coach is gonna play us like this the whole season?" Jake said to Nate a few minutes from the end of practice, the two of them walking back to the huddle, Jake getting the last snaps of the day.

"Unclear," Nate said. "For now I think Coach is just seeing what the rest of us are, that this all is bringing out the best in both of you, much as I hate to admit it about him."

"I feel like all eyes are on us, every play."

"Well, *yeah,*" Nate said, dragging out the last word like a piece of gum he was stretching out of his mouth. "Both of you boys are quarterback of the Cowboys, so you can't be surprised at people looking at you, because Granger High's no different than Granger when it comes to their quarterbacks: They're fascinated by where you *spit*."

"I don't want it to be like this," Jake said.

"Like what? Hard? Boo hoo."

Jake's last throw of the day was to Spence Tolar, left sideline, Spence having snuck out of the backfield like a decoy. Jake led him perfectly, Spence gathering the ball in clean, running into the end zone.

Coach McCoy blew his whistle, motioned for everyone to come gather round him.

"Good work today," he said. "In fact, good work all week. See y'all tomorrow."

He started to walk away, came back, and said, "By the way, I think we'll change things around, let Jake start tomorrow."

Then he walked away from them for real.

Two games into his freshman year, Jake was the starting quarterback for Granger High, at least for one game.

In a low voice, Bear said to Jake, "All those people callin' the radio all week, and in the end there was but only one vote that counted."

Nate and Bear said they had to do something to celebrate. Jake said only a plain fool would celebrate the night *before* the game. Nate said he just meant they should all go out and get something to eat.

Jake said, "I sort of knew you meant eating," but explained to both him and Bear that he'd promised to eat at home with his mom tonight; his dad was already in Austin for the UT-Baylor game tomorrow afternoon.

"If I rally after dinner," Jake said, "you and Bear can come get me."

The three of them were outside the locker room, Jake not even having bothered to shower, trying to do his level best to stay away from Casey Lindell. The last thing he wanted today was another scene.

"Dude," Bear said, "you got the job. You're allowed to at least look happy."

"I *am* happy," Jake said. "But it doesn't mean squat if I can't *do* the job."

They all went and piled into Bear's truck. Sometimes Jake thought that when he remembered high school, he'd remember the front seat of this pickup, squeezed in between Bear and Nate, as well as he'd remember school or sports.

His mom was in the kitchen, cooking up some of her mean Texas tacos, when Jake walked in. Soon as he did, she looked over at him and said, "Sweaty, dirty boy."

"Had to make a fast getaway after practice."

"And why is that?"

"Didn't want to get into it again with Casey."

"Something new happen between you two?"

Jake couldn't help himself now, couldn't keep the smile down.

"Coach said I'm starting tomorrow."

His mom was across the room in a blink, wiping her hands on her apron, smiling herself now, putting her arms around him.

"Well, look at *you*," she said.

"We're still both gonna play," he said.

"Jacob," his mom said, "John McCoy didn't shuffle the deck this way because he thinks you're *not* up to the task."

"I guess," Jake said.

"I know," she said. "Now go take a shower."

He went upstairs, but before he got into the shower decided to do something he'd been thinking about doing since practice ended, really since Coach told him he was starting.

He decided to private-message Sarah on Facebook. But then lost his nerve.

Sometimes one victory a day was enough.

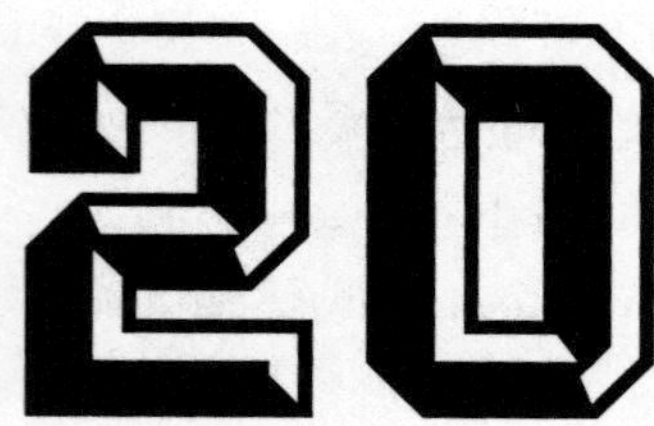

START OF THE FOURTH QUARTER AGAINST THE CHIRITA WILD-cats, Granger up a touchdown, 28–21, ball on the Cowboys' forty after a Chirita punt, officials' time-out because a kid on the Chirita punt return had to be helped off after twisting an ankle.

Casey and Jake had each thrown a touchdown pass today and both had moved the ball. Both had felt pressure on every series, knowing that the next snap, next throw, next play, might be the one that either kept them out there or moved them to the sidelines. Maybe that was John McCoy's plan all along, make them challenge themselves and each other at the same time.

And Jake was okay with that. He was. Just kept reminding himself, even when he was watching Casey run the team, where he'd started out this season and where he was now.

On this day, Casey had even run for some big gainers, the first time all season he'd pulled the ball down, almost like he was trying to show the coaches Jake wasn't the only one who could scramble around when he had to.

Casey's biggest run was for twenty-five yards to the Wildcats' three—but it had also been his last. He'd fallen awkwardly, rolling his ankle when he tried to slide to avoid getting hit. Even though he said he could stay in there, Coach McCoy told him to go sit down for a bit, told him Jake could hand the ball off from there, which Jake did, Spence finally diving in from the one, putting the Cowboys ahead by the touchdown that now separated the two teams.

So here was a chance for the Cowboys to stretch their lead and maybe put this one away.

As the punt return team headed back to the sideline, Coach McCoy went over and spoke to Casey, who'd been sitting on the bench with his leg up since he'd come out of the game, holding ice to his ankle. Jake could see Casey trying to make his case to go back out there, but Coach finally shook his head, came back over to Jake and said, "Lindell says he's good to go, but Doc says we should let him sit."

"Yes, sir," Jake said.

"Wasn't looking for your approval, son," Coach McCoy said. "Now *git*."

Jake ran out, knelt down in the huddle, thinking it hadn't been all that long ago he'd been in this huddle as a varsity QB for the first time. But somehow, even under the gun every time he was in here, it felt natural to him now. He hadn't been great today, or even close—had even thrown an interception in the first half, his first turnover of the season. Still, he felt like he belonged. Like he was supposed to be here, even if the only reason he was here right this minute was because Coach was playing it safe with Casey.

Business at hand? First-and-ten at the Granger forty, all that green in front of him and the Cowboys, a chance to finish off Chirita in front of the home fans, including—as usual—Jake's mom, but not his dad.

Three straight completions moved the ball to the Chirita thirty-two. A short run by Spence and an incompletion to Justice made it third-and-eight. The call was a ten-yard curl route to Calvin on the right sideline, a throw that had been there for both Jake and Casey all game long.

The Wildcats, sensing a pass play coming and needing to force an incompletion, came on a blitz, the middle linebacker coming up the chute, the corner from Justice's side knowing he had the safety behind him, the outside linebacker charging from Calvin's side. Nate took care of the middle linebacker, and Mo Hanners, now the Cowboys' starting right guard, moved over and cleaned out the outside linebacker, no problem. But the cornerback, who hadn't been quick enough to cover the wideouts today, but was big enough to be a linebacker and could hit like one, made it through.

Maybe it was the pick Jake had thrown earlier. Maybe there was a part of him thinking he couldn't scramble every single time he was under pressure, that he could stand in there until the last second and make the kind of throw Casey could when *he* held on to the ball as long as he could.

So Jake stood in the pocket until the very last second before throwing the ball, the big cornerback just exploding on him. Jake took the hit from the side, flying through the air, feeling all the air come out of him at the same time.

He'd see later on film that somehow the throw had been a dart, Calvin catching it in stride, two yards past the first-down marker, exactly where he was supposed to be, money. Jake had suspected the play was good from the reaction of the crowd, even though the cheer sounded as if it was coming from the other side of town.

That was because the real noise, along with what his dad had always called brain hurt, was inside of Jake now, in the area of his ribs. Thinking to himself this was about the biggest lick he'd ever taken in football.

Nate was there first, of course, Jake still on his back.

"Talk to me, brother," Nate said. "You all right?"

"Compared to what?" Jake said.

Nate grabbed Jake's left hand without asking, not knowing that was his hurt side right now, Jake turning his head so Nate couldn't see him wincing. He was pretty sure he hadn't broken anything. He knew what a broken rib felt like—oh man, did he ever—from the time when he was twelve and had been thrown from one of his dad's cutting horses.

This hurt wasn't *that* hurt.

But would do.

"I think you need to take a seat," Nate said.

"I'm good," Jake said.

Now it was Nate who said, "Compared to what?"

Other players gathered around as Coach McCoy and Coach J came toward them, along with Doc Mallozzi.

Coach McCoy said, "Where's it hurt, son?"

"He got me good, Coach," Jake said. "But I think it looked worse than it was." He forced a grin and said, "Once I got permission to land."

Doc Mallozzi said, "Let's get you over to the sideline so I can check out your rib cage. That's where he got you, right?"

"Doc, I'm fine. If I was hurt bad, I'd say."

More sure than ever that he wasn't. Hurt bad, that is. His breathing had started to come more easily.

The lead ref came over and said, "Gotta game to play."

Coach McCoy studied him for what felt like a long time and then said, "I'm gonna trust you."

Doc Mallozzi looked Jake in the eye and then nodded his head.

Jake's breath came even easier.

"Let's go put this baby away," Coach said before leaving the field.

Jake knew it was going to take more than a hit to the ribs to send him to the bench.

They ran the ball twice for eight yards, down to the twelve. Spence brought in the third-and-two call, what was supposed to be a quick slant to Justice on the left. Supposed to be. But the Wildcats blitzed from that side again, and this time Jake saw it coming and got out of there.

He ran to his right, waving at Calvin as he did. Calvin let fly in the same direction and Jake led him perfectly on the run. Calvin caught the ball at the two and continued into the end zone.

Jake wanted to celebrate, but that scramble had brought back the pain. Much as he had wanted to, Jake couldn't hide it.

When he got to the sideline, Coach McCoy told him he was

done for the day, that Casey was going back in. Jake saw Casey testing out his ankle behind the bench. He looked fine.

"Sir, you don't have to baby me," Jake said.

"Go sit," Coach said. "You did good today. Specially *after* you took that hit. That's when you showed ever'body somethin' about yourself."

He went over and took a seat next to Nate, wishing his dad had been there to see it, too.

THE NEXT THURSDAY NIGHT, TEXAS FACED KANSAS IN Lawrenceville for a prime-time televised game. Troy and Libby Cullen flew up to Kansas to watch. Unfortunately, Wyatt Cullen, enjoying his own dream freshman season, finally played a nightmare of a game.

Jake watched it in his dad's den with Bear and Nate and couldn't believe what he was seeing from his brother.

Four picks, just one touchdown pass, not even two hundred passing yards, finally getting benched in the fourth quarter, the Longhorns losing 31–7, the TV announcers wondering if the 'Horns might go from number four in the country all the way out of the top ten.

When it was over, Bear and Nate fixing to leave, Nate said, "Looked like one of those identify-theft deals to me."

"No, it was my brother," Jake said.

"Holy crap," Bear said, "you mean he's . . . *human*?"

On the phone afterward, calling from his hotel, Troy Cullen said to Jake, "You watch?"

"Course I watched," Jake said.

"The whole darn country watched," Troy Cullen said. "Tell me again who you got tomorrow night?"

"Kersey."

"Well, can you at least get the family one win this weekend?" Jake's dad said.

Jake said he was sure going to try.

The Cowboys did get another win the next night against Kersey, Casey throwing for two touchdowns, Jake running for one on a sweet bootleg. It ended up 28–13, Granger. They were starting to roll now. Jake felt he'd come back from playing the way he had against the Chirita 'Cats and the hit to the ribs he'd taken, felt like he was about to get on a roll himself.

But when Jake was riding around with Bear late Saturday morning, the callers to the radio weren't talking about the Cowboys in Granger, how good the Cowboys were going, even whether or not they liked Jake better or Casey.

Most of them were still talking about how bad Wyatt had looked against Kansas.

Amazing, Jake thought.

It was still all about his big brother, even when the other team did everything except throw him down a flight of stairs. When Jake and Bear finally showed up at Stone's Throw for lunch, first thing Bobby Ray said when they walked through the door was, "Some game."

"Sure was," Jake said.

Only Bobby Ray Stone didn't mean Granger vs. Kersey.

Bobby Ray said, "Never saw your brother throw that bad in his life."

Amazing.

The 'Horns came home and had a hard practice on Friday—Wyatt saying on his Facebook page that "Coach made us practice soon as the plane landed"—but then their coach gave them Saturday off. So Wyatt drove home in the morning, showed up in time for lunch, Jake thinking that his brother hadn't lost a football game since his junior year at Granger, wanting to see how he'd react, getting knocked down on national television.

Right away he saw that this wasn't Wyatt the cocky college boy he'd seen the first time he'd come home from Austin, everybody gathered around him at Amy's.

"Just needed to get away from Longhorns football for a day," he said when they were all at the table. "Man, I forgot what it was like to get thrown down a flight of stairs like that."

"That's exactly what it feels like, a spit-storm like that," Troy Cullen said, "like you're just fallin' all over yourself and can't do a thing to stop it."

"I knew everything wasn't going to go right all season," Wyatt said. "I just didn't think it would go *that* wrong."

"Just one game," his dad said. "Good wake-up call, that's the way I look at it. Now you got time to regroup before the Red River game. Just one game."

Texas-Oklahoma, as big a regular-season rivalry game as there was in college football.

Wyatt said, "You listen to the callers on the radio, they already think that Chris Bishop ought to be back in there by then." So he'd been listening, too, maybe all the way home.

Chris Bishop had briefly started for Texas the season before as a sophomore, but Wyatt had flat beat him out in the preseason, the way he'd ended up beating out all the other quarterbacks on the roster. Chris hadn't done anything except mop up in Texas victories until the Kansas game.

"Oh, don't listen to that bull," his dad said, everybody at the table knowing he wanted to say more, and worse. "Don't be listening to those people. Most of 'em don't know whether a football is blown up or stuffed with horsefeathers," Troy Cullen said.

Finally Wyatt grinned.

"Gee, Dad, none of us ever heard that one before," he said, and they all laughed.

Jake said, "Though I do believe that when Mom's not around it's not feathers."

"By the way," Wyatt said, "how's little brother doing? I heard you got flattened by a sixteen-wheeler against Chirita."

"Wasn't so bad."

"Man, the only thing scares me more than a blind-side hit like that is snakes."

"The kind that used to make you squeal like a pig when you saw one?" Jake said.

Wyatt said, "Were you this funny when you were younger?"

"I was," Jake said, grinning at him. "Leastways when I was allowed to talk at the dinner table."

Then they were all back to talking about the Kansas game, Troy Cullen mostly, acting like it was his job to make Wyatt feel better about it, somehow convince him it wasn't as bad as he thought it was. But Wyatt, to his credit, wasn't having any of it, finally quoting his dad about how game film never lied and neither did the stat sheet.

"Still only counts as one loss in the standings," Troy Cullen said.

"Am I allowed to change the subject to a game that our other son *won* last night?" Libby Cullen said.

"Not only allowed," Wyatt said, "but encouraged."

"Boy's lookin' more comfortable back there all the time," Troy Cullen said, then turned to Wyatt and said, "Which is the way you're gonna feel when you get back at it against Oklahoma."

Jake shot a quick look over at his mom, saw her smile and shake her head, as if in that moment she and Jake weren't even there.

Or as if she was just giving up for now.

Whether she wanted to accept it or not, at this table, in this family, there was no quarterback controversy, because Wyatt came first.

Win or lose.

The best Jake had ever figured, his whole life, from the first time he started thinking about these things, was that his dad loved him *differently* than he did Wyatt. Who *had* come first, no way around that. Who was the *real* QB-1 in the family, least in all the ways that mattered. Who'd been the best player in town from the time he was seven years old. Who'd become the star at Granger High. Who now had the job that their dad had always dreamed about having, quarterback of the Texas Longhorns, all the way up to number four in the country. It was big-time, Jake had to admit.

When lunch was cleared, Wyatt and Jake went into their dad's study to watch the Notre Dame game with him while Libby Cullen went off to play doubles with some of her friends at the tennis club, a rare day off for her from football.

It was at halftime that Wyatt said to Jake, "You want to go out behind the barn and throw the ball around, see if I can remember how to do that proper?"

Jake said, "Been waitin' for you to ask, brother."

On their way through the door, they each tried to hip check the other into the door frame, same way they had been trying to do that to each other their whole lives, Troy Cullen calling after them not to screw around when they got outside and get themselves hurt.

"If something does happen to me," Wyatt said to Jake in the hall, "you think Dad could step in against Oklahoma?"

"I heard that," Troy Cullen said from the study.

"You were supposed to," Wyatt said back to him.

"You think Archie Manning takes this much lip from his boys?" Troy Cullen yelled as his boys headed through the kitchen.

Wyatt said, "I think we established a long time ago that we aren't Peyton or Eli. And you *sure* aren't Archie."

Then Wyatt laughed again, like he was starting to feel better. The sound of his brother's laughter made Jake feel better, too. Maybe this was what his mom meant when she called him a pleaser, Jake wanting to help his brother let go of the Kansas game, same as their dad did.

This was a corner of the pasture that had always belonged to Wyatt and Jake, one their dad made sure was mowed nice for them. It wasn't as long as a real football field, maybe seventy-five yards. And as football-crazed as their dad was, he'd never painted yard lines out here or put up goalposts.

Still, you could have a solid touch football game out here, and run solid pass routes. It was here, Jake knew, that he'd first learned about being a quarterback, just watching his dad work with Wyatt.

Troy Cullen would work with Jake when he was bigger and older, teach him the same fundamentals, telling him that this was the way he'd done things when he'd played. Or just flat telling him to do them the way Wyatt did. Like they were supposed to be the same player. It wasn't until Jake had started working with Coach Jessup that he really heard somebody telling him to be himself.

Jake wore Granger blue shorts and an Ole Miss T-shirt he'd bought online, in honor of Eli. Wyatt had changed out of his jeans after lunch and wore an old pair of khaki shorts, an orange Texas T-shirt with the famous horns on the front.

After they'd warmed up for about five minutes, soft tossing, Wyatt said, "You changed your motion."

"Didn't think you'd notice."

"You kiddin'? Been watching you since you could barely see over the center in peewee ball."

Jake explained how it had been Coach J who'd done it, and how once he tried dropping down just a little, it felt more comfortable, and now he was sticking with it because it was working for him.

Jake said, "Dad was none too pleased when he finally saw me throwing like this in a game."

They moved back a little now, putting more on their throws, Jake smiling to himself, thinking that it wasn't just his brother out here with him, it was the quarterback of the Longhorns.

"Shocker about Dad," Wyatt said. "What'd he say, that you'd stopped throwing like me?"

"Pretty much."

"Course you know that's just code for him telling you he wants you to throw like *him*."

"Yeah." Jake threw his brother a tight spiral, putting some snap on it.

"Looks good to me," Wyatt said.

Now Wyatt threw hard, the ball stinging Jake's hands, like Wyatt showing off *his* arm. An unspoken contest that had been going on for as long as Jake could remember, even being four years younger. Never just a game of catch, not with him.

More like a game of catch-*up*.

Jake said, "You better move back. I can see you're babying that college arm of yours, but I feel like I got my good heater going today."

"Babying?" Wyatt said, and threw one now like he was throwing into double coverage, like he wanted to knock his kid brother down if he could.

"Oh," Jake said, "so it's gonna be like that?"

Wyatt grinned. "Hasn't it always, little brother?"

Jake knowing that Wyatt was always going to call him that, even if Jake ended up being bigger than Big Ben Roethlisberger.

They started running pass patterns for each other after a while, both of them starting to air the ball out big-time, Jake realizing—maybe for the first time in his life—that he had as much arm as his older brother did.

When they finally took a break, both of them hitting the water bottles they'd brought out here with them, Wyatt said, "I forgot how much losing sucks."

"Dad's right," Jake said. "One game."

"You start to think that college is gonna go the way high school did, that you're just gonna crush it," Wyatt said. "Till you go and *get* crushed."

"Oklahoma better look out," Jake said, "goin' up against a highly motivated Cullen boy."

They both lay back in the grass, staring at the sky, sun on their faces, neither one of them saying anything until Wyatt broke the silence. "Daddy tries to change your throwing back, call me. I'll talk to him."

"Aw, man, you know his deal. He's been stuck my whole life on me doing it like you."

"Not as stuck as he is on me being him," Wyatt said. "I know you think it's been hard being you, having to follow me."

"Just part of it," Jake said.

"You ought to try being me sometimes, having to live out Dad's dream about quarterbacking the by-God Texas Longhorns."

They'd never really had conversations like this, maybe because of the difference in their ages, brother-to-brother or heart-to-heart or whatever you wanted to call them. Wyatt wasn't that kind of talker, never had been, letting you in on his feelings, what he was thinking. As popular as he'd always been, even becoming the kind of star he'd become at Granger High, as many friends as he always had in the pack around him, Wyatt had always hung back. Like he was always waiting for the world to make the first move.

Holding back so much of himself, even from his own family. As Libby Cullen liked to say to Jake, "The difference between you and your brother is that you actually tell me things."

Lying in the grass next to Wyatt, neither one of them in much of a hurry to get back up and start throwing again, Jake said, "You're telling me you're the one feeling the pressure in this family? Heck, look at me right *now*. I'm feeling more pressure than I ever did in my life, just trying to hold on to my part of the job."

Wyatt really laughed now. "Are you serious? I think if I'd told Dad that I wanted to be a receiver or a running back he would've told me to go find another family in Granger, go live with them, have a nice life."

"Did you? Want to play another position?"

"Don't be stupid, I always wanted to be a quarterback, even if I didn't have a choice. By the time I was ten I knew I was better than anybody else in town. I just didn't realize until later, when I got to high school, that I was always going to have to be better than my best."

Jake turned, grinned. "I have no idea what that means."

"I had to be better than Dad had been," Wyatt said. "Heck, I'm the quarterback of the 'Horns as a freshman, and I already know that's just the start of it."

"You've only played college football for one month, only lost one game," Jake said.

"Big Troy's already wondering—out loud of course, only way he knows—if I should come out after my junior year. Already got his eyes on the pros."

No wonder Dad can't see me, Jake thought. *Not only is he watching Wyatt this close, he's already trying to see down the road with him.*

"By the time you're a junior, they'll be talking about you for the Heisman," Jake said, "if you haven't won one of those already."

"Yeah, yeah, yeah," Wyatt said. "Listen, I know Dad means well. It's just he feels like he got cheated, all those hits to the head. I just wonder if he ever sees that he doesn't want all this for me as much as he wants it for himself."

He wasn't talking to Jake like Jake was just this annoying kid brother now, the kid brother who'd always been looking for attention as much from Wyatt as he had from his dad.

He was talking to Jake, for the first time Jake could ever remember, like they were equals.

"Dad loves you more than anything," Jake said.

"Tell me about it."

Wyatt rolled over now, put his elbow in the grass, propped his head in his hand. "You havin' fun? Even with all that terrible pressure you were just crying about?"

Jake couldn't help it. He grinned. "Mad fun."

"You know why? Because this wasn't *expected* of you. Wasn't supposed to happen for you, at least not this soon, even if you end up sharing the job the rest of the way. Coach McCoy told me one time, one of his chatty moods, 'There ain't no timetable for sports that anybody can see.' Said that sports has this big clock only *it* can see. And somehow this season, all the stuff happened on the team, it just decided it was your time."

"Never thought of it like that," Jake said.

Wyatt said, "Maybe even Sarah will give you a second look one of these days."

"Whoa, who told you about Sarah?" Jake said. "Not that there's anything to tell."

"Mom."

"Nothing going on there," Jake said. "Less than nothing."

"Make your move, little brother."

"Probably all she sees," Jake said. "Your little brother."

Wyatt jumped up suddenly, like changing the subject, ball in his right hand. "Okay, you've been showing off your fancy new motion; let's see who can chuck it the farthest." Wyatt tossed the ball to Jake, saying, "You first."

"Running start?"

"Whatever edge you think you need, high school boy."

Jake windmilled his arm for show, gave himself five yards to gain some momentum, threw the ball with everything he had in the direction of an old spruce that was at least sixty yards away. Gave Wyatt a stare, not saying a word, ran and got the ball, brought it back, tossed it to his older brother.

Flexed his arm, like he was showing Wyatt his muscle.

"Like it," Wyatt said. "Chirping on me without saying a word. That was a good throw, to that old tree," he said. "Excellent."

Then took a few running steps himself, let the ball go.

Flew it past the old spruce by ten yards, at least.

Turned to Jake, smiling, and said, "See what proper mechanics will do for you?"

Jake put a shoulder down, put an easy tackle on him, both of them rolling around in the grass the way they always had, laughing, trying to pin each other.

When they stopped, they got up, headed back to the house. As they passed the barn, Jake said to Wyatt, "I know you think it's hard, Dad fixed on every little thing you do. But sometimes I feel like he's not seeing me at all."

Opening up to his brother now the way his brother had opened up to him.

"I feel you," Wyatt said. "Like I joke with dad: Neither one of us pulled ol' Archie Manning in the dad draft."

Jake said, "From what I've read, on Eli especially, doesn't seem like he ever felt like he got overlooked by *his* dad."

"You were always the smart one with all the A's. Not like me. I think you might've surprised our daddy the way you surprised yourself a little bit this season. Comin' on as quick as you did. Almost like he wasn't ready for you."

"Think he ever will be?" Jake said.

"Yeah, I do," Wyatt said to Jake. "Just keep on keepin' on, little brother. You'll make him see eventually." Gave Jake a little shove and said, "Whether he's ready for you or not."

Jake wasn't sure if he was right about that. But they'd done enough talking for one day.

"Race you," Jake said now, and they both took off for the house, Jake starting to ease up so Wyatt could pass him, then laughing as he pulled away at the end.

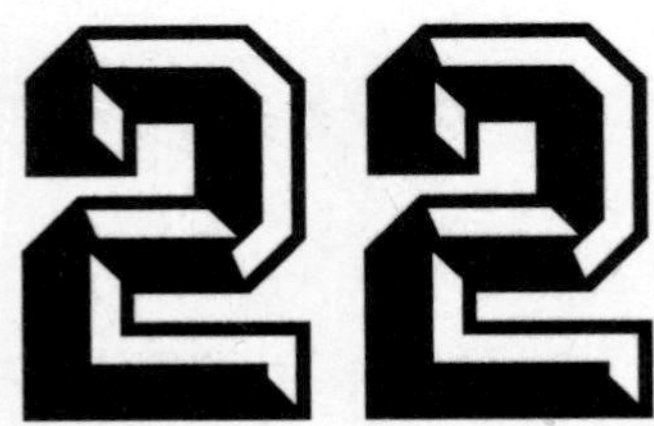

JAKE KEPT LOOKING FOR SIGNS THAT THINGS HAD CHANGED between him and Sarah, just because of the way she'd run out to the parking lot that night at Stone's. But, man, if there were signs, he was missing them; more than ever he wished that he could read girls the way he could read defenses.

She was nice enough to him when they'd see each other at school, and he didn't feel nearly as tongue-tied with her as he had at the start of the year. There were even a couple of times when he and Nate and Bear sat with Sarah and her friends at lunch.

The only good news? She wasn't with Casey anymore that Jake could see, in the cafeteria or anyplace else. Maybe Jake had read *that* wrong, too; maybe they'd never been hanging out at all, maybe Casey just wanted it to look that way.

But one thing hadn't changed, far as Jake could tell, and never would: Sarah was a sophomore and Jake was a freshman, and even if he was a freshman playing quarterback for the Granger Cowboys, that was never going to change, the way it was never going to change that sophomore girls might be nice to a freshman every so often, the way Sarah was at Stone's, but that's as far as it was ever going to go.

Jake kept thinking of it in terms of sports: Her being one year older took him out of her league.

So he concentrated on the only league he could do anything about, the Lone Star League, Division 1AA, Texas high school football. As the Cowboys got ready to play Morgan Creek on Friday night at Cullen Field, they were nearly halfway through their regular season.

They'd beaten Bancroft the previous Friday night on the road, an easy win for them. The Cowboys had been up 28–3 by halftime. Casey had been the better quarterback on this night, throwing two touchdown passes while Jake had none—even though Casey had also thrown an interception on a pass he never should've attempted. Jake, meanwhile, had struggled most of the night, forcing a couple of throws, one of which *should* have been picked at the goal line.

Jake ended up sitting most of the second half, watching Casey run the team, wondering if they'd go back to having votes on the radio this week, which quarterback the fans of Granger liked best.

Wondering if he'd already had the best chance he was going to get to establish himself as the starter, and if maybe Casey had passed him now.

But even with all that, Jake couldn't help but see where this team was, how far it had come. If they somehow beat Morgan Creek tonight, they'd still have just one loss for the season, still be a game out of first place, no matter which of his quarterbacks Coach John McCoy liked best this week.

"Turns out what was supposed to be our rebuildin' year might just involve us *buildin'* ourselves another title," Coach Jessup was saying.

"I need to play better," Jake said, "or I'll end up watching us do it."

"You were gonna throw in a stinker, that's inevitable for even the great ones," Coach J said. "Don't start doubting yourself now."

"You act as if I ever *stopped* doubting myself," Jake said.

"You got more belief in yourself than you let on," Coach J said. "I saw that in you from the start. So did Coach McCoy; it's why he brought you along fast as he did."

"I know why you got behind me," Jake said. "But why did he?"

"Because your old coach is the one who taught me that a quarterback's brain really *is* as great a weapon as his arm," Coach Jessup said. "That some have gotten by on talent alone, but not many he ever coached. He saw that kind of brain in you, son, and heart to go with it."

"I didn't know he was watching me that close."

Coach J said, "Now that's a dumb comment from somebody with the kind of brain we're talking about. Because the thing you got to be able to see about John McCoy is that *he* sees everything. And what he saw from the git-go with you was a guy could be a game manager for him, whether he was a freshman or not."

"Good quarterbacks hate being called game managers," Jake said.

"Well," Coach J said, "football coaches just flat love 'em to death."

"Usually means you don't have the arm," Jake said.

"Or maybe it means that you've figured out that there's ten other guys out there with you, that not everybody in the world loves your arm as much as you do."

"Now we're talking about the other quarterback on the team," Jake said.

"No," Coach said. "We're just making an observation."

They were in Coach J's cramped office, two hours before the game, looking at more film on the Morgan Creek Lions.

Jake and Coach J were spending more and more time in this office, usually after practice when everybody else was gone, Jake wanting to know as much as he could about how the Cowboys' offense needed to attack whatever defense they were going up against. This was Texas high school football, after all, so teams scouted one another the way the real Cowboys scouted the Giants and Eagles and Redskins.

Right now they were looking at blitzes. The Lions loved to blitz, Jake constantly asking Coach J to freeze the picture on the old-fashioned pull-down screen he had. They could have done it on a laptop, but Jake just thought he saw things better like this.

Coach J finally said to him, "Can see why you're an A student. You must study this hard in school, too."

"I read up on Peyton and Eli," Jake said. "Tom Brady, too. And Aaron Rodgers. Sounds to me like they all spend more time in the film room than they do on the field."

"Smart quarterbacks get smarter as they go."

On the pull-down screen, the Lions were coming with an all-out blitz, from the Shelby quarterback's blind side.

"Run that again, please?" Jake said. "You see how the middle linebacker moves a step to his right before they come all-out from my left? I got to give Spence and David a heads-up on that, so they can pick it up, too."

"Yes, coach," Coach J said.

They went back to studying the Morgan Creek blitz packages in the small dark room that was the real beginning of all the noise, the bright lights, that were waiting for them later at Cullen Field.

Jake couldn't wait. As much as he'd thought he loved football coming into this season, turned out he loved it even more. Even when he messed up. Even when Casey was better.

Even in here.

"Run that again," he said to Coach Jessup.

Jake and Bear were on the field stretching before the Morgan Creek game, Bear pointing down to where the Morgan Creek Lions were stretching at the other end of the field, having just shown up in a huge bus that Bear thought might be bigger than his house.

"They're big," Bear said.

"Been seeing that on film," Jake said.

"And they're good," Bear said. "They were about to beat Redding until one of their guys dropped a punt in the last two minutes."

"They are good," Jake said. "But I'm gonna let you in on a little secret."

"What's that?"

"We're better."

Casey got the start tonight, played all of the first quarter and then into the second, the longest Jake had sat since the first game of the season. But then Casey, always in love with his arm, stared at Calvin all the way throughout the second series of the second quarter, gunslinging a throw even though a linebacker and safety had read his eyes and drifted over to blanket Calvin. The ball was intercepted and returned almost twenty yards, setting up a Morgan Creek field goal that gave them a 10–0 lead.

Coach McCoy told Jake he'd be going in when the Cowboys got the ball back.

When he got out there, he wanted to make something good happen right away, wipe away the memory of the way he'd played last weekend, the way he'd opened the door back up for Casey.

But on his fourth play, he didn't pick up one of the blitzes he'd been studying with Coach J, flat missed it and got hit just as he threw. He was on his back when the ball was intercepted, Calvin having to save a touchdown by catching one of the Morgan Creek corners from behind.

"Well, look at me," Jake said, still steamed, standing next to Nate after they came off the field. "I'm not just trying to hand the game to Morgan Creek, it's like I'm trying to hand the quarterback job to Casey on a big old steak platter."

"Relax," Nate said.

"Easy for you to say," Jake said. "You know you're going back in next series. I sure don't."

Nate moved in front of Jake now, his back to the field, the big man blocking out the game and about half the stadium, his way of getting in Jake's face, the two of them nearly face mask to face mask.

Nate said, "I've never heard you feel sorry for yourself about anything, not one time since we been friends. We still have us a game to win. So don't you start now. You hear?"

"I hear."

"We're clear then?"

"Well, yeah," Jake said, grinning at him. "But only because of how scared I am of you."

Coach decided to stay with Jake when the Cowboys got the ball back. Jake wasn't sure why he was showing this kind of confidence in him, not the way he'd just turned the ball over. But Jake was determined to reward that confidence.

And he did, all the way until it was 27–10 in the fourth quarter. The Lions had come at him with a couple more blitzes, but Jake had read them all, releasing the ball quickly, even changing one of the plays at the line of scrimmage and finding the open receiver. Twice that receiver was Calvin, who took the throws and ran them in for touchdowns, Jake certain that nobody was able to cover Calvin one-on-one, the kind of receiver that could make any quarterback look good. All he needed was the right play call so that the defense couldn't triple-team him in coverage.

The last score of the night, the game-ender, was just a straight fly off a play-action fake to the running back. It came on a third-and-one from midfield, when the Lions were stacking the line of scrimmage, certain the Cowboys would be running the ball to eat up some clock. Jake stuck the ball in Spence Tolar's belly and then pulled it out, straightening up and throwing it as far as he could, like he was trying to get it to the old spruce in the pasture.

Still, Calvin had to slow up to catch it.

He'd end up with twelve catches for two hundred and twenty yards, three scores. One of those nights when Calvin looked like a man among boys.

When Coach finally pulled him, middle of the final drive, Calvin got the biggest and loudest ovation Jake had heard at Cullen Field since Wyatt had thrown the game-winner at the end of the state championship game against Fort Carson the year before.

Calvin hugged Coach Jessup, high-fived a bunch of the defensive guys, finally took his helmet off, came and stood next to Jake at the thirty-yard line, and put his arm around him.

"Gotta tell you something," he said to Jake. "You're not your brother."

Jake couldn't help it—he laughed.

"I love you, too, Calvin," he said.

"But turns out," Calvin said, "in light of the events that transpired here tonight, you're close enough to suit my purposes."

"I'll take that as a compliment," Jake said.

"Take it any way you want."

Gave him a smile as bright as the lights.

"Damn," Calvin Morton said. "I'm good."

Jake laughed again. Calvin pulled him closer, into a hug, Jake thinking that the only reason he was doing it was because he couldn't hug himself.

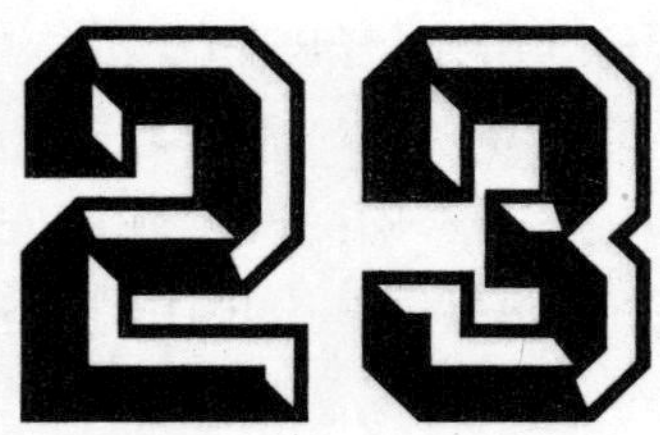

IT WASN'T UNTIL JAKE HAD SHOWERED AND MADE HIS WAY outside that he found out his dad had left at halftime, hadn't seen the best of Jake's game.

"He said to tell you he was sorry," Libby Cullen said.

Jake immediately wondered if that was true, or if it was something his mom thought she had to say to make him feel better.

"Wyatt called from Dallas, said he needed to see him," she said, "so he drove right down to the Red River game tonight, not even stopping at home for clothes. Told me he'd meet us there in the morning."

"Did something happen to Wyatt?" Jake said.

Nate and Bear, he could see, were across the parking lot, waiting for him over by Bear's truck.

Jake's mom said, "I just think he needed a pep talk from his biggest cheerleader. Or amateur psychologist. The Red River rivalry's pretty big stuff for a freshman QB."

The next morning Jake was supposed to drive with both his parents to Dallas to see Texas play Oklahoma in the Red River game, one of college football's biggest rivalries, held annually in the Cotton Bowl stadium.

Suddenly, though, he wasn't so sure about that.

"So Dad drove all the way down there tonight just to, like, prop Wyatt up?" he said to his mom. "Wyatt's never needed propping up by anybody his whole life."

Libby Cullen smiled at him, shrugged. "I guess he had a bad week of practice, and then the other quarterback got more snaps with the first team than usual. I just spoke to him briefly before I handed the phone to your father. He just sounded worried about tomorrow, like he might lose his job if he didn't play well, even though he didn't come right out and say so."

"I played bad against Bancroft," Jake said. "Dad didn't seem too worried about how I was doing. I'm fighting every week to be the number one QB on this team. How come Dad never gave me one of his famous pep talks?"

"Maybe he didn't think you needed one," his mom said.

"And how would he know that?" Jake said.

In that moment, Jake was thinking about when Wyatt had been home, Wyatt telling Jake not to worry, he'd make their dad really see him sooner or later.

Well, not if he wasn't around.

"I think I get it," Jake said. "The game Wyatt hasn't even played yet was more important than the one I was playing right in front of him."

"It wasn't like that."

"Usually I'm the one making excuses for Dad over stuff like this," Jake said. "Not you, Mom."

"He felt bad, Jacob, really he did."

"Well, guess what, Mom? Sometimes I do, too, whether I show it or not. You know what I think sometimes? That I can't win with him, even when I *do* win."

"Do you want to ride home with me and take a little time to regroup?" she said.

"Gonna ride into town with the boys. Some of them are going to Amy's," he said.

"Now remember, don't stay out too late," his mom said. "The two of us have to leave pretty early for Dallas."

"You know what, Mom?" Jake said. "I think I might pass, do my regrouping tomorrow while I watch the game on TV."

"Now, Jacob," she said, "you've been saying all week how much you were looking forward to the game. You haven't seen Wyatt play a game in person since last year's championship game."

"I can catch him later in the season," he said. Kissed her on the cheek and said, "But right now I gotta bounce."

"Bounce back, how about that?"

"Didn't think I'd have to, not the way we played tonight. The way I played."

"Wyatt didn't do this," Libby Cullen said.

"He never does," Jake said. "Does he?" Smiled as he said that, one he didn't feel and didn't mean. But he didn't want to make his mom feel as if she'd done anything, either.

Because at least his mom had been here. For the whole game.

Jake gave her one more quick kiss on the cheek, walked toward Bear's truck, the lights of Cullen Field still bright behind him, the sound of music, loud, coming from a car somewhere behind Bear and Nate in the parking lot.

Jake knew he should have been hearing something else still, the cheers he and the Granger Cowboys had heard all night long.

But no matter how hard he tried, he couldn't.

He decided not to tell Bear or Nate about his dad. No reason to bring them into it, do anything that might put a dent in their night. All they'd done was help their team win the game, Bear getting more time at outside linebacker tonight than he had all season, all pumped up about that, about finally being a real part of the team.

But when his boys started talking up the game on the way to Bear's truck, like they wanted to replay it here and all the way into town, Jake decided, just like that, that he wasn't ready to leave yet. Didn't want to leave all that had happened, the good parts, at Cullen Field just yet.

Just wanted to go inside and be alone there for a few minutes, maybe see if he could hear the cheers again if he tried hard enough.

Told his boys to go ahead, he'd get a ride into town from Coach J if he had to. He always stayed after the game, looking at game film right away.

"Don't know what's going on, 'cause you're not sayin'," Nate said. "But we're not leavin' you."

"You know our rule," Bear said. "No Cullen left behind."

"I don't remember us passing that rule," Jake said.

"We did it just now, you were talkin' to your mom," Nate said. "So go do what you got to do to get yourself right. Bear and I will just sit here and keep goin' through our own personal highlights." Nate smiled. "Mine mostly."

"So please don't be long," Bear said.

Jake walked back through the tunnel, out onto the field, not sure when they shut off the lights after a game—he'd never stayed around long enough on even Wyatt's Friday nights—walked across some of the more chewed-up parts of the grass, walked right past what he knew was the exact spot where he'd been pulled down on the ten-yard line after a third-down scramble that set up a slant to Calvin that was one of the best throws he'd made all year, even if it couldn't have traveled more than five yards, the space he'd had no wider than the front of Calvin's jersey.

Thinking: *What would Dad have thought about my throwing motion on that one?*

If he'd been in his seat to see, that is.

He wanted to rally now, clear his mind. That was what he was really in here to do, not let this ruin the rest of his night or let it steal his joy. Wanting in the worst way to get himself an attitude adjustment before he saw Sarah.

Of all the games his dad missed, why did this one bother him so much? He knew a big part of it: Jake was playing tonight and Wyatt wasn't, so he didn't have the excuse of choosing Wyatt's college game over Jake's high school game, the way he had been.

Tomorrow for Wyatt being more important than tonight for Jake. Again.

Jake stopped and looked at the field again, walked up to where he'd cut one loose to Calvin for forty yards, smiled now.

That cheer he could hear.

Went over now and sat himself down on the bench.

"Damn, they should name this place after you. No, *wait*. They already went and did."

Calvin.

Again, Jake hearing him before he saw him. Guy had a gift for it.

Jake turned and saw him sitting in the front row of the stands, bright white sneakers up on the railing in front of him.

"Calvin, what in the world are you still doing here?"

Calvin leaned back, cool like, put his hands behind his head, showed Jake teeth almost as bright as the sneakers he was wearing.

"Was tryin' to make my own top ten highlights, just about me," Calvin said. "But couldn't cut the list *down* to ten was the problem." Motioned for Jake to come over. "Come sit awhile 'fore my ride comes. Tell me what the last star Cullen in Cullenville is doin' out here his own self."

"One condition," Jake said. "No Cullen stuff tonight. Okay?"

Calvin said, "You tellin' me this night has to be different from all the others? Doesn't work that way. Carry the name, deal with the fame. And all the other stuff comes with it."

Jake hopped over the railing, sat down next to him, said, "Ask you something, Number One? You ever ride my brother this much about being a Cullen?"

"Whether I did or didn't, doesn't matter. Told you already, you're not him."

"Sometimes," Jake said, "I forget." Turned and looked at Calvin and said, "What are you really doing out here, with everybody else gone?"

"Do it every game, you just never came and saw me. Really do go over the game in my mind. What I did good and the few things I did bad." Grinning as he said the last part. "I look at film same as you, more than you know. But I first got to see it inside my head, while it's still fresh. And I can still hear the roar of the crowd, baby."

Him too, then.

"But the difference between you and me right here is that I'm feeling soooo good about myself. And you look like you lost the game tonight. Or maybe your best friend."

Jake took a deep breath, let it out. "Between us?"

"You can trust me here the way you trust me out there."

Then Jake told him about his father leaving the game when he did. Not sure why he was telling Calvin this when he didn't tell his best friends, when he thought he wanted to be alone with all of it. Here he was, anyway, in here looking for quiet time and now telling his secrets to the loudest guy he knew.

"It was like my dad telling me, straight up, no more getting around it, that Wyatt will always matter more than I do, leastways when it comes to football," Jake said. "I knew it inside me already. But this time it got to me more than the others."

For once, Calvin Morton was silent, face serious. Not saying anything until he said to Jake, "That it? You done now?"

"Pretty much."

"You waitin' for me to respond, am I right?"

"Yeah, I guess I am."

"Boo hoo," Calvin said.

"Huh?"

"I said, boo hoo. Let me ask you a question, Cullen, now that you're feelin' so sorry for yourself. You ever even seen *my* daddy around here?"

"Now that I think of it, no. Just your mom."

"Right, just my momma. That's because my dad hasn't ever come to one of my games ever, is why."

In that moment, it occurred to Jake how little he knew about Calvin's life away from football. Or school. He knew Melvin was his cousin, he'd seen Calvin with his mom in the parking lot after games. He knew some of the girls he liked, because there was never just one with him. But that was it. Jake didn't even know where Calvin's dad was.

"Is he around here, your dad?"

"He's *never* been around, from the time I was six and he walked out, said he was going out for a quart of milk and went and lived with his girlfriend and the family he'd already started with her, as it turned out, over there in Plano. Put it another way, Cullen: It isn't like I sit around on my birthday every year waiting for a call or a card."

"I'm sorry," Jake said, because he was. And because he didn't know what else to say.

"I don't want your sorry," Calvin said. "You're missin' my point here. What I'm tryin' to do is tell you to stop feelin' sorry for yourself. So your daddy showed up and then left tonight. So he missed the last two quarters. How about my own daddy missin' *all* the quarters, like he's tryin' to set the Texas state high school record for that? How about him doin' that my whole damn life?"

The lights suddenly dimmed at Cullen Field and the sprinklers started to come on, one after another, in formation, moving down the field, the sound of the water being sprayed on the grass the only sound in here right now.

"I didn't know any of that," Jake said.

"Lot you don't know about me," Calvin said. "But you still got time to learn." Now he smiled again. "About me and from me."

He pulled his sneakers back off the railing, noticed a speck of dirt on one of them, wet a finger, cleaned it off, and stood up.

"Got to be someplace," he said.

"Me too," Jake said.

Calvin looked at him and said, "You ain't nearly as good as you're gonna be, Cullen. And maybe ain't *ever* gonna be as good as you want to be. But you ought to appreciate what you got, next time you want to throw yourself a damn pity party."

Calvin didn't wait for an answer. Just hopped over that railing now, graceful as a cat jumping off a couch, managed to stay clear of the sprinklers—not even hurrying when it looked like the water might get him—walked out of Cullen Field and into the tunnel and never looked back.

Leaving Jake in his dust the way he had the Morgan Creek Lions.

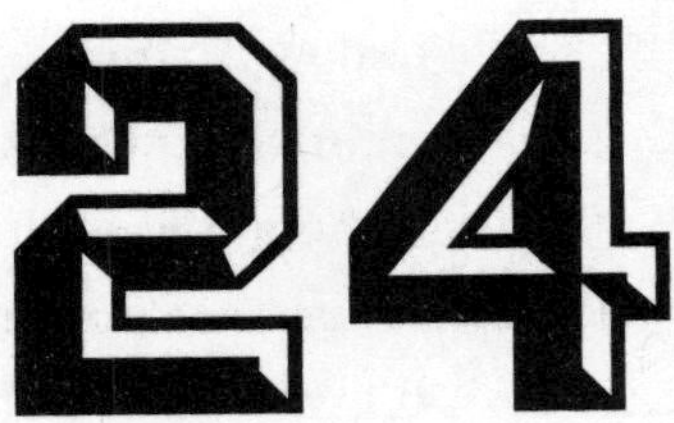

WYATT CULLEN DIDN'T PLAY GREAT AGAINST OKLAHOMA IN the Red River game, not by a long shot. But he was way better than he had been in that loss to Kansas, throwing a touchdown against one pick and scoring the winning touchdown on a quarterback sneak after the defense—which had carried Texas that day—had caused a fumble deep in Oklahoma territory.

When Troy Cullen did get home, of course he thought that the pep talk he'd given Wyatt the night before the game had made all the difference.

He had grinned and said, "Looks like I can still get 'er done in the big game."

"Yes, dear," Libby Cullen had said. "I'm surprised they didn't give you one of the game balls."

"Have your fun," Troy Cullen had said. "Wyatt would tell you, not that I'd ever want you to bring it up, that I got his head back to bein' screwed on right." He looked at Jake and said, "You missed a good one."

"Wyatt didn't need me there when he had you."

Knowing he could always get by telling his dad what he wanted to hear.

Troy Cullen never said anything about leaving Jake's game early, and Jake never asked him about it, maybe because he knew the answer, knew that in that moment, his dad had just decided that Wyatt needed him more.

"Well, I hope you're all rested up now," Troy Cullen said. "Because it's startin' to look like you boys could still win the whole God-darn thing."

The Cowboys still had just that one loss, in their opener. It was why they were sitting right there in the standings, second place still, behind the Shelby Mustangs. There probably wasn't a guy on the team who would have said it after they lost to Shelby the way they did—or maybe even thought it in their wildest dreams—but in a season when the Cowboys were supposed to be going nowhere, they were starting to get the idea, not so crazy anymore, that they could go all the way.

And it was Jake's mom who'd always said that the problem with a good idea was that once it got inside your head, it was almost impossible to get it out.

Now it was the Thursday night before the Niles game, what should have been a school night but wasn't because of teacher conferences the next day. So Jake was supposed to meet Nate at Sal's for an early pizza, Bear being forced to stay home and study. He was doing that badly in English and history—his parents didn't care if he had off the next day or not, they were threatening to take the keys to his truck away if he didn't pick it up in school.

So Libby Cullen drove Jake into town, Jake knowing a lot of guys on the team would be around, telling her he'd call later if he needed a ride home, but he didn't think he would since there'd be plenty of rides around.

Right before she dropped him at Sal's, Nate texted him, saying that Bear had done all his work and been sprung, and that they'd be maybe forty-five minutes behind Jake. The next text said there'd been a change of plans: Bear wanted—no, needed—one of the five-napkin, double-cheese, extra-bacon specials at Ed's Burgers, just up Main Street from Sal's.

Jake said fine with him, was ready to go get a table at Ed's and wait for them until he looked through the window at Sal's and saw Sarah Rayburn sitting there by herself.

"This seat taken?" he said.

She looked up, surprised to see him, but smiled right away, the way she'd smiled at him at Stone's that night and got him to thinking he might actually get somewhere with her someday.

"No, sir," she said.

"I saw you through the window. Thought you looked lonely."

"My friends are late," she said. "Shocker."

"Mine too."

Sarah smiled again and said, "Now if I see one more pizza come out of the oven, I'm about to die, I'm so hungry."

"Me too," Jake said.

Sarah said, "How about we tell our friends they're on their own and order something for the two of us?"

"Great," Jake said.

They went and sat in a booth, Jake thinking that whether this was an accident or not, this might be as close as he ever got to having a date with this girl.

Somehow he managed to not sound like a complete idiot making small talk about the season, about the Niles game, and how things had worked out better for the team than anybody could have thought when they'd gotten their doors blown off in the opener the way they had.

"Back then," Jake said, "I got the feeling people in town wanted to just call *off* the season now that Wyatt wasn't the quarterback anymore."

"But that was before they found you," Sarah said.

"I don't know about that," Jake said. "Me and Casey, the two of us, still don't make one of Wyatt."

"I think you've done great," she said.

"Thank you."

"Be serious," Sarah said. "You ever think about pinching yourself to make sure this is all real?"

"You mean being here?" Jake said, the words out of him before he could stop them.

"I said you had to be serious," Sarah said. "I guess what I'm asking is if you ever thought you'd be one of the stars of the team in your first year?"

Jake, a noted blusher, felt himself start to redden, nothing he could do to stop it.

"There's only one star on this team," Jake said. "Calvin."

"I don't know about that," Sarah said. "My dad says that someday you're going to end up being better than your brother."

Her hair was pulled back tonight, showing off even more of her face than usual. Dark blue shirt, light green jeans, cool blue sneakers, Jake had noticed, the old-fashioned kind with no laces.

Jake said, "All due respect to your father, but has he already forgotten what Wyatt did last season?"

"Just telling you what he says," Sarah said. Now she made her voice deep and Texas, imitating her dad, and said, "You mark my words, young lady, that Jake Cullen is gonna pass his brother someday the way Eli passed Peyton."

"I think you'd find a lot of people with a fair argument against that one." He grinned. "And about Eli being anywhere near as good as Peyton."

"Daddy likes to count Super Bowl wins ahead of everything else."

"Either way, I think Wyatt and I are a long way off from being the Manning brothers. Even with the way Wyatt brought the Longhorns back against Oklahoma last week."

"That must have made everybody in the family happy," Sarah said.

"Mostly my dad," Jake said. "Listening to him when he got home, I thought he was the one who'd quarterbacked the 'Horns."

Jake started thinking about what Wyatt had said in the pasture, how he wondered if their dad would ever see that he was trying to live out his own dream through Wyatt.

Suddenly, Sarah said, "Hey you, Mr. Quarterback. Am I getting boring already? Feel like I lost you there."

Jake smiled and said, "Busted."

"What were you thinking about?"

"Can I tell you the truth," he said, "and get you to promise you won't make fun of me?"

Sarah reached across the table and put out her hand. Jake took it, knowing she just wanted to shake on it, but Jake didn't want to let go.

"Deal," she said.

"I was thinking that lately, first time in my life, I haven't wanted to be my brother."

Saying something to her he hadn't said to anybody else, not his mom, not Nate or Bear, not Coach J. Nobody. Talking like this to a girl he'd been afraid to talk to since the school year started.

"Well, that certainly sounds sensible enough to me," Sarah said.

He went to the men's room, texted Nate, told him what was going on, told him to go ahead to Ed's, he'd catch him whenever. Sarah had already called her friends, told them she'd eaten with Jake, would meet them at Amy's later for ice cream if it didn't get too late. Or they could go to Stone's for pie.

"You sure you don't want to go meet them now?" Jake said after he'd paid up, refusing to take up Sarah's offer to split the bill.

"I'm good," she said.

"You want to walk around a little bit or something?"

Without hesitating at all, Sarah said yes, she'd like that.

There were a lot of nights like this, always during the football season, when Jake just knew, mostly with his heart, that he wouldn't want to be anywhere except Granger, Texas, a place where you knew just about everybody and everybody knew you on Main Street at seven thirty the night before another big game.

A couple of Jake's teammates, Chad Mauro and Raheem Johnson, walked into Sal's as Jake and Sarah were leaving. Raheem raised his eyebrows soon as he could see Sarah wasn't looking. Jake shook his head and mouthed, *Shut up.* And kept walking. Nate and Bear had texted him from Ed's, telling him they'd just ordered and would be a while.

Through the front window of Amy's, Jake could see the front room was already filled with Granger Cowboys. It would be different in an hour or so in these places, up and down Main Street; the players would all be gone, Coach McCoy having told them at the end of practice that even though there was a school holiday tomorrow, he'd better not see any of his boys still out and about late if he got a hankering for a burger or one of Amy's milkshakes himself.

For now, Jake and Sarah walked.

It was Sarah who finally said, "This is nice."

"A nice surprise," Jake said. "Seeing you there at the counter, I mean."

Sarah said, "Can I say something to you, *you* promise you won't take it the wrong way?"

She didn't know she could say anything she wanted, anything at all, and Jake would happily take it. He still couldn't believe she was with him right now.

"This something bad?" Jake said.

"No, silly, it's not like that. It's just that . . ."

"Keep going."

"You seem older than you really are," she said.

A laugh came out of Jake, he couldn't stop it.

"You said you wouldn't take it the wrong way!" Sarah said.

"No," Jake said. "I laughed because my mom has always said the exact same thing."

"Well, we're both right. I don't mean that you're all serious or whatever. You just don't act like . . ."

"A freshman?" Jake said.

"Sometimes you don't act like you're in high school at all! The other kids in your grade, even my grade, they act plain goofy at times. You never do."

They were coming up on the park now.

Jake said, "Maybe it's just a thing happens to you, you grow up in a small town like this, knowing people are watching you, because of who you are, and your daddy, and your brother. Makes you think twice about putting on a clown suit, especially when you're out in public. Or looking at third-and-eight."

"You said you don't want to be your brother," Sarah said in a soft voice, "but the conversation keeps finding its way back to him, doesn't it?"

"That it does," Jake said. "You know what they always said about ol' Wyatt Cullen: You can't stop him, you can only try to contain him."

"You don't have to tell me what it's like," she said. "I had an older sister who was Little Miss Perfect, too."

"Wyatt was Little Miss Perfect?"

"Wow, aren't you the comedian?"

Jake said, "All I know about your older sister is that she is old enough to already be through college."

"The college being Yale," she said. "Drama major." Sarah's eyes got big and she said, "But then she's been a drama major her whole life. In addition to being a soccer star. She was always the one. I was never much good at sports, unless you think of cheerleading as a sport. Do you, by the way?"

"Absolutely!" Jake said.

She punched his arm and called him a big liar.

"No way," he said. "I can't believe some of the stuff you guys do."

"Anyway," she said, "she was Miss Perfect, and I'm leading cheers. But I have fun doing it, and it makes me feel like a part of the team. And, who knows, maybe I'll end up being a dancer someday."

"Really?"

"There's a lot you don't know about me," she said. "But at least now you know that *I* know a little bit about having the spotlight be on somebody else growing up."

"Thank you," Jake said.

"For what?"

"For telling me that."

They heard some laughter now from across the street as they got to the entrance to the park, saw some of the guys from the team leaving Amy's. And then some of the offensive linemen, Buddy Herzlich and Dicky Grider, coming out of Ed's.

Big-game Thursday night on Main Street, not just kids out

there, but adults, too, waving and calling out to Jake and telling him to have a good one.

If he wasn't officially the number one quarterback now, he felt like one on this night. And realized that people in this town weren't just looking at him, they were looking *to* him. Wanting him to make them proud, make it all right that they cared about a high school football team as much as they did, at Ed's and Amy's and Sal's and Stone's, and on J. D. Frederick's radio show and of course at coffee shops and filling stations in the morning.

David Stevens and Spence Tolar, his two running backs, came up to him and said, "You ready?"

"Let's go play 'em right now," Jake said.

David said, "Can I digest my five-napkin Ed's burger first?"

He and Spence moved on. Aaron Saunders and Justice yelled at Jake from across the street. Jake waved at them and Aaron yelled over, "Sarah, what are you doing with that loser?"

Now Sarah yelled back at him and said, "Did you forget how to keep score?"

Jake and Sarah sat down on a bench, and Sarah slipped her arm through his like it was the most natural thing in the world.

"You guys really seem to like one another," she said.

"Good teams don't need to have every single guy like one another," Jake said. "But it sure doesn't hurt when it happens that way."

He was so focused on Sarah that he didn't even notice Casey Lindell until he was standing right in front of them.

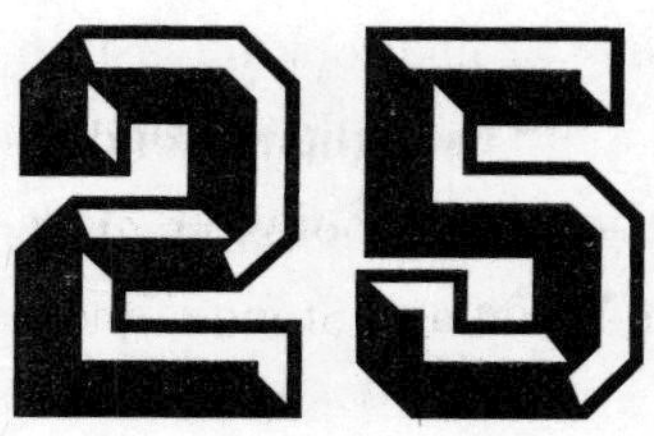

25

HE WAS STANDING WITH HIS HANDS ON HIS HIPS AND IGNORING Sarah, not even saying hello to her, focused on Jake.

"Well, look at you," Casey said. "Having a nice night?"

Jake, keeping his own voice down, said, "Everybody's been having one."

Casey was wearing a Spurs T-shirt with the sleeves cut up to his shoulders. Faded old jeans. Boots.

"Just not as nice as you're having," he said. "Like you're the mayor of Granger."

"Now, Casey Lindell," Sarah said, smiling up at him, leaving her arm where it was. "*You* be nice."

"I kept thinking I was wrong, that we'd both get the same chance," Casey said to Jake. "But I can see where this is going, no matter what I do." Casey shook his head, like he was sad. "Coach and them said all along it would be a fair fight. But we both know it's not."

"We're both playing quarterback for the Cowboys, last time I checked," Jake said.

"We both throw a pick, but you're the one left in. Now you're starting against Niles."

"And you started against Morgan Creek. Seems to me it's who finishes that counts. I'm the starter tomorrow night. Nothing more."

"In the biggest game of the year so far," Casey said. "So I'm all the way back to where I was when I got to this town. A backup. To a *freshman*."

Making it sound like that was some kind of dirty word.

"I kept trying to tell you it wasn't ever a fight," Jake said. "The only one ever saw it that way was you."

"Doesn't matter that I'm a better thrower of the ball than you'll *ever* be," Casey said. Voice rising up, like he wanted everybody on Main Street to hear. "Why wouldn't I think the quarterback job in this town is just something gets passed from Cullen to Cullen?"

"Casey, we played this out already. You're wrong about all this, mostly about me."

"I got two years of high school football left," Casey said. "I was willing to wait my turn even though everybody could see I was a better quarterback than Tim from the time we got to camp. Even if you backed me up for two years, you'd still have two more after I'm gone. But nobody in this whole town, including our old coach, seems to think you should ever have to wait your turn."

"You don't know me," Jake said.

"You're Jake Cullen," he said. "Everybody knows you."

"You think I didn't wait my turn behind my brother?" Jake said in a quiet voice. "You think I didn't wonder if my turn would ever come?"

"I don't want to hear about your problems," Casey said.

"Didn't expect that you would," Jake said.

Casey nodded at Sarah and said, "Far as I can see, you're overcoming your problems just fine. Guess any Cullen'll do."

Jake could feel Sarah's hand gripping his arm.

Jake stood up anyway. Like at Stone's. Just feeling different this time.

"You say what you want to me," he said. "But you're being rude to Sarah, and I'm gonna have to ask you to stop now."

"You know what everybody says, right?" Casey said. "She couldn't get near your brother so now she's with you."

Jake took a step.

"Enough."

"Or what?" Casey said. "You finally gonna man up about all this?"

Jake could see guys from the team watching from the other side of the street. Some started to cross Main Street now. Sensing that something was about to happen with their quarterbacks.

Jake heard a laugh then.

"Lindell, what in the world do you know about how to man up?"

Calvin Morton.

Standing there with his cousin Melvin. The two of them having come out of the park from Jake's left, Calvin for once not announcing his own arrival.

Until now.

"Sorry, didn't mean to interrupt, but I couldn't listen to none of this for even one more minute," he said to Casey. "You talkin' about being a man and acting like a little boy."

"This doesn't involve you, Calvin," Casey said.

"See now, that's where you're wrong," Calvin said. "Ever'thing involving this team and its general well-being involves me. Specially if I see somebody doesn't seem to *care* about its general well-being."

"You're going to give me some kind of lecture now about being a good teammate?"

"Matter of fact, I am," Calvin said. He'd been smiling, but now he stopped. "Because I *am* a good teammate. No, that's not quite right, now that I think about it. I'm a *great* teammate, and so is he." Nodding at Jake. "He's a better teammate than you and a better all-around quarterback, and he beat you out this job fair and square. Starting with him knowing that there's more to being a quarterback than being a thrower."

Casey opened his mouth and closed it. Maybe starting to realize there was no way out of this now, not with his swag, anyway.

"Now drop this right here and right now and move along," Calvin said. "And one more thing? Between now and tomorrow night, you decide whether you want to be on this team or not."

Sarah still sat on the bench, not moving, watching the scene being played out right here in front of her. Jake hadn't moved. He could see a few guys from the team, Spence and David, Dicky and Buddy, maybe halfway down the block. Nate and Bear had suddenly appeared, too. Melvin was right where he had been, behind Calvin.

Somehow Calvin was between Jake and Casey now, Jake not even sure when it had happened.

"You've done taken this as far as you're gonna take it," Calvin said to Casey. "We both know it, to the point where there isn't nothin' left to say and no reason for you to be here."

And in that moment, there wasn't for Casey Lindell, who turned, shot one last glare toward Jake, like he had to get in a last word, and walked alone into the park.

When he was gone, Calvin turned to Melvin and said, "Let's bounce."

To Jake he said, "See you tomorrow."

"Yeah, man," Jake said.

Calvin gave a little bow and said, "Night, Sarah."

"Night, Calvin."

Calvin looked back at Jake then, grinned, reached out, cool-like, put out his fist. Jake bumped it. Then Calvin and his cousin walked across Main Street, knowing all eyes were on him, strutting like he did when he wanted to put it on.

The real mayor of Granger, Texas.

BEFORE SARAH LEFT, SHE SAID, "WHAT DO YOU THINK WOULD'VE happened if Calvin hadn't happened along?"

"Probably something dumb."

"Casey's not a bad guy," Sarah said. "Not really."

"I know," Jake said. "His ego gets in the way, for sure, on *and* off the field. But he's like me, he just wants to play. And when I think about it, I can see how maybe he thinks the deck got stacked against him."

"I was just afraid that fight he was talking about was going to turn into a real one," Sarah said.

"I'm hoping he would've backed off," Jake said. "But it was like I told him, I wasn't gonna stand there and let him insult you."

"I can take care of myself," she said.

Jake grinned and said, "I don't doubt you can."

Then Sarah Rayburn smiled at Jake one last time tonight, before she said. "I've got an idea. Next time we want to come to town together, we should make an official plan. Maybe after we beat Niles."

"Do we have to invite Casey?" Jake said.

"No," Sarah said. "I don't believe we should," and then she ran off to find her friends.

On the ride home, Nate and Bear had wanted to know exactly what had happened with Casey and Calvin.

"Just a bunch of stuff that has nothing to do with us winning the game tomorrow night," Jake said.

And it didn't.

The score was 21–0 for Granger after the first quarter, Jake having thrown three touchdown passes already, two to Calvin. By the start of the fourth quarter it was 35–7, a certified beatdown, and it was only then that Casey Lindell got into the game.

And when he did, it was mostly to hand the ball off the rest of the way, because Coach McCoy was never going to let one of his teams run up the score.

Casey hadn't said a word to Jake about what had happened at the park from the time they'd both showed up in the locker room, didn't say a word to him on the sideline even when Jake would come off from throwing for another score. But Jake didn't have time to worry about the other quarterback because of the way he was playing himself, against a good team that nobody expected the Cowboys to blow out, but sure did.

There wasn't a defense the Broncos threw at him that surprised him, there wasn't a read that he missed. It was as if all the time he'd spent watching film with Coach Jessup had paid off big-time. He knew it wasn't like some final exam, he knew there was still more football to be played if they were going to have another shot at the state championship.

But Jake knew it would sure do for now, standing on the sideline with Bear, watching the clock run down in the fourth quarter, baseball cap on his head, big old smile on his face that nothing or nobody was going to wipe off.

His dad wasn't there, as usual. Texas was playing on the road the next day against Notre Dame in South Bend. But Libby Cullen was in her seat and Sarah was down the sideline, waving to Jake a couple of times when the Granger defense was on the field.

This was a big win over Niles, even bigger than the Cowboys knew. Because later on in the fourth quarter came the news that began on Twitter and had soon made its way from the stands to the Cowboys' bench. The Shelby Mustangs had lost to Redding.

The Cowboys were now in a three-way tie with them for first place.

First place. For now, at least.

Notre Dame upset Texas on national television the next afternoon. Wyatt threw two picks in the first half, one his fault, one the fault of his tight end, who bobbled a sure completion so badly, the ball finally bounced into the hands of one of the Notre Dame safeties, who ran it sixty yards for a score that put the Longhorns into an early hole from which they never did climb out.

When Wyatt threw another interception halfway through the third quarter—this one all his fault—the coach benched him. Chris Bishop, the backup, almost brought the Longhorns back from three touchdowns behind, even had a Hail Mary in the end zone on the last play of the game that got knocked down.

Fighting Irish 34, Longhorns 27.

Jake watched the game at home with his mother. He found himself wondering what his dad was going through, sitting in the stands and watching it all happen to Wyatt this way, in front of the whole country, again.

But also wondering, when it was over, if the only starting quarterback in the family now might be him.

Jake was out behind the barn around noon on Sunday, practicing his throwing, a half-dozen balls in the bucket he brought out with him, dropping back sometimes, rolling sometimes, to his right and to his left, trying to hit as many fence posts as he could. Hitting a lot of them, like he was still as hot as he'd been on Friday night against Niles.

He was picking up balls when he saw his dad coming around the barn, Jake knowing he'd driven up to Chicago from South Bend, stayed the night at an airport hotel, flown to Dallas in the morning, and driven home.

Jake watched him come, in an old gray sweatshirt, a pair of his Wranglers, his Justin Boots, and tried to remember the last time it had been just the two of them out here.

"How about you take a little rest and we sit for a spell?" Troy Cullen said.

Jake put the balls in the bucket, went and sat in the grass next to his dad, who looked tired today. And maybe a little old.

"Your mom and me just had a talk," he said. "Well, she did most of the talkin', to be honest, lit into me pretty good about how I got two sons playin' football seasons, not just one. And how it ate you up a little bit the time I left your game early to head to the Red River."

Jake shrugged. "I got over it."

Jake waited. Not only couldn't he remember the last time his dad had been out here with him, he couldn't remember the last time they'd had a real sit-down about anything other than the game they were watching.

But he knew they were about to have one now.

"You feel the same as she does?" Troy Cullen said. "About how she says I favor Wyatt sometimes?"

Sometimes.

Maybe it was the game Jake had just played or the season he was playing. Maybe it was the confidence he could feel growing in him with each game as the Cowboys' quarterback and—yes sir—the confidence he'd gotten being with Sarah Rayburn. Maybe it was all that and the way, as Bear kept telling him, he'd gotten all growed up in front of the whole town's eyes.

Jake turned himself so he was facing his dad and said, "I've always felt that way, you want to know the plain truth."

"Well, you're wrong."

It was Jake's call now. Drop this or keep going with it.

"No," he said, "I don't think I am."

In a voice that surprised Jake, as small as it was, Troy Cullen said, "I love you both."

"Never said you didn't," Jake said. "But you've got to know that Wyatt comes first."

He couldn't believe they'd gotten here this fast; his dad hadn't shown up but a couple of minutes before. But Jake wasn't backing down now any more than he had with Casey the other night at the park. Hadn't done it then, wasn't going to do it now. There'd always been the joke in their family, when he and Wyatt were both a lot younger, his dad saying, "Don't make me take you out behind the barn."

It had never happened. Until now. Here they were. Only question in Jake's mind was which one of them was going to get taught a lesson.

His dad smiled. "Well, technically he *did* come first."

"You know what I mean, Dad," Jake said. "If there's one thing I learned about you growing up was that you do what you want to do and nobody in this world, not even Mom, really makes you do something other than that. Or go someplace you don't want to go. That night you left, being with Wyatt is where you *wanted* to be."

"You and your mom must have gotten your stories straight," Troy Cullen said, "because that sounds a lot like the earful I just got from her."

In a quiet voice, Jake said, "I don't need Mom explaining my life to me."

"Something wrong with your life now?" Troy Cullen said. "That what this is about?"

Not in a mad way or mean way. Acting genuinely surprised.

"That's not what this is about, and you know it," Jake said, keeping his voice nice and even. "And what you have to know is that things between you and Wyatt are different."

"I love you the same," Troy Cullen said, like that was his story and he was by-God sticking to it.

"No," Jake said, "you *don't*."

"All 'cause I left one game and then missed your best?" Troy Cullen said. "We've gone over this. He needed me."

"Almost as much," Jake said, "as you wanted to be needed."

"I'd be there for you, you really needed me," his dad said. "But up to now, you never have."

"And how would you know that, exactly?"

Maybe five feet of grass between them. Still like they were going toe to toe. Like on this one Sunday afternoon this was the hottest place on the whole ranch, or maybe the whole town.

"I just—"

He stopped. Like he wanted to get this right. Maybe like he was changing a play at the line of scrimmage.

"You surprised me this year," he said. "Getting this good this fast. Wanting it as much as you did. I just . . . What I'm trying to say is that you were ready for it all before I was ready for you to turn into this kind of quarterback this fast. Does that make sense to you?"

Now Jake was the one surprised. "Actually, Dad, it does."

Neither one of them spoke until Troy Cullen said, "So we good?"

Jake could have let it go, could have let his dad put a smiley face on their talk, like you did with a text message sometimes. But he wasn't out here to be a pleaser today, he'd come too far to just let him off as easy as that.

"The *good,*" Jake said, "is that maybe you're finally finding out who I am, even though you never tried very hard."

"I know who you are," Troy Cullen said. "You're my *son*."

"Yeah," Jake said. "The other one."

"That's not fair."

"Maybe what's not fair is your own father thinking you're not good enough."

"You've always been plenty good, son. You've got a brain on you could power a football stadium at night. You don't think I can see that?"

"You're right," Jake said. "I figure you can see that. But what you've never done is act like it's all that important to you. At least not as important as having an *arm* could power a football stadium at night."

"Maybe it's the only kind of power I can understand."

His voice sounded a little sad as he said it, looking away as he did.

"And maybe you just made my point for me," Jake said.

He got up then, picked up his bucket, told his dad he had to go, that Bear and Nate were going to be coming for him. They were going to watch the games over at Bear's this afternoon, maybe all the way through the Sunday night game.

Truth was, Bear wasn't coming for another hour. But Jake

knew there was nothing left to say, not now. Jake knew his dad well enough to know he wasn't going to back up, either. Or admit Jake was right.

Because that would have meant Troy Cullen was wrong.

Jake started walking in the direction of the barn.

His dad, though, wasn't quite done yet. He never wanted to let anybody have the last word, except Libby Cullen sometimes.

"Well, you're right about one thing," Troy Cullen said, calling out after him, trying to keep his tone light. "Sometimes I *don't* know you."

"Sure you do," Jake said. "I'm a Cullen."

FINAL REGULAR SEASON GAME. GRANGER COWBOYS VS. THE Redding Bulldogs. A win combined with a Shelby win would leave the two teams tied for first. But since Shelby won the head-to-head matchup, the tiebreaker would fall Shelby's way. If the Cowboys had any shot at going to the playoffs, they would need a win combined with a Shelby loss.

The second part, Coach McCoy reminded them, was out of their control. First things first, and that meant taking care of their own business. What Shelby did wouldn't matter if the Cowboys couldn't come away with a win.

For Jake, that meant not getting ahead of himself. Even knowing that Wyatt hadn't been able to lead Granger to the sectional finals as a freshman, that he was chasing something even the great Wyatt Cullen hadn't done.

He looked over in the stands, saw his mom there. His dad was supposed to be there, too; the Longhorns weren't playing until Saturday night, home game against Texas Tech, so there was supposed to be no conflict for Troy Cullen tonight.

Maybe he'd decided there was another Wyatt emergency and had driven down to Austin.

Is what it is, Jake told himself. If it was one more game his dad missed, nothing he could do about it. Nothing he'd ever been able to do about it. Neither Jake nor his dad had mentioned the conversation they'd had behind the barn since it happened, not one time. Things seemed pretty much the same with the two of them, as though nothing had changed.

Maybe because nothing ever really would.

The rest of the stands were full, the crowd already loud. As calm as Jake always felt in the heat of the game, he had to admit that even his heart was trying to come right out of him tonight.

Jake wasn't thinking about his brother or his dad now, just about Redding, about this chance at first place, the chance to keep playing, telling himself that the only thing that could spoil a game like this and a night like this and a chance like this was a loss.

Coach McCoy, as always, had kept his pregame talk brief, Jake by now knowing brief was all his old coach had; if this was his last season, he wasn't going to suddenly turn as chatty as a TV man. He told them stuff he'd told them before, about how the other team was gonna want it as much as they did, how he'd had other teams that had come this close to winning a title before but they couldn't stay on the horse.

"This game we're about to play out here," he said, "has got nothin' to do with the season we thought we were gonna have back in September. Got even less to do with the season we might still have if we win tonight. It's about the one thing sports is always about: ever'body in this room reaching down and finding the best in himself, so we can find out about the best in *our*selves."

Then he just walked out of the room, like he always did when he had nothing more to say. The Granger Cowboys had followed him, waiting until they got into the tunnel before they started yelling their heads off, the tunnel loud and excited, but not nearly as loud and electric and excited as Cullen Field was when they ran out of that tunnel and into a sound and feeling that was just purebred Texas high school football.

The Redding Bulldogs were a little bit like the Cowboys: Their starting quarterback had gotten hurt in their second game, but his replacement, a senior named Brett Conroy, had become a surprise star for them, same as Jake had been for Granger. Brett had a good arm and had proven to be a solid leader.

The Bulldogs also had a fullback as big as a tackle or guard named Jarryd "Moose" Mosedale, who could get them short yards when they needed them, and sometimes a lot more than that.

But the most important thing about Redding was this: They had just one loss, same as the Cowboys. And they were the team that had beaten Shelby last week. So now they had the same chance to steal the whole league on this last Friday night of the regular season. A win against Granger and the league title was theirs since they would own the tiebreaker over Shelby.

The Cowboys won the toss, Jake finished with his warm-up throws, happy they were getting the ball to start the game. As he waited in front of the bench, standing next to Nate, nervously shifting his weight from one leg to the other, Coach Jessup came over, got in front of him, put his hands on both sides of Jake's helmet.

"As much as you've given me so far," Coach J said, "I know you got more in you."

"Thank you for believing in me," Jake said.

"We ain't done yet."

"No, sir."

"All the work we've done, we done it for a reason."

"Yes, sir."

Coach J said, "But you'll make a play tonight that has nothin' to do with the way you've prepared, all the time we spent lookin' at film. It'll just be about the *gift* you have to make a play when you have to. That magic I believe you got inside you. Trust it." Sounding like Nate, another one who'd always talked about magic.

Then he walked away, and Jake jogged out on the field after Melvin Braxton returned the kickoff to the thirty-five-yard line. On the third play of the game, he scrambled to his right after the pocket started to collapse, started to run out of field, then saw Calvin break free, running down the middle with that great speed of his. Jake had enough time to stop and plant and throw the ball as far as he could. Calvin had to slow up slightly, break stride just a little, waiting for the ball to come out of the night sky and the lights. But once the ball was in his hands, he ran away from everybody for a sixty-yard score. The kick was good. They hadn't played two minutes yet, and it was already 7–0.

Calvin came over to Jake on the sideline and said, "It was worse waiting for that ball than it is for class to end. That all you got?"

Grinning at Jake.

"Pretty much," Jake said. Then bumping his helmet on Calvin's.

But Coach McCoy was right about this game the way he was right about a lot of things. The Bulldogs *did* want it, too—did they ever. And they were good. Brett Conroy came right back at them, completing the first seven passes he threw, like he was never going to miss, took his team down the field and finally handed it to Moose Mosedale, who piled in from the one.

It was 7–7, and Jake was as excited as he'd been coming out of the tunnel, as if the game was starting all over again. This was why you played. This kind of night, this kind of opponent, stakes like these. Didn't matter whether you grew up in Granger or Redding, Laredo or Huntsville or Abilene. This was the kind of game you grew up seeing somebody else play at the same time you were dreaming about playing it yourself. This was Texas, Jake knew, as much Texas as anything else in the whole big state. This was the town in the stands, families, friends, and strangers alike, every one of them feeling like they were a part of something, that they were going to somehow help you win tonight.

The defenses settled in after the Redding touchdown and it was still 7–7 at the end of the first quarter.

It was 14-all at the half.

By the time the fourth quarter began, the teams were tied again, 21–21, the league championship still out there on that field, waiting for somebody to just take it.

After giving up that opening touchdown pass, the Bulldogs had been putting double and sometimes triple coverage on Calvin all game long, holding him to just three more catches—none for longer than ten yards. Now, on a third-and-four, four minutes left in the game, Jake faked a handoff to Spence to freeze the linebackers and safeties, and looked up to find Calvin with some daylight on a slant route. It had big play written all over it. But the Bulldog cornerback saw the play developping and closed the gap quickly, just getting a hand in at the last second, knocking the ball loose, incomplete. Another punt for the Cowboys.

Now Brett Conroy's chance to eat up some field and maybe the rest of the clock, get another score, and take the night back with him on the bus to Redding. If so, the Bulldogs would be going to the sectional finals and the Cowboys would be going home.

Jake knew he could be that close to the end of the season, 3:54 showing on the scoreboard clock.

Brett got his team moving, short passes mostly, out to their forty, then past midfield. Then all the way to the Cowboys' twenty, third-and-three, a minute-fifty left. Cullen Field was as quiet as it had been all night, Jake standing there at the fifty, nothing to do but watch the other quarterback.

He'd had a lot of practice at that, watching his brother when he was a high school quarterback, now watching Brett Conroy as he tried to take Jake's season, maybe before Jake ever got to take another snap.

Calvin standing there with Jake now.

"This *ain't* the way the movie's s'posed to end," Calvin said. "For me *or* for you, Cullen."

"Tell me about it."

"Somebody's got to stand up and make a play," Calvin said, "so we can get back out there and finish our unfinished business."

He said it Texas-style.

Bidness.

Of all the players, it was Bear Logan who stood up. The Cowboy defense was expecting a run, the Bulldogs this close to scoring, guessing the offense would play it safe while eating up more of the clock. And sure enough, Brett Conroy put the ball in Moose Mosedale's belly. But then he pulled it out, straightened up, saw his tight end open in the left flat. What appeared to be a perfect play-action pass.

Paid no attention to the fact that Bear Logan was spying him.

Paid no attention to Bear at all, who, despite getting in on a couple of tackles hadn't done much to make the Bulldogs pay him much mind.

Bear waited until Brett Conroy released the ball, stepped in front of the Redding tight end, and made the first interception of his life, going all the way back to when he and Jake played Pop Warner together. He didn't even try to advance it, for fear he'd fumble, just wrapped his arms around the ball and fell to the ground. But when he got up, more excited than Jake had ever seen him on a football field, he held the ball over his head like it was a trophy and got a huge cheer out of the Granger fans.

Cowboys' ball at their fifteen-yard line, Jake with two time-outs in his pocket. Minute-forty left. As he ran out on the field with the offense, Bear coming off, Jake took time to wrap his arms as far around him as they'd go.

"I knew you had it in you, big man."

"Well, I sure didn't know," Bear said.

"Can't believe you didn't think about puttin' on a couple of juke moves like you were Calvin."

"The only move I got is the one I just showed you. I fell down."

Coach Jessup had sent Jake out with four plays: a quick out to Roy, a sideline route to Justice, a screen to Spence, then a deep cross to Calvin if Justice could do his job and legally pick the Redding safety without ever making contact with the kid.

But Jake didn't want to wait to put the ball in Calvin's hands, Despite how tight the Redding D had been playing him.

He grabbed Calvin when the huddle was breaking, said, "Can you get loose?"

Calvin just smiled.

"Sorry," he said, "I didn't realize that was a serious question."

"Gonna fake it to Roy," Jake said, "and then see if we can go big."

He dropped back into the shotgun, took Nate's snap, faked a throw to Roy on the left sideline, then rolled to the opposite side. The fake had drawn the extra defenders off Calvin, who streaked across the field and got away with a pro-style shove-off on the safety closest to him. He then broke his route and cut to the inside of the field, running hot. Jake's throw wobbled a little more than he would have liked. So did Eli Manning's sometimes. The ball still found Calvin in stride at the forty. Jake thought for a second he might break all the way for a score, but the corner on Justice's deep route down the right sideline saw what was happening, ended up with a good angle on Calvin, and brought him down from behind at midfield.

Just like that, they'd cut the field in half, brought the crowd to a roar, and brought a little panic to the Bulldog defense.

Jake hurried the offense to the line and hit Justice on a sideline route from there, another first down, stopping the clock. He then threw the screen to Spence, who tried to get out of bounds, but couldn't. Jake had no choice but to burn his second time-out. Thirty seconds left.

He knew the Bulldogs would be guarding the sidelines tight, so he took a chance and squeezed one in to Calvin over the middle, who took what the defense gave him and went down.

Jake immediately called his last time-out.

Twenty-one seconds left, at the Redding twenty. Too far to count on making a field goal.

As Jake started toward the sideline, Coach McCoy and Coach J came out to meet him.

"Spread 'em out," Coach McCoy said. "Then just pick out the one you like the best."

He nodded.

When Jake got back to the huddle, Nate pushed back his helmet just far enough so that Jake could see the big smile on him.

Nate said, "This is more fun than eating pie."

Jake couldn't argue with that.

He spread out his wides and went for it all with Calvin on first down, but overthrew him, the ball sailing overhead. It was the worst throw he'd made all night. The incompletion stopped the clock again.

On second down, Justice and Roy were covered deep. Calvin was double-teamed, as usual, but recognized that while the defense wasn't about to let him get into the end zone, there was a soft spot in between. Jake hit him with a bullet at the twelve and Calvin sprinted out of bounds. Clock stopped.

Third-and-two.

Ten seconds left. Just enough time to run another quick play and get out of bounds to stop the clock for a field goal attempt. Or going for it all with a play into the end zone.

Jake looked over at Coach J, who put an index finger up near his nose.

Number 1.

Just somehow get the ball to Calvin. There was no logic to Jake's belief in him, at least right now. The Redding defensive backs, even though a couple of them looked like they were a head shorter, had done the best job covering Calvin that any team had all season. And now the field itself was shorter, giving Calvin less room to improvise—at a time when everyone on the field knew that Jake would be looking for him.

Maybe his belief was just based on something as simple as this: Calvin would make a play when he had to.

Jake knelt in the huddle and called the play. Told the guys they were going to complete the pass and walk off the field winners.

Went with a quick count. Straightened right up. But just as his arm came forward, just as Calvin made his move, the Bulldogs' middle linebacker, number 50, took a step to his left. Either lucky or smart, it didn't matter, he was standing where Calvin was headed, and if Jake threw it anyway, he might pick the ball off the way Bear had just intercepted Brett Conroy's pass.

Jake pulled the ball down and circled back to his right, arm up, looking for somebody, anybody, to throw it to. But Calvin was still jammed in the middle, Roy Gilley had slipped and fallen in the middle of the end zone, and Justice was in the far corner, covered.

And then Jake saw a lane.

Saw that the defense was more afraid that he'd throw than run, the linebackers having backed up, trying to cover everybody at once.

Jake decided he could beat them all to the pylon.

Pulled the ball down, stopped faking the throw, and ran to the five-yard line. Then the three.

Saw a safety coming straight at him, saw number 50 coming from his left. Decided the best thing to do was dive for it, not take a chance on getting hit hard by either one of them, coughing the ball up.

Jake thought: *Let's see if I can fly.*

He launched himself toward the pylon, not knowing that number 50 had launched himself at the same time, like some kind of missile in a helmet and pads. Jake never saw him coming, didn't know he was coming until he got hit in midair, felt himself helicoptering around, somehow not twisting around but twisting *over,* which was why he landed on his back, his helmet snapping hard against the turf, the last thing he remembered as the Friday night lights of Cullen Field went out on him.

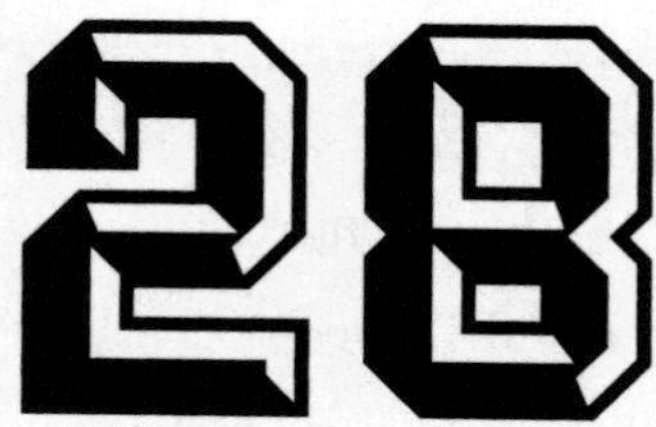

JAKE NEVER BELIEVED HE'D BEEN KNOCKED OUT. THE DOCTORS would tell him later it was just hitting the back of his head, even with the protection of his helmet, that made everything go dark on him, even though he could hear another huge cheer come up out of Cullen Field.

When he opened his eyes, he saw Coach McCoy looking down at him, and Coach J, and Nate. And Doc Mallozzi.

But the face closest to Jake belonged to Troy Cullen, looking as scared as Jake had ever seen him, mostly because he'd grown up believing his dad wasn't scared of anybody or anything.

"Dad," Jake said, "what are you doing here?"

"Where the heck else would I be?" Jake could see the hurt in his face. "My son just got leveled."

"Dad, I'm okay."

"That's what I'm down here to find out," Troy Cullen said in a rough voice. "Was like that boy dropped you out a window 'n' you landed on your head."

In that moment, Jake realized the football was still in his right hand.

"Did I score?" he said.

"Yeah," his dad said. "Yeah, you did."

"I'm okay," Jake said.

"Course you are," Troy Cullen said. "You're my son."

Nobody at Cullen who'd seen the play, nobody who'd talk about it all week on the radio, could believe that Jake had managed to hold on to the ball, not after the hit he took and the way he'd spun around in the air—like John Elway in a Super Bowl one time; Jake had seen the play on the NFL Network—and especially the way he'd landed, no time left on the clock.

Jake?

He still wouldn't be able to believe afterward how fast his dad had made it down out of his seat, where he'd apparently been all game, and onto the field, almost as quickly as the coaches and Doc Mallozzi had.

At home later, when Jake would ask his dad where he'd been before kickoff, Troy Cullen would say, "Can't a man use a restroom?" and Jake would smile.

But for now, out on Cullen Field, the lights still shining bright, his dad let Doc Mallozzi take over. Doc asked Jake if he felt well enough to sit up. Jake told him he thought he did, that he just felt a little dizzy, was all.

Doc and Coach J slowly pulled Jake up to a sitting position, and then Doc started asking him questions, asking him the last thing he remembered, if he remembered the play he'd called, asking him if he'd heard the cheer from the crowd that went up after the refs' arms went up and signaled the touchdown.

Jake said he did.

"How many points you guys score tonight?" Doc asked.

"Enough to win," Jake said. "Twenty-seven. Unless everyone's waiting for an extra point?"

Doc nodded and shined a light into his right eye, then his left, asking if the light hurt. Jake said, "No. My head hurts a little, is all."

"A little or a lot?"

"Little," Jake said. "I'm okay, really. Can I stand now and celebrate with my team?"

Nate and Bear were there, helping Jake slowly to his feet, and it was then that Cullen Field exploded into as big a sound as Jake had ever heard there, for his brother or for anybody else.

He walked between Nate and Bear up the sideline to the Cowboys' bench, his dad right behind him with a hand on Jake's shoulder.

Jake still had the ball under his right arm, the ref having told him before he left the field to keep it, because he'd by-God earned it.

Jake watched the scene play out and wondered if he could be dreaming and wide awake at the same time.

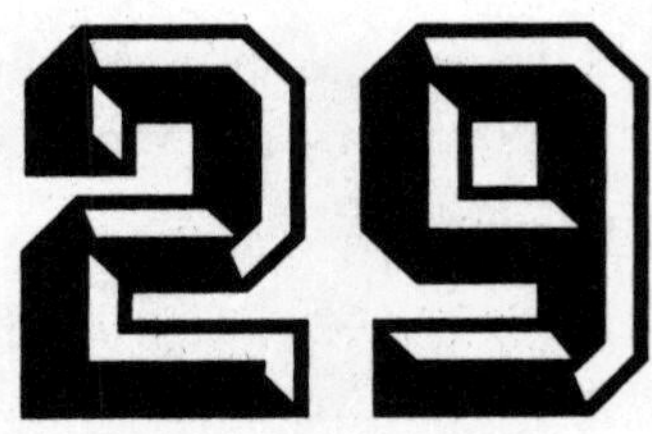

THE HEADACHE BEGAN THE NEXT MORNING WHEN JAKE WOKE up, and it stuck around.

He should have felt on top of the world. When news came the previous night that Shelby had lost in overtime, Jake went to bed knowing he had quarterbacked the Cowboys all the way back to to playoffs, the sectional final against Sierra that could lead Granger to the state finals.

Yet, sitting in Doc Mallozzi's office Saturday afternoon, Jake felt anything but great. Not only was his head pounding, but Doc had just told him that he would have to sit out next week's game.

It meant that if they lost, Jake had lost his own season by winning last night's game for his team.

"Jake, it's a low-grade concussion," Doc said. "I can't write it up for Coach McCoy as anything but. And the rules of our league say that if you get even a low-grade concussion, you have to sit out the next week's game."

Jake said, "I feel fine. It's just a little headache."

"No such thing as a little headache after the hit you took. You blacked out for a moment there."

Libby Cullen said, "And you were sick to your stomach all last night, even though you never did throw up."

Jake was on the examining table, legs hanging over the side, nearly touching the floor. He looked at his mom and said, "Mom, you *told*?"

Knowing he sounded like he was ten.

"Your father played when he shouldn't have played. You're not going to."

Jake looked over at his dad.

"She's right," he said to Jake.

Jake said, "You know you would've made them let you play, if it was you."

"And I'd've been dead wrong," Troy Cullen said. "Those of us who played, in the day, only wish we knew then what we know now. Turned out I was one of the lucky ones, because even as hardheaded as I was about head injuries, I wasn't so hardheaded that I kept playing after my docs told me that I'd get to the point where I couldn't remember what I had for breakfast."

Jake started to say something. His dad held up a hand.

"I see how a couple of my teammates ended up," he said. "I consider myself lucky I only forget some of the things I do, get the headaches I do sometimes."

Doc said, "Jake, we haven't even talked about how sensitive your eyes still are to light today, and how tired you clearly are, even though you tried to give me a head fake and say you weren't."

"It's a chance to go to the state finals!" Jake said.

"And if the Cowboys get to the states," Doc said, "somehow figure out a way to get 'er done without you next week, then we'll see where we are."

"Wait a second," Jake said, "you're telling me that I might not even get to play in the state finals if we get there?"

Doc said, "We're gonna examine you every other day, which means the next time I see you is Monday after school. Put you through what we call protocols, which is a fancy word for testing, things like balance, and keep doing neurological assessments. But no contact, obviously. Maybe some light running as we get near the end of the week. This is your brain we're talking about, son. It's the only one you got."

"The only thing hurting my brain is what you're telling me," Jake said.

"Not only do doctors get to tell you things, you have to listen to them when they do," Jake's mom said. "It's a rule that got passed a while back."

He knew the voice. Her game-ender.

"Can I at least go to the game?" Jake said.

"Of course," Doc said. "Root your boys home."

"I'm not cut out to be a cheerleader," Jake said.

His mom smiled. "Sarah can teach you."

He wasn't just cheering on his team now, he was cheering on Casey Lindell.

Jake and Wyatt had grown up hearing their dad say that people could talk about running the ball and defense all they wanted, but football was a quarterback's game, even in high school. So

Casey had to play well against Sierra and their fancy offense, the highest-scoring team in the state this year, or the Cowboys wouldn't win the sectionals, wouldn't make it back to the state finals.

So the quarterback Jake had finally beaten out this season was the guy Jake needed to save his season.

Go figger, as Bear liked to say.

Of course it wouldn't just be Casey. Maybe in the end it would come down to Calvin making a play or a catch. Jake knew enough about sports to know that most of the time when a game looked even to you, it was best to put your money on the best player on the field.

That would be Calvin Morton Friday night, the way it was most Friday nights.

Still, Calvin needed Casey to throw him the ball. Which meant that *Jake* needed Casey. The guy who'd gone out of his way to make himself Jake's nemesis.

Amazing.

A lot had changed for Jake across this season, so many things on and off the field, they could have made Jake dizzy *before* he'd landed on his head. Now, at the end of this week, he was going to have to watch somebody else quarterback Granger in the big game.

"Just pretend that he's Wyatt," Bear said at Tuesday afternoon's practice, "and you're rooting for your brother."

Jake turned and looked at him. "Which one of us got the concussion, me or you?"

"Now listen up," Bear said. "You wouldn't even root against

Casey when him and you were competing for the same job. So nothin' has changed, you ask me; you're just being the same kind of teammate with your pads off you were with your pads on."

In a voice only Bear could hear, Jake said, "I want to *play*."

"Next Friday night," Bear said. "Not this one."

"If Doc lets me."

"He will."

"Don't be so sure. I passed all the tests, flying colors yesterday, and all he said when we were done was, 'See you in two days. And no running till I do.'"

But Bear wasn't listening now; he was staring at Casey, shaking his head, saying, "Are we sure Casey is still right-handed?"

This was the second day in a row that Casey was wild throwing the ball. And today was worse than yesterday. His arm was still as strong as ever, and every few minutes he'd manage to make a throw that reminded everybody that arm strength was never a problem for him.

At the moment, accuracy was.

Big-time.

When he wasn't missing high, he was missing wide. Or the ball would be too far out front when he was trying to lead somebody. One time he threw it a yard behind Justice, and when Justice reached back, he got popped good by Melvin. And when Justice got up he said to Casey, "Man, you tryin' to get me killed?"

"Sorry, man," Casey said. "Working out the rust."

All season long Casey had let everybody, starting with Jake, know how much he wanted to be the man on this team. Now, for this one game, he was officially the man. Had the job to himself.

Only he seemed to be pressing more than he ever had. Like moving to the bench had shaken his confidence.

On the field now, Calvin broke open on a deep post, having just dusted Melvin with a filthy fake to the inside. Casey overthrew him by ten yards, easy.

Bear said, “Well, it’s still early in the week.”

Bear was right, it didn’t matter how you looked on Tuesday afternoon long as you brought it Friday night.

“Tomorrow will be better,” Jake said.

“Damn straight.”

Only it wasn’t. It was just more of the same; Jake could see that as soon as he got to practice after his latest appointment with Doc Mallozzi, having gone through all his tests again, Doc saying to come back the next day and maybe, just maybe, he’d be able to do some light running on the weekend.

Today he decided to watch practice from the top of Cullen Field, thinking that might take some pressure off Casey, not make him feel as if Jake was standing right there looking over his shoulder.

But the view wasn’t any better from up there, because Casey was still acting like a baseball pitcher who’d completely lost the strike zone. Or an outside shooter in basketball firing up one brick after another.

The Cowboys were maybe half an hour or so from finishing when Jake saw Sarah waving at him, heading up the steps.

“I’m sorry,” Jake said, “this seat is taken.”

“Oh,” she said, “like the seat next to *me* was taken that night at

Sal's?" She tossed her backpack in the aisle, sat down next to Jake, and said, "How's it going?"

"Terrible."

"Oh, does your head still hurt?"

Jake pointed at the field. "It doesn't, but it's going to start hurting all over again if Casey doesn't start throwing better."

Sarah said she'd heard some of the guys on the team talking about that in study hall. "What's that thing our parents are always telling us? Be careful what you wish for? Maybe that's Casey."

"That," Jake said, "is exactly what I'm afraid of. That maybe he just wants this so much, it's eating him up."

On Thursday, after Jake aced all Doc's tests again, Doc Mallozzi told Jake he could start running again.

"But if you feel yourself getting tired, stop," Doc said.

"No chance of that happening," Jake said. "After not doing anything all week, I've got enough energy to run all the way to Highland Junction."

"You can run, and you can throw, and that's it, young man. Are we clear?"

"I feel good enough to play tomorrow night," Jake said.

"Not happening," Doc said. "Go."

Libby Cullen dropped Jake off at school. He went straight to the locker room, put on his football pants, spikes, and a T-shirt. Happy to be just doing that, knowing this was a step closer to him being back in full football clothes.

But only if the Cowboys won on Friday night.

Only if Casey could do the job against Sierra. *Do his job,* Jake thought, *so I can get* mine *back*.

When he got out on the field, he threw behind the bench with Justice, who'd taken a hit yesterday on an already-sore knee, Coach giving him the day off to rest it. Both of them would stop every few minutes to watch today's seven-on-seven drills, every play call a pass, like Coach McCoy and Coach Jessup were giving Casey as many throws as possible for him to find his form before they all got on the bus tomorrow for the ninety-minute ride to Highland Junction.

But Casey seemed to be pressing even more today than he had been all week, pacing after every missed throw, talking to himself, hanging his head when he wasn't slapping the sides of his helmet with his palms.

Justice came over and stood next to Jake and said, "I better stop watching now, before I get too overconfident."

"My dad has an expression that covers this," Jake said, not adding that Troy Cullen thought he had expressions that covered pretty much everything under the sun.

"Is it gonna make me feel better about what I'm watching out there?" Justice said.

"Probably not."

"Give it to me anyway."

"Casey Lindell," Jake said, "is tighter than new boots."

Justice finally asked if Jake wanted to throw a little more, saying that at least one quarterback on the team was accurate this afternoon. The two of them tossed the ball around until they could see that Coach McCoy was about to wrap things up for the day.

It was then that Jake had one of those good ideas his mom talked about, the kind that refused to get out of your head once they got in there.

Even knowing that Doc had said only light running today, Jake sprinted toward the locker room.

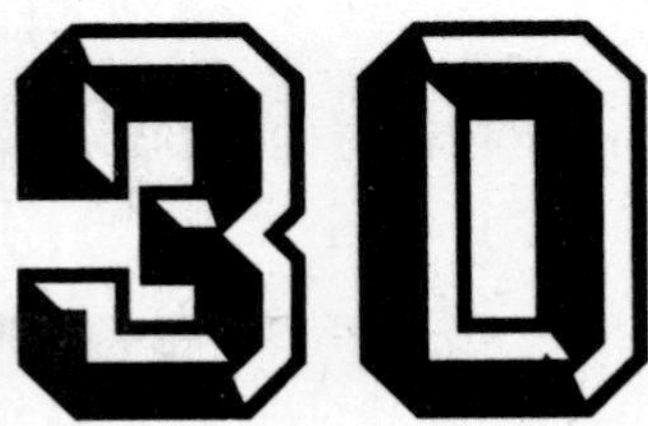

JAKE, BEAR, AND NATE WERE IN THE PASTURE BEHIND THE BARN a little after five o'clock.

Bear said, "I'm not a receiver. The only thing I catch on a regular basis is grief, from the two of you."

"Seems to me," Jake said, "you were enough of a receiver to make your first—wait for it—career interception not so long ago."

"It was one catch!" Bear said. "And forget about whether I can catch a ball or not. I still can't believe you dragged me over here, dragged *both* of us over here, after we already practiced once today."

"Speak for yourself," Nate said. "I *like* catching passes." He was wearing high-top basketball sneakers, cargo shorts, a T-shirt that read "Not Lucky. Just Lucky To Be This Good." Nate said, "You both know if I wanted to, I could be the best tight end on our team."

"You keep tellin' yourself that, big man," Jake said.

"You told me yourself once," Nate said.

"I must've wanted something."

"You mean like you want something now?"

Jake said, "This is a good thing we're doing."

"I sure hope so," Bear said. "We got nothing to lose, 'cept the game, of course."

Jake looked past Bear to the corner of the barn. "I knew he'd come."

Casey Lindell, wearing baggy shorts and his football spikes. As he got closer to them, Jake saw he was wearing an old black Spurs cap and a gray T-shirt that had "Granger Football" stenciled in white letters across the front.

"Got your note," Casey said. "Didn't even know people left actual notes anymore."

"The personal touch," Jake said.

Casey shrugged. "Don't see as how things could get any more personal between us than they already are."

"But you came," Jake said.

"Yeah, I did," Casey said. "I thought you were crazy at first, the part about me maybe needing to get away from practice *to* practice. But the more I thought on it, the more sense it started to make, maybe because I got no clue right now."

"We *noticed,*" Nate said.

The way he said it, so much feeling in his voice, made them all laugh. Casey included.

"And you think you can help me?" Casey said, looking right at Jake.

"I do. But not just me."

"And you *want* to help me?" Casey said.

"Only if you want to be," Jake said. "Helped out, I mean. Start throwing strikes again, like we all know you can. Get your mojo back."

"These days I don't feel like I ever had it," Casey said.

"That's why we're here," Jake said. "Me and your two receivers here."

"What, all the good ones in town were busy?" Casey said, grinning, at least showing some of the old Casey, not the whupped dog he'd been all week at practice.

Then he looked back at Jake and said, "Might as well put this on the table right now. After all the stuff I said to you this season, you want to be my quarterback coach?"

"Actually, I don't," Jake said. "But I went and found you one who thinks he's the best quarterback coach in the world."

He turned Casey around and pointed him toward the barn, because here came Troy Cullen.

He got right to it, saying to Jake and Casey, "The two of you good?"

It was Casey who said, "Good as we're gonna be, Mr. Cullen."

"Good enough for me; I ain't out here to be your guidance counselor," he said. "You ready to work?" Nodding at Casey.

"Yes, sir," he said. "For the life of me, I can't figure out what's happened to me."

"Hell's bells," Jake's dad said. "*Football* happened to you, son, the way it happens to all of us sooner or later. The big game happened to you, and even that happens to the best of 'em. You think it hasn't? Go back and take a look at that last Super Bowl ol' Tom

Brady lost to the Giants. He missed a big throw to that little Welker, one that would have changed everything. A throw he could have made with his eyes closed."

Then Jake's dad grinned and said, "But I'm getting ahead of myself. For now all you have to understand is that somethin' don't have to be broke to need fixin'."

Jake was a little bit behind his dad, so Troy Cullen couldn't see him smiling. But then maybe this was just funny to Jake, him having brought his dad out here to work with a guy who'd spent the whole season trying to beat him out of a job.

His dad out here, at Jake's request, after all the times in Jake's life when he would've given anything to see him come walking out from the barn toward him.

Troy Cullen and Casey began to warm up now, soft-tossing to each other, his dad's motion as clean and classic as it had always been, same as it was with Wyatt.

When Casey announced that he was ready, Troy Cullen brought Bear and Nate into it, telling them to go stand about twenty-five yards down the pasture, a little bit apart.

Jake said, "And what do I get to do?"

His dad grinned. "Watch and learn."

At first Troy Cullen kept things simple, just having Casey drop back, quick three-step drop, and yell either Bear's name or Nate's, just asking Casey to hit stationary targets, Casey doing that with no problem.

"So far, so good," Jake's dad said.

"With receivers not running around," Casey said, "and nobody running at *me*. It's not just that I feel like I've lost my location, Mr. Cullen. I feel like I lost all my timing."

"Nah," Troy Cullen said. "It's like I told my other boy, Wyatt, before the Red River game: You've just misplaced it, is all, like I do all the time with my reading glasses."

Eventually Bear and Nate ran patterns, simple ones, outs and slants and hooks, nothing deep. Sometimes Casey would take a snap from Jake, acting as his center, sometimes Jake—a pretty good snapper—would give it to him in the shotgun.

And Casey started to miss now.

Not by a lot, but by enough. Jake could see him, even out here, start to squeeze the ball like he did when things started to get sideways in practice, reminding him of a Little League pitcher who couldn't throw a strike if his life depended on it.

Same old, same old, Jake thought. Harder he tried, worse it got. After one overthrow to Nate, Casey looked at Troy Cullen and said, "What do I do?"

Troy Cullen said, "Close your eyes."

Troy Cullen told Jake and Bear they could—his words—sit and take a load off, all's he needed were Casey and Nate for the time being. Sending Nate ten yards down the pasture and explaining that the idea for what they were about to do came from *his* dad, a golfer whose putting always drove him crazy.

"Not a thing in the world he was afraid of, 'cept that little putter in his bag," Jake's dad said. "Couldn't putt under pressure to save this ranch. Finally the pro at his club took him to the putting green one day and made him start making short putts with his eyes closed. Two-footers, then five-footers, then back to ten, even. Told him to see the hole, see the ball, close his eyes, let 'er go. Told him not to worry about the result, just the process. And before long, damned if it didn't work."

"Let me get this straight," Casey said. "You want me to throw *with my eyes closed*?"

"Yes, son, I do," Jake's dad said. "It may sound crazy, but I'm here to tell you it works. Worked for me in college one time I got scatter-armed. And it will work for you, I promise."

Jake said, "How come you never did this drill with me?"

"Because the one thing you always did was hit what you were throwin' for," his dad said, then smiled at Jake and said, "No matter what motion you used."

At first, Casey was as off throwing to Nate with his eyes closed as he had been when they were wide open. He'd miss short, bouncing the ball in the grass, or wide, or high.

Troy Cullen just told him to stay patient, it would come.

And eventually, to Casey's amazement—and Jake's—it finally did.

Casey started to get it, suddenly throwing one spiral after another, Nate going five minutes sometimes without having to move a single step. Every few throws, Jake would watch Casey's eyes to make sure he wasn't cheating. But he wasn't.

"Yeah," Casey would say when he'd open his eyes and see another ball in Nate's hands. *"Yeah, man!"*

Troy Cullen started to move Nate back, five yards, then ten.

"You're seein' him now," Troy Cullen said, "like your eyes were open instead of closed." He'd had Nate running simple patterns, telling Casey that Nate was going to run ten steps, or fifteen, then cut left or right, telling him to close his eyes on the cut, see in his mind's eye where he wanted the ball to end up.

"Trust it," Troy Cullen kept saying, and then Casey Lindell would complete another pass.

He didn't hit every one, but hit most, his passes looking better now than when he'd gotten here. When he had been throwing with his eyes wide open.

In a quiet voice only Jake could hear, Bear said, "You actually think he can do this tomorrow night?"

Jake grinned. "Think I'll close *my* eyes and imagine it happening just that way."

It was starting to get dark, they'd been out here in the pasture that long. Not that the fading light was bothering Casey any; Nate was the one having trouble picking up the ball now. So finally Troy Cullen said, "One more." Nate started to back up, and Troy Cullen said, "Nah, let's have some fun here 'fore we call it a night. We'll split Jake out this time, like him and Casey here are both in the game runnin' one of those fancy wildcat plays, kind where one QB throws it to the other one. Nate, snap it to him in the shotgun. Bear, pretend you're the tight end. Jake'll take off down the sideline and Casey'll hit him deep. Wait and see, you boys'll want to call up John McCoy, tell him to put it in his playbook."

"You want *Jake* to be a receiver, and for me to throw him a deep ball?" Casey said. "With my eyes still closed?"

"Pretty much," Jake's dad said. "I know my boy can't run like Calvin, but he can move it pretty good when somebody's chasin' him."

"Thanks, Dad," Jake said. "I think."

Casey said, "I don't want to end the night on a miss."

"You won't miss," Troy Cullen said. "Like I said: Just trust it and let 'er go."

Casey did.

The ball sailed through the twilight like a shooting star until it came down in Jake's hands, Jake gathering it in, running about twenty more yards, spiking the ball. Pretending he *was* Calvin.

"Lindell to Cullen," Casey said. "Didn't see that coming when I woke up today."

Troy Cullen said his work here was done and started toward the barn, until he stopped, turned, grinned at Jake, and said, "I still got it."

THE HORSESHOE-SHAPED STADIUM AT HIGHLAND JUNCTION wasn't as new or as nice as Cullen Field. But it seemed to be a little bigger, had a big scoreboard at the closed end, and, the Cowboys found out, a spacious visitors' locker room that had a flat-screen TV and carpets on the floor. *Texas high school football,* Jake thought, *with all the trimmings*.

Bear said, "Looks like we got all the comforts of home."

"All we need to make it better is pie," Nate added.

"Beat Sierra," Jake said, "and I promise to buy you all the pie you can eat afterward."

Nate thought about that, his face serious, and said, "There isn't that much pie."

Jake went and sat with Coach Jessup as his teammates started to get dressed, knowing the only part of his uniform he was wearing tonight was his jersey, over a pair of jeans. He came out about fifteen minutes later, walked over to Casey's locker, and said, "We got this."

"We're not playing behind your barn," Casey said.

"Just keep telling yourself that you are," Jake said. "Tell yourself it's like when you're out playing in the yard or the street and you get called for supper and you don't want to stop because you're having too much fun. That's the fun of it tonight. Playing to just keep playing."

Jake didn't wait for an answer, afraid he might not like it, just went outside and walked around the field as the stands started to fill up, seeing the sky start to get darker, feeling the threat of rain in the air, worrying about a sloppy field and a sloppy game, then shook his head, like he was trying to get the worries about the conditions out of there before they could settle.

"Control the things you can," his mom had always told him, one of her favorite lines, "then leave the rest to God and Texas."

Jake walked by the cheerleaders now, where they were warming up, so he could say hi to Sarah.

"You gonna be okay tonight?" she asked.

"No, but it'll be worth it," he said. "Long as we win."

He walked slowly back to the locker room, feeling the night begin to start without him, stood just inside the locker room door as Coach McCoy addressed the Granger Cowboys, nobody knowing if this was his last season or not, Jake realizing that if it was, and they didn't beat Sierra tonight, this might be Coach's last game.

When he quieted them down and had their attention, Coach said, "Sometimes, you get to this point in the season and realize you got nothin' original left to say. So I guess all I got tonight is a question: You boys done yet?"

In a good, loud voice, the Granger Cowboys shouted, *"No, sir!"*

Coach said, "Good, 'cause I sure ain't done," and that was it, all he had. He turned and walked out the door. The Cowboys followed him, Jake high-fiving as many as he could as they walked past him, waiting until all the guys who were playing the game were out of the room, every last one.

Then he followed them. This was going to be the hardest game of his life. And he wasn't even playing in it.

The Sierra Broncos had led their league in scoring, done that by a lot, mostly riding the arm of their senior quarterback, Tommy Chavez, son of a famous tie-down roper named Freddie Chavez. Tommy had already committed to Baylor next season, people saying he was going to light it up there like he was the second coming of RG III.

But it was all throwing with him; he couldn't run like RG III or Johnny Manziel. Couldn't run to save his life. But Tommy Chavez had thrown twenty-eight touchdown passes in ten games, the Broncos having won nine of those games, seven by double digits. Coach J told Jake they didn't have just one stud receiver like Calvin; Tommy had thrown touchdown passes to *seven* different players.

He was six four, looked like he went two-twenty easy, and wore number 1, just like Calvin—like it wasn't just a number on his jersey, it was a grade.

"What I hear about Tommy," Nate said, "is he thinks God has to check with him before the sun rises in the morning and sets at night."

"Whatever," Jake said. "My money's on our number one tonight."

"All's we need is somebody to throw it to him," Bear said.

"Casey'll be fine," Jake said.

"How you gonna convince us of that," Bear said, "when it sounds like you haven't even convinced your own self?"

It wasn't that Jake didn't think Casey couldn't come out of his slump tonight. He just didn't want this to turn out to be a quarterback's game, because if it did, then the Cowboys were going to be in trouble—Tommy Chavez was that good.

Yet for all the pregame talk about him on the radio and in the newspaper, all the talk about what an aerial circus this game was going to be, it was the defenses, from both teams, that dominated early. The defenses and nerves, actually. Even from Tommy Chavez. *Especially* from him. Making a prophet, in the first half anyway, out of Coach J, who'd said to Jake before the game, "Tommy's a talented kid. But he's still a kid."

Melvin intercepted him on the Broncos' first series of the game, the Broncos having driven to the Cowboys' thirty. Then it was the Cowboys driving, Casey hitting his first three passes, all short ones, the coaches trying to get him into the flow of the game that way.

But the first time he tried to stretch the field, like the coaches were ready to get him off training wheels, he eyeballed Calvin all the way, same as he had at the start of the season. The Broncos' strong-side safety read the play like a book, stepping in front of Calvin for the interception, breaking some tackles, getting all the way back to midfield.

Three Tommy Chavez passes and a couple of runs later, the Broncos were up 7–0.

Casey started missing now, forcing throws even when everybody in the place could see his intended receiver was covered. It was one three-and-out after another for the Cowboys, out of the first quarter into the second. Jake thought that even if their defense could continue to contain Tommy Chavez, the best the Cowboys could hope for would be going into the locker room at halftime down a touchdown.

But with under a minute left in the half, third-and-two from the Cowboys' thirty-five, Coach Jessup decided to put the ball—and the game—into Calvin's hands in a slightly different way.

Jake was standing with Coach J and Coach McCoy when he heard the play call, then Coach J turned to him and winked and said, "More than one way to skin a Bronco."

Casey spun away from center, stuck the ball in Spence Tolar's belly for what looked like a simple off-tackle play, sold the fake a lot better than he'd been throwing the ball, pulled the ball out and flipped it to Calvin Morton, flying around from where he'd split out wide on the left.

An end-around.

First one they'd run all season.

And it caught the Broncos completely by surprise, Jake seeing what everybody in the stadium at Highland Junction saw: that nobody was going to catch Calvin once he got to the edge and turned upfield. The Cowboys' number 1, on his way to the house.

It was 7–7 at the half.

Jake stayed away from Casey in the locker room, stayed away from everybody, just took his place by the door. Part of the night but not part of it; in the locker room with his teammates but feeling like some fan who'd snuck in. Listening as Coach McCoy said there was no doubt in his mind, none, that the boys on defense were just going to keep bringing it, saying they were going to keep mixing it up on Tommy Chavez, dropping extra guys into coverage, blitzing him enough that he didn't get too comfortable.

"We're tied with those boys on the other team," he said, "and we haven't even taken our cuts yet."

As the Cowboys were walking out of the room, Casey Lindell came over to Jake.

"I'm letting you down," Casey said.

"No, you're not," Jake said. "Like Coach said, we haven't come close to playing like we can, and it's still seven to seven."

"I'm probably making your dad want to close *his* eyes," Casey said.

"You made some great throws," Jake said, trying to do anything to pump the guy up.

"That fun you talked about?" Casey said. "When does it start?"

Put his helmet on, walked past Jake.

Not good, Jake thought.

Not good at all.

But it was still tied at the end of the third quarter, 14-all. Tommy Chavez had put the Broncos ahead with a ten-yard bullet, but with the Bronco defense over-playing the run, Casey suddenly found his form, nothing to indicate that he was about to do it, hitting Roy, Justice, and Calvin in succession. Then, with the defense loosened up and looking for a pass, Spence ran twenty-five yards, straight up the middle for a touchdown, on a draw, nobody touching him. So the game was even again. One quarter to go.

The rainstorm blew into Highland Junction then. Jake had been thinking that as bad as the sky looked, maybe the storm would hold off until the game was over, but it came now, came hard and fast and mean, the way storms did in Texas, the rain howling, blowing across the field in sheets. What Troy Cullen called Bible weather.

Tommy Chavez got hit, fumbled the ball, and Michael Pinkett recovered it for the Cowboys.

David Stevens fumbled it right back, the ball coming out of his hands as he was running free around right end. The aerial circus everybody had predicted just turned into mudball now, both teams still trying to throw, but neither having much success.

Meanwhile, the clock kept moving, Jake wondering what kind of shape the field would be in if they had to keep playing into sudden death overtime.

Late in the fourth quarter, the Cowboys got the ball back at the Broncos' forty-seven. The Broncos' punter had slipped in the mud as he planted his lead foot and had kicked the ball only twenty yards, nearly getting blocked by Bear Logan.

Two minutes left.

"What are we gonna do?" Casey asked Coach J.

"That end-around to Calvin where you roll to your right and he comes behind," he said. "Then hope the misdirection makes ever'body slip 'cept Calvin."

It worked just like that, Casey flipping Calvin the ball as he came behind, Calvin putting the ball in his left hand, making the turn without sliding around, running twenty yards until a safety knocked him out of bounds. Just like that, the Cowboys were in business at the Broncos' twenty-seven.

Then, Coach J brought Calvin into the backfield—first time they'd done *that* all year. Casey pitched it to him, and Calvin ran ten more yards until he got shoved out of bounds.

Jake said to Coach J, "You think we could kick a field goal if we had to?"

"No," Coach J said. "No way we can get off a snap, hold, and kick in these conditions. We need a score."

"You got something good?" Jake said.

"I got Calvin, is what I got."

They ran Calvin again from the backfield for six, down to the Broncos' eleven. Then, everybody on defense watching for Calvin, the Cowboys ran a direct snap to Spence, who ran for five more. They were at the six-yard line now, with under a minute to play, first and goal to go.

Casey rolled out, hoping to find Calvin in the end zone, but Casey was pulled down from behind, Jake nearly dying as the ball came loose before it slid out of bounds at the ten.

Clock stopped, forty-one seconds left.

Pitch to Calvin, smothered, no gain.

The Cowboys called their last time-out.

Coach J decided to throw for it. The play was for Calvin to push the corner and the safety on him a few yards deep into the end zone, then curl toward the sideline. Casey was supposed to roll with the pocket to buy some time in the mud and get it to him somehow.

Before Casey went back on the field, Jake went over to him and said, "You can do this."

"Don't tell me with my eyes closed."

"Not gonna," Jake said. "You got hot before. Get hot for one more throw."

Nate snapped him the ball and Casey moved carefully to his right behind Nate and the right side of the line. Calvin drove the guys covering him into the end zone, planted without slipping, started back for the ball.

Then for the first time, he slipped and went down. Worst possible moment, just as Casey was about to release the ball. Somehow Casey, even with that wet ball in his hands, was able to hold on to it and stop his throwing motion. He pulled the ball down and kept rolling to his right, buying himself more time, waiting for Calvin to pick himself up.

Locked on Calvin one last time.

Calvin got up. Problem was, his momentum had brought him all the way out to about the three-yard line now. Casey let the ball go anyway, threw the best pass he had all day even if it was a short one, a tight spiral through the rain that landed in Calvin's hands.

As soon as Calvin had his hands on the ball, he was already turning his body, squaring himself up, knowing he was short of the end zone, knowing he had to get there somehow.

And it made the cornerback closing on him miss, go sliding

past. Now there was enough room and time for Calvin to lunge forward with the ball, doing whatever he had to do to get it to cross the plane at the goal line.

Just as he did, the linebacker closest to Calvin hit him from the side, put a great lick on him, direct hit.

The ball came loose. And squirted into the end zone.

Jake saw it all the way, even from where he was, saw the ball go skidding along the ground until it disappeared underneath the rain and mud and two Texas high school football teams.

The refs went running in. Jake heard a whistle over the noise of the rain and wind, saw the refs trying to separate bodies, see who had the ball at the bottom of the pile.

Jake should have known.

Should have known that the man with the ball, the last man up, showing the refs and the world that he had the ball, was the strongest guy Jake had ever met.

Nate Collins.

Nate, who got up and signaled touchdown before the ref closest to him did, the touchdown that meant Granger had won this game, that meant Granger was back in the state finals.

When Nate finally got to the sideline, covered with mud and as much pure joy as Jake had ever seen on a football field—and after what he was pretty sure was the first touchdown of Nate's whole career—he took off his helmet and hugged Jake, covering Jake in mud now.

Nate pulled back now, still smiling, and said to Jake, "I believe you owe me some pie."

JAKE GOT THE CLEARANCE TO PLAY FROM DOC MALLOZZI ON Monday, right after school, and his mom took him straight from Doc's office to practice. Jake set a world's record getting his pads on and into uniform, began to prepare himself for Granger's rematch with Fort Carson in the 1AA finals, even though he'd been preparing himself since Nate recovered that fumble in Highland Junction.

Jake didn't care if it was last year's opponent or not, whether Wyatt had been the quarterback in that game or not. This was his own season now, this was his game.

There was no rust on him after a week off; he came out firing on Monday, had a good day throwing, had a good *week* throwing at practice, and an even better week in Coach Jessup's office looking at film on Fort Carson.

"Coach McCoy tells me even your brother didn't spend as much time at the movies as you," Coach J said when they finally called it a night on Thursday, nothing more to see on Fort Carson's defense, or say about it.

"I told you all along," Jake said, "I want to learn."

"You're ready for your final exam," Coach J said. "Now go home and relax."

"Well, *that's* not gonna happen," Jake said.

He ate dinner with his parents. When he and his dad were cleaning the table, Troy Cullen poked him and said, "You want to go out in the pasture, throw it around for a little?"

Jake didn't. He just wanted to wait for Bear and Nate. They were going into town to just hang out for a little while, Jake meeting Sarah at Amy's for ice cream.

Yet he smiled at his dad and said, "Let's go."

They walked out of the house and past the barn, Jake knowing it was as important to his dad to make the offer as it was for Jake to accept it.

His dad said, "You don't know how glad I am you're feelin' better, son. That you haven't had none of those aftershocks I ended up with."

"Thanks, Dad."

His dad smiled now. "Don't want you to end up like me."

"Wouldn't be the worst thing in the world," Jake said.

Then Troy Cullen took the ball out of Jake's hands and told him to go out, and make sure he didn't step in any holes—it would be a shame to have his head back screwed on tight and then roll an ankle the night before the big game.

An hour later, Jake was telling Sarah about it, the two of them sitting on their bench at the head of the park, watching the parade of Granger players walk past them, both sides of the street. Small-town Texas—Granger, Texas—the night before the state final.

"He's trying," Sarah said. "Your dad."

"He is," Jake said. "He always says we're not that much alike, so it's funny when you think about it. It took me getting dropped on my head to make us closer."

They sat there for a few minutes now, neither saying anything, until Sarah said, "You seem pretty calm."

"We call that misdirection in football."

"Don't you think it's crazy that a year later, it's the same team playing us in the final, in the same place at Texas State?"

"Been thinking it would be nice to see Boone Stadium again at this time of year," Jake said.

Sarah smiled. "Now you get to win the same game Wyatt did."

Jake smiled back, knowing she didn't mean anything by it, Jake understanding—even here and even now—that if he was going to be compared to his brother, this was the best way.

"He had his," Jake said. "This one's mine."

"You're right," she said.

Jake said, "You know, all my life, there was a part of me wondering if I ever *would* get outside Wyatt's shadow, no matter what I did. But I finally realized something this season."

"And what is that?"

"You spend too much time worrying about somebody else's shadow, you never have time to make one of your own."

It was only an hour's drive to Boone Stadium at Texas State, Coach saying the bus would leave from school at four o'clock. The football players had been let out of school early, skipping their last classes, Coach telling them to go home for a couple of hours and shut off their phones and laptops and brains and start getting themselves ready for Fort Carson.

"Because by seven thirty," Coach had said, "you know the volume'll get pumped up pretty much all the way."

Jake took Coach's advice after school, went straight upstairs to his room, telling Libby Cullen he'd eaten at the cafeteria before he left school.

At the bottom of the stairs, his mom said, "I'm happy for you, Jacob."

"Mom," he said, "we haven't won anything yet."

She smiled at him, like there was something else on her mind, but all she said was, "Didn't say you had. Still happy for you."

Jake closed the shades in his room, stretched out on his bed, and closed his eyes, knowing it was impossible to shut off the football part of his brain, impossible to stop himself from imagining the first series of plays he already knew they were going to run tonight, already playing the game inside his head, when he heard his door open and saw his brother, Wyatt, come walking in.

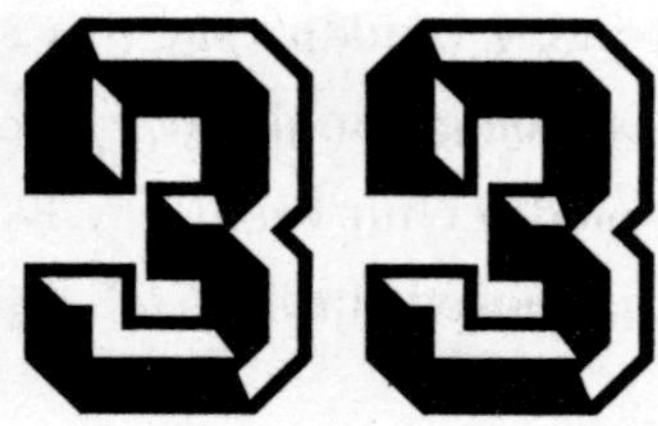

"WAIT A SECOND," JAKE SAID. "DON'T YOU HAVE A GAME tomorrow night?"

"Yeah, little brother," Wyatt said, "but I believe you've got one tonight."

Then he explained that the 'Horns had practiced early today, finishing their day-before walk-through about one o'clock, and his coach had given him permission to go to Jake's game as long as he was back in Austin, only ninety minutes south of Texas State, by midnight.

"It's not Coach's first rodeo," Wyatt said. "He knows that not one of us is in bed by midnight whether we've got a game the next night or not."

"Sounds like you and the coach are getting along better," Jake said.

He was sitting up on his bed, glad to see his brother, trying not to show him how much. Wyatt had pushed back Jake's chair, had his feet up on Jake's desk, wearing an orange 'Horns T-shirt, jeans, and sandals.

Wyatt said, "He likes me better now that we've won three straight, even though it's been more about our running than my passing."

"Well, somebody's quarterbacked you all back into the top ten."

"Man," Wyatt said, "it's been a grind. I wouldn't say this to Dad, because it would be the same as teeing him up for one of those motivational speeches he says would get him big money. But college football is *hard,* dude. I've never looked at this much film in my *life*."

"Not gonna lie," Jake said. "I love watching film."

"I imagine it comes a lot easier to you than it does to me. The studying part always has."

"Come on," Jake said. "*None* of this comes easier to me than it does to you."

"Gonna let you in on another secret," Wyatt said. "I mostly just always wanted to play. Get out there and figure it out, and trust my arm to do the rest."

Jake sat there listening to his brother, the one he'd worshipped pretty much his whole life, talking about himself like he was just an older—and better—version of Casey Lindell.

Wyatt said, "You were always more like Mom, the brains of the family. I always knew that, same as Dad did."

"Oh, yeah, sure he did," Jake said.

"No, it's true. You want to know the by-God truth? I think he's always been a little intimidated by you. He never thought he was much of a brain when it came to football, either, as much as he acts like a know-it-all. You'd do something in a game, far back as Pop Warner, and he'd say, 'That's the Libby in him showin' itself right there.' Mom being somebody who's intimidated him since high school."

Wyatt paused and then said, "You can't really understand our dad till you understand that. He's supposed to be the big, loud star of everything in our family. Only he's the one living in a shadow. *Hers.*"

Quiet now in here. Jake looked at the clock radio on his nightstand. Maybe ten minutes until Bear would show up in his truck.

"Long as we're telling each other stuff," Jake said, "Dad told me he thought you needed him more this season."

"Well, the old man had that one right," Wyatt said. "I did. More than I ever thought I would. And another thing you got to know about our dad is, he *needs* to be needed. He just didn't know you needed him till this year."

Jake said, "You came all the way from college to explain Dad to me? Coulda done that with an e-mail." Grinning at his brother.

"Hell's bells, no!" Wyatt said, doing his dead-on impression of Troy Cullen. "I came here to be the one *givin'* the motivational talk this time, so my brother can beat Fort Carson."

After that it was just football in Jake's room, Jake telling Wyatt what he'd seen on film all week, Wyatt telling everything he remembered from last year's game, breaking down Fort Carson's tendencies, sounding to Jake like his own football brain was working pretty well.

TWO MINUTES BEFORE THE OPENING KICK, THE BIG SCOREboard at the closed end of Boone Stadium counted down the seconds, the Fort Carson Hawks having won the toss, and electing to receive.

Jake was behind the Cowboys' bench, alone, taking it all in, more nervous than he'd ever been for any kind of game in his life, after all the times when he'd been praised for his calm. Guys on television were always talking about good nerves in sports, how you could use them, the way you could use your fear of failing. Jake didn't know if the nerves he was feeling were good or not. They were just *there*.

Same as his own fear of failing.

So he looked around, hoping to calm himself down, or maybe store up some memories. He saw Sarah's face, smiling at him from the end zone; his mom and dad and Wyatt in their seats, right above him at the fifty-yard line; Coach McCoy in front of him, squinting at his laminated play card; Nate and Bear, to Jake's left, seated at the end of the bench, no jokes between them now, no laughter, the two of them just staring out at the field.

Under a minute to the championship game.

This, Jake knew, was what it looked like when you were on the inside of a night like this, not up in the stands where he'd been one year ago, in the seat next to Troy and Libby Cullen where Wyatt sat tonight.

Playing it himself, at the end of a season when he really hadn't pictured himself playing at all.

Going up against the Fort Carson Hawks, so many of whom had been here a year ago in the loss to Granger, starting with their senior running back, Artis Dennard, the best back in the state this season, on his way to UT next season to play in the same backfield as Wyatt Cullen.

"He's their Calvin," Nate said as they watched the kick teams for both sides lining up.

"Nah," Jake said. "There's only but one Calvin."

From behind them, Calvin Morton said to Jake, "See, that comment right there shows me how much smarter you got since the start of the season."

Jake turned around, lightly pounded Calvin's shoulder pads with both fists. "All you tonight, C."

Calvin shook his head. "Every year, I got to tell a Cullen the same thing," he said. "I might as well be sittin' up there in the stands if you don't get me the ball."

"It's like my dad says: I'm all bowed up and ready to go."

Calvin's face was all business now, as they could feel the whole place rising as the ball was kicked into the air. "You remember what I'm tellin' you, Cullen. Whatever it takes tonight. You got that? Whatever it takes."

"Let's come out firing," Jake said.

Cap pistols, as it turned out. They couldn't move it in the first quarter and neither could the Hawks, until Artis Dennard busted one sixty yards for a score with about five minutes left in the half. Then on the next Cowboys series, Jake did something he'd done a couple of times already tonight, bailed out against an all-out blitz, got rid of the ball way too soon, made this weak back-foot throw in Calvin's direction that seemed to float in the air like one of those television blimps.

The cornerback covering Calvin said thank-you-very-much, stepped in front of him, returned the ball thirty yards for a touchdown without being touched.

In about a two-minute span, the Cowboys had managed to get themselves behind 14–0.

When Jake came out after the pick, Coach Jessup was waiting for him, as hot as Jake had seen him all season.

Just not about the throw.

"There hasn't been a single part of this that's scared you from the start," he said. "Don't you start playin' scared now. If you're afraid of gettin' hit again, tell me right now."

"I'm not scared of getting hit," he said.

"Then show me," and walked away looking at his laminated play card.

When Jake turned around, Nate was there, saying, "Man might have a point."

"You think I've been playing gun-shy?" Jake said.

"Little bit," Nate said. "Bear said you've had those happy feet going in the pocket a few times."

"Remember when we talked about how Casey had to be afraid of what he was wishing for?" Jake said. "Maybe I'm that guy now."

"How's about we just do a better job of givin' you time, and you do a better job throwin' that thing?"

"Sounds like a plan," Jake said.

He nearly got the Cowboys into the end zone on the very next series, mixing runs and quick passes, killing the clock a couple of times with spikes when they got under a minute. But then with the Cowboys out of time-outs, he tried to get some extra yards, give Bobby a chance at a field goal, and didn't run out of bounds when he had the chance at the Fort Carson fifteen. Then he couldn't get his teammates lined up in time so he could spike it.

They ran out of time and went to the locker room still down two scores. Jake was not entirely sure, with the way he'd played, that he'd get to start the second half, thinking that Coach McCoy, with one half left in the season unless they ended up in overtime, might reshuffle the deck with his quarterbacks one more time.

But he did not.

What he said when everybody was inside: "You boys don't need me to tell you that we broke bad out there. But it wasn't *so* bad that we can't fix her in the time we got left. Now y'all know I'm not much for making predictions, but I'm gonna give you one right now: We may not play plumb perfect the second half, as my grandma used to say, but we're gonna be perty near. We're gonna get the ball to start the second half, we're gonna make it 14–7, and then look out for the Cowboys after that."

Never a rah-rah guy, not one now. Not raising his voice—talking to them like he was talking on the telephone, looking at them and saying, "Anybody else got anything they'd like to add?"

Calvin, who'd been sitting on a long bench between Melvin and Justice, slowly stood up, came over, and stood next to Coach McCoy in the middle of the room.

"I got another year of Friday nights," he said. "But not everybody in this room does, and that might even include Coach. And I was thinking, listening to him just now, that when you start playing high school ball, you never think you're gonna run out of Friday nights like this one. Not one of us has any guarantee that we're ever gonna get another like this. So I say we go back out there on that field and make this the kind lives *forever.*"

Then he led them out of the room, Calvin Morton as sure of himself as ever, even in a two-touchdown hole.

On the first play of the second half, Jake stood tall and strong in the pocket, would have stayed there all night if he had to, threw a strike to Roy Gilley over the middle even though he got popped good as soon as he'd finished his follow-through. He was on the ground when he heard the Granger side of Boone Stadium tell him, big and loud, that Roy had made the catch.

Nate pulled Jake up. "How'd that feel?"

"You want to know the truth, big man?" Jake said. "It felt plumb perfect."

Jake scrambled for another first down on the next play. Then he hit Spence Tolar in the flat for a gain of eight. Stayed in the pocket and threw a deep post to Calvin—no nerves now, good or bad, no fear—put it right in his hands even though the cornerback was running with him stride for stride.

Calvin did the rest from there, forty yards on the play. Bobby made the kick. 14–7.

On the next Fort Carson series, Bear hit Artis Dennard from the side on a sweep, Melvin hit him head-on at pretty much the same moment, and the ball came loose. Melvin fell on it. Cowboys' ball.

On the very next play, Jake looked at Calvin the whole time, suckered the defense that way, then turned at the last moment and threw one into Justice's hands a yard from the back of the end zone.

It was about to be 14-all, a brand-new game at Boone Stadium, until Bobby Torres caught his spikes stepping into his kick and hit a low, ugly hook that went so wide, Jake thought it might be on its way to Dallas.

So it was 14–13 instead.

When Bobby came off the field, Jake grabbed him and said, "Don't worry about that point. It won't mean nothin' in the end."

But that point kept getting bigger as the defenses started playing bigger. Both offenses were still moving the ball, but neither side could close the deal.

Calvin dropped a sure completion from Jake on one third down. Punt.

Then Fort Carson's tight end, their best receiver, had a drop of his own. Another punt.

It went like that out of the third quarter, into the fourth, the score still 14–13, Jake starting to feel as if the seconds on the clock were racing down again, the way they had before the start of the game. Then Artis broke another long one, this one for fifty yards, and even though the Cowboys' defense kept them out of the end zone after a first down at the five-yard line, their kicker made a field goal that was barely longer than an extra point, and Fort Carson led 17–13.

It stayed that way until the Cowboys stopped Artis on a third-and-one and the Hawks punted one last time. The Cowboys took over at their thirty, with two minutes and ten seconds left.

When Jake got to the huddle, before he told them the play and the count, he tipped back his helmet, smiled at the Granger Cowboys, and said, "How about we play ourselves some football?"

He was going to Calvin. The defense knew it, too, had to know it. Didn't know the call was for an inside cut. But the corner covering Calvin, the safety helping, they had to know the ball was coming their way. And this was a moment when it was about Jake's brain, about all the time he'd spent in the film room with Coach J. Slowing the game down, even in the pocket, trusting your blocking the way you trusted yourself, having the patience to stand back there and look off the defense until the last second, trick them into believing that what they knew was the obvious call—Calvin—suddenly wasn't.

So that is what Jake did, even feeling the pass rush, eyes locked on Calvin, body angled toward Calvin's side of the field, counting down the few seconds he knew he had to release the ball, finally turning at the very last second to where Justice had broken free in the middle of the field, Jake's arm taking over now, putting the ball right on him, money.

The Fort Carson defense knew the one thing they couldn't do was give up a big play, so they dropped their safeties back and their cornerbacks guarded the sidelines. Again Jake took what the defense gave him, hitting Roy over the middle. They were at midfield, that fast.

Jake was supposed to throw a screen to Spence on the next play, but never got the chance. His blocking broke down and he got hit hard from the right side before he had time to react or release the ball, was lucky he held on to the ball. Got up shaking his head. Saw Nate staring at him.

"Your head okay?"

"Hard as ever," Jake said. "How many times we got to go over that? Family trait."

Minute and twenty left now. The pass rush came again, and this time he did get out of there, slipping out of the pocket, his eyes downfield. Calvin broke a pattern and came back for the ball, then spun and broke a tackle, got twenty out of the play before the two safeties could bring him down.

Fort Carson thirty-five yard line. Coach John McCoy called his second time-out.

One minute, straight up.

Coach J thought he could trick the Hawks with a draw, but the defense read it all the way. Spence was lucky to get back to the line of scrimmage. Second-and-ten, clock disappearing fast.

Jake hurried the offense and took the snap, found Calvin making his cut about fifteen yards down the field. Jake knew Calvin's speed would get him some separation, but he got excited and rushed the throw, led Calvin by a couple of yards too many.

And as Calvin stretched for the ball, laid out for it, defenseless in that moment, he got blasted by the safety making a play on him and the ball from the other direction.

Clean, hard, legal hit.

Calvin went down and stayed down. Jake couldn't remember a time all year when he'd been really hurt, when he didn't get right up no matter how much of a lick he took.

He stayed down now, the big clock on the scoreboard stopped with thirty-five seconds left. They all ran to Calvin, Doc Mallozzi telling them to back off, give him some room, talking to Calvin in a quiet voice, asking him the same questions he'd asked Jake when he'd gotten hit like this.

Calvin talked right along with him, telling Doc yeah, yeah, yeah, he didn't have time for no quizzes, he was fine.

It was Coach McCoy, crouched next to him, who said, "You need to come out, catch your breath, son."

"Only thing I want to *catch,* Coach, is the ball."

"I'll get you back in," Coach said, quickly adding, "If I'm sure you're all right."

"Get me back in *when,*" Calvin said, "next season?"

But it was a fight he was going to lose. He knew it, Coach knew it, Jake knew it. Coach and Doc walked him off, into a long, loud ovation from the Granger side of the field.

The third-and-ten play was to Justice, Justice getting the double coverage now, their best receiver with Calvin on the sideline. It was a throw Jake had been making to Justice all year long, into any kind of coverage, Justice going hard down the right sideline, then turning as Jake made a back-shoulder throw.

He made it now, Justice doing what he did all the time, giving the corner closest to him just a shove to create separation, catching the ball at the fifteen, stepping out of bounds.

Only this time he didn't get away with the shove. The back judge was standing right there, throwing his flag, making the pass interference signal.

Pointing at Justice Blackmon.

Not only did it mean a fifteen-yard penalty for the Cowboys, it meant something even worse than that:

Loss of down.

Just like that, twenty-three seconds left, it was fourth-and-twenty-five for the Granger Cowboys.

Even though the clock was stopped, Coach McCoy called his last time-out so they could all talk about it. Jake went running over, seeing Calvin with his helmet back on, rolling his shoulder, moving his head from side to side, obviously coming back in for what might be the last play of their season.

When Jake got to the sideline, Coach J said to him, "Son, you know this offense as well as I do. What do *you* think is our best chance?"

Jake had been asking himself the same question on the way over, had already come up with the answer.

First, he turned to Calvin.

"You said whatever it takes, right?"

"I did."

Then Jake turned back to Coach J and Coach McCoy and said, "Our best chance is something that isn't *in* our offense."

He told them what he thought they should do. Nobody said

anything right away, even as Jake could see one of the refs jogging in their direction.

It was Coach John McCoy who said, "It might just be crazy enough to work."

Turned around then and yelled at Casey Lindell to put his hat on. He was going in at quarterback.

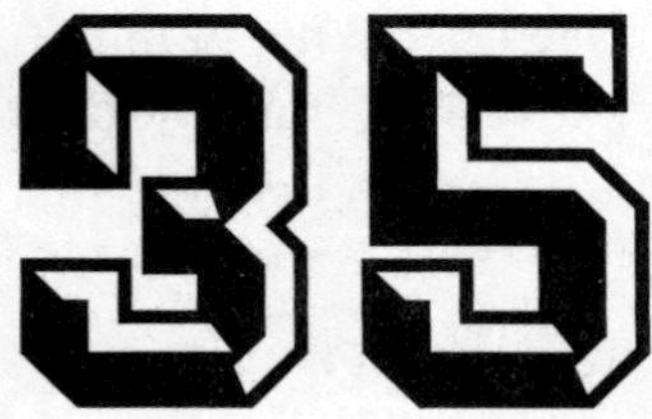

"LINDELL TO CULLEN?" CASEY SAID AS THEY JOGGED TOWARD the huddle, Calvin a couple of yards ahead of them. "On fourth down? In the championship game? Really?"

"We've done it before," Jake said.

"We did it behind your barn!" Casey said.

"Trust it," Jake said.

"I haven't thrown a ball since I warmed you up at halftime," Casey said.

"This time when you close your eyes," Jake said, "picture yourself making the greatest throw of your life."

"And I'm gonna be a damn *decoy*?" Calvin said.

"Yep," Jake said, then knelt down in the huddle and told everybody they were going to try something a little different to save the day, on three.

As soon as Casey lined up at shotgun, guys on the defense started yelling, "Wildcat!" Jake went out and lined up next to Calvin on the right, Justice split out on the left with Roy Gilley, David Stevens in the slot. Jake looked at the defense with quarterback eyes, saw the safety and corner come up on Calvin, saw the extra defensive backs backing up, knowing the Cowboys needed a mile for a first down.

As soon as the ball was snapped, Calvin took off hard for the middle of the field, angling toward the left, where the other receivers were. Jake ran at half speed toward the sideline, the outside linebacker on his side eyeballing him, trying to see Jake and Casey at the same time.

But Jake was eyeballing him, too, and as soon as the kid turned his head, wanting to see if Casey had thrown the ball yet—he hadn't, he was eyeballing Calvin one last time this season, the way Jake had told him to—Jake ran as hard as he could down the right sideline.

The outside linebacker scrambling to catch up with him.

Too late.

Because now Casey turned his attention to Jake Cullen, his intended receiver all along.

Letting it go.

One of the extra DBs saw what was happening, but he was also too late, ended up seeing what everybody at Boone Stadium saw: the ball coming out of the night sky and into Jake's hands, Jake telling himself to look the ball all the way into his hands, catching it at the fifteen, almost losing his balance at the eight-yard line, recovering to break a tackle at the five, lunging forward with one Fort Carson Hawk grasping at his legs, finally getting tripped up.

But not until he fell into the end zone with the touchdown that made it 19–17 for the Granger Cowboys.

A Cullen making a catch this time instead of a throw to win the big game.

The rest of it was pretty much a blur, Jake handing the ball to the ref, getting mobbed by the guys as soon as he did, Bobby making his kick, Fort Carson getting off one play after the kickoff, a Hail Mary pass that Melvin batted down like he was spiking a volleyball.

Scoreboard said 20–17, Granger.

Like Calvin said:

Forever.

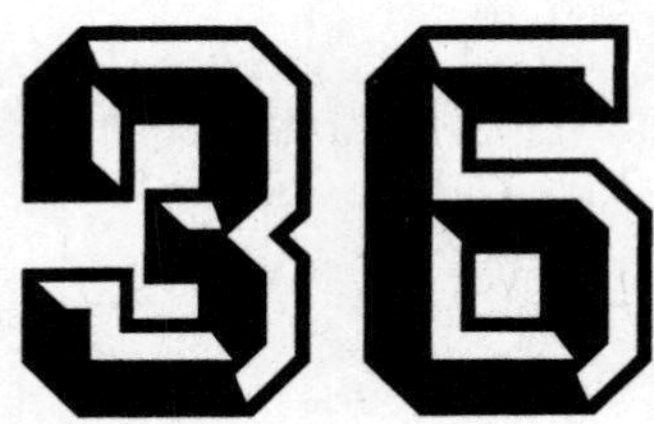

WHEN IT WAS OVER, JAKE MANAGED TO GET HIMSELF LOOSE from Bear and Nate, both of them shouting that they wanted to stay in high school forever, and made his way through the crazy celebration in the middle of the field. There he found Calvin Morton standing alone at the forty-yard line, cool as ever, smiling, helmet in his hand, taking it all in.

"Sorry you didn't get to make the score this time," Jake said.

"Only score that matters is the *final* score."

"Must be getting old for you, C," Jake said. "Winning these championships like you do, no matter who's throwing you the ball."

"No, Cullen," Calvin said. "I don't believe it's *ever* gonna get old."

"You feeling all right?" Jake said. "I almost got you killed with that pass."

"Didn't you, though?" Calvin said. "And me tellin' ever'body who'd listen how accurate you are."

"Sorry," Jake said.

"I'll let it go just this one time," Calvin said. "Specially since it appears that I'm stuck with you for my immediate future."

Calvin to the end: not *their* future, *his*.

Jake said, "I'll get better."

Calvin gave him a long look, then leaned forward, touched shoulders with him, and said, "Yeah, I expect you will."

Calvin smiled now, put his arms around Jake, and said, "Just remember goin' forward: You throw. *I* catch."

"Got it," Jake said.

Calvin said he was going to find Melvin now, would see Jake at the trophy presentation. Walked away. Or strutted. Probably depended on your point of view.

A few yards away, waiting for Jake to finish with Calvin, was Casey Lindell.

Jake walked over to Casey now, who put out his hand right away. Jake shook it, and Casey said, "Congratulations, dude. You did it."

"We did it."

"You did the heavy lifting," Casey said. "And the play calling."

"All's you did was come off the bench cold and complete a fourth-and-twenty-five that if you'd missed, we would've gone home losers," Jake said. "No, man. *We* did it."

"Just wanted to keep playing a little while longer," Casey said.

"What it's all about," Jake said.

"You know I'm gonna come after you next season."

"Wouldn't have it any other way," Jake said.

Then Coach J was on Jake, out of nowhere, clean blind-side hit, lifting him in the air, like a kid himself now, yelling, "Maybe I should make you a wide receiver next season!"

"No, sir," Jake said. "I'm a Cullen, which means I'm a quarterback."

Jake looked past Coach J and saw his parents, Wyatt, and Sarah behind the Cowboys' bench. Somehow he made his way back through the players and fans and photographers and the reporters on the field, even a couple of television cameras. When he got to them, Sarah jumped over the bench, like it was one more of her cheerleader moves, and jumped into his arms, hugged him for all she was worth. Hugged him for the first time. Then got on tiptoes and kissed him.

When she let him go, she took a step back, frowning, almost suspicious.

"Who came up with that last play?"

Jake shrugged. "Guess I did."

"You let Casey be the quarterback?"

"I did," Jake said. "Gave us our best chance to win."

"Wow," she said.

Then she was running off to find the other cheerleaders, Jake watching her go, saying to himself, "Yeah. Wow."

He felt a little shove from behind now, turned and saw Wyatt smiling, shaking his head.

"And the guy gets the girl, too," Wyatt said. "I'm gonna have to step it up a little."

Jake grinned, gave him a little shove and said, "Good luck with that."

Libby Cullen gave Jake a hug of her own then, and said, "I knew you had this in you, Jacob. I always knew."

Wyatt laughed. "Well, I sure didn't." Then put out his right fist, pounded his brother some skin. "Seriously? I'm proud of you, little . . ." Shook his head. "Proud of you, brother," he said. Then: "Who called the wildcat?"

"That would be me," Jake said.

"Put the ball in the other quarterback's hands? On fourth-and-forever? Are you insane?"

"I gave him the ball," Jake said. "But I didn't let him keep it."

Libby Cullen said she was going to run over to congratulate Coach McCoy. Just Troy Cullen and his two sons now behind the bench at Boone Stadium.

Jake saw his dad smiling, but thought his eyes might be a little redder than normal, thought his voice was a little shaky when he finally said something.

"Good thing I had you and ol' Casey run those wildcats in the pasture that night."

"Good thing," Jake said, smiling at his dad.

Then Troy Cullen was pulling Jake close to him, those strong arms around him, wrapping Jake up, Jake trying to remember the last time his dad had done that. Now saying something, over the noise and music and cheering, something that only Jake could hear.

"Sure glad I saw this one," he said.

"Me too," Jake said.

Then they were walking toward where Libby Cullen and John McCoy were, the field somehow opening up for them. A photographer would snap a picture of the three of them, freezing that moment, Troy Cullen with an arm around the shoulders of each of his sons that would run in the *Granger Dispatch* on the front page, one that would eventually wind up framed at Stone's.

Maybe it was just the angle, or the fact that they were walking so close together. But it would look in that picture as if the three Cullen boys had somehow cast a single shadow in the lights of Boone Stadium.

Turn the page for a preview of

Mike Lupica's

FANTASY LEAGUE

One

HERE WAS CHARLIE GAINES, KING of the pro football fantasy leagues even at the age of twelve, not just watching the second preseason game for the Bengals and Giants as much as studying it.

His mom had come in a few minutes ago and said, "I can't tell, are you watching the game or searching for clues?"

"Both."

As soon as she'd come in, he'd paused the screen, freezing on the Giants' rookie quarterback out of Ohio State, Rex Tuttle, as he dropped back into shotgun formation.

"I'm not distracting you, am I?" she'd said. Charlie had turned, saw her smiling at him, both of them knowing what his answer was going to be.

"Yes," he'd said.

"Talk to you after the Super Bowl in February," she'd said, and left.

Charlie had the remote on one side of him on the bed, laptop on the other. He pointed the remote. The game came back to life, the announcers' voices came back into his room.

All the company he needed when there was a game on, Charlie happy being alone with football. Good at it. He really preferred watching the games alone unless he was watching with his friend Anna, the only person he knew who loved football as much as he did.

But then Anna's family owned a team.

It was different with Charlie Gaines; he felt as if the whole league belonged to him, the players and their stats and where they were in their careers and how much Charlie projected they had left in them. Sometimes his mom said that when he dropped his backpack on the table in the front hall, she expected decimal points to come spilling out.

"How many leagues are you in this season?" she'd said at dinner that night.

Meaning fantasy leagues.

"Just counting mine?" he'd said. "Or all the ones I help my friends with?"

She'd given him a long look. "You still have time for real life, right?"

Real life to his mom meant three things: friends and school. And his own football team in Pop Warner.

"Mom," he said, "I know you think sometimes that I've turned into some kind of football geek, that it's all I think about or talk about. But last year I had my best year ever at school. And you know I've got all the friends I could want *from* school."

"I'm allowed to worry about my guy," Karla Gaines said to her son. "It's what moms do. If we didn't have worrying, we'd have to do more yoga."

"I'm fine," he'd said. "And by the way? How can you worry about me and fantasy leagues when you're the one working in what you call the world of make-believe?"

They lived in Culver City, California, where Sony Studios was located. His mom worked there as an executive assistant for one of the top production guys, still believing she was going to be a movie producer herself someday, constantly on the lookout for what she called the "right script." He'd asked her once, one night last weekend when she was reading a script while Charlie watched one of the first preseason games, if she'd rather have the right script or the right man, having divorced Charlie's dad a long time ago.

"Script. If it's the right one, it doesn't leave."

At dinner tonight she'd said, "I just want your life to be great, pal."

"It is," Charlie Gaines had told her. Grinning. "How can it not be great? It's football season."

Most football fans thought the preseason was a waste of time. You hardly got to see the best players, and coaches were afraid of getting their stars hurt before they ever got anywhere near September.

Charlie didn't care, he loved it all.

It *was* football season again. From August all the way through the Super Bowl in February, it was when he was happiest, when his life *did* feel great.

He didn't have to watch tonight's game alone. He could have invited Anna over, but he was going over to her house tomorrow night to watch her team—and his—the L.A. Bulldogs play the Bears in Chicago. And he could have invited one of his boys, Kevin Fallon, to come over—Kevin only lived two blocks away. The only problem with that was Kevin wanting to do his own play-by-play of the game; he hardly ever shut up.

It was better with Anna. She focused on games, especially Bulldogs games, the way he did. Maybe it was why she knew more about the sport than any guy Charlie knew, certainly any guy their age.

Any guy except for Charlie.

Charlie Gaines knew real games the way his friends knew video games. And wished that Anna's uncle, the general manager of the Bulldogs, knew the league that well. Or at least better than he did.

The Bulldogs were an expansion team still playing like one four years after they'd brought pro football back to Los Angeles. They were so bad, still not managing to have won more than four games in a season, that the sportswriters and the bloggers and the radio host and the fans on Twitter liked to say that pro football *still* hadn't come back to L.A.

But as pathetic as they were, Charlie still loved them, not because he had to the way Anna did, but for the only reason that mattered in sports, or had ever mattered: They were his first team. And were going to stay his team, even though they weren't getting any better and looked like they might never get better—there would be Sundays a month into the season when the stadium Anna's grandfather had built for his team would be half-full.

If that.

One of Charlie's football fantasies about his Bulldogs? That someday Bulldogs Stadium would be totally full, of noise and excitement, for a big game at the end of the season, instead of just playing out the string again.

The other day Charlie had read a review by one of the sports columnists in the *Los Angeles Times,* read it because he read everything about the Bulldogs no matter how bad it was. And it was bad:

> **It was so important to our city that we got it right when we finally did get pro football back. Only the people running the team, the Warrens, have done the opposite. Gotten it exactly wrong. Thanks for nothing.**

The columnist was talking about Joe Warren, Anna's grandfather, the owner of the team. And her uncle Matt, the team's general manager. They were about as popular in L.A. heading into another season as traffic.

The Bulldogs were named after an old independent team out of the city's football past, the L.A. Bulldogs of the 1930s. Charlie had read up on them and everything else that had ever happened in pro football in L.A. until the Rams left for St. Louis.

So he knew that the NFL had thought about bringing the

league to the city when the first Bulldogs were playing, but found out that teams from the east and the Midwest didn't want to take trains all the way across the country to play a game, even if they were only coming from Chicago, which Charlie knew used to have two teams and not just one. And cross-country flights were still sketchy in those days. So the city didn't get a team until the Rams in 1946, and then didn't have a team for nearly twenty years after the Rams left in 1994.

Now they had the brand spanking new L.A. Bulldogs. Except that wasn't what most people called them now.

People had taken to calling them the L.A. Dogs.

It was because they just kept losing. They either drafted the wrong players or traded for the wrong players or signed the wrong free agents, doing it as consistently as Charlie Gaines kept picking the right players in his fantasy leagues. And when they did draft the right players in a given year, it seemed like they always got hurt.

That column in the *Times* said that one of the reasons fantasy football was so wildly popular in Los Angeles is because any kind of fantasy ball was better than the grim reality of the L.A. Dogs.

Charlie Gaines still loved both.

He'd read somewhere that fantasy football was at least seventy-five percent luck, people comparing it to playing blackjack, saying that you could have your system all you wanted, but the game still came down to what cards the dealer turned over. Maybe that was true. Charlie was fine with the element of luck—what happened on the field after you'd made your calls on which players you drafted and which ones you might slot in on a given Sunday, or Monday, or Thursday night.

He'd take his chances with the twenty-five percent that wasn't luck. Then it *did* feel like a video game to him, like he was playing *Madden* not just against a friend, but against a whole fantasy league.

And he was the one with the controller in his hands.

Controlling it like a champ.

Then it was all about brains and study and hard work. About searching for clues, even if you had to go back into the past looking for them. And maybe something else, too, what Charlie's buddy Kevin Fallon called Charlie's "gift."

When Kevin would say that, Charlie would tell him it sounded like something he'd unwrap on Christmas or on his birthday.

Kevin would come back at him: "You know what I mean. You're, like, a genius. It's why I started calling you Brain."

Charlie would come right back at *him*, ask how come somebody who studied hard and aced a test didn't have a gift. Wasn't called Brain.

"But you ace all the tests in football. It's why I don't know whether I should call you Brain, or just Freak."

"You know I'm not all that crazy about Brain. But let's go with that."

Charlie and Kevin went to Culver City Middle School—getting ready to start the seventh grade in a few weeks—and played football together for the Culver City Cardinals in Pop Warner. Kevin was the team's star running back, already talking about being in the backfield for USC or UCLA or even Stanford someday. Charlie? As much as he loved football, Charlie pretty much thought of himself as a scrub. Backup linebacker last season, probably a backup linebacker this season. Special teams player, which he told Kevin was misleading, since there was nothing special about his game.

He had enough size, that wasn't the problem. The problem was he just wasn't quite big enough, or fast enough, or strong enough. One time Kevin, being serious, asked Charlie what he thought his best position was and Charlie had said, "Blocked."

"I mean it," Kevin said. "What do you think your best thing in football is?"

"Probably holding a clipboard."

This was when they were playing sixth grade football. Charlie didn't ever actually hold a clipboard but did spend a lot of time on the sideline standing next to their coaches. Occasionally he'd have the nerve to point out something he thought they'd missed. But mostly he was there to study them. See what they were seeing. And what *he* might be missing.

Trying to learn.

TRAVEL TEAM

Danny may be the smallest kid on the basketball court, but no one has a bigger love of the game. When the local travel team cuts Danny because of his size, he's determined to show just how strong he can be. It turns out he's not the only kid who was cut for the wrong reasons. Now Danny is about to give all the castoffs a second chance and prove that you can't measure heart.

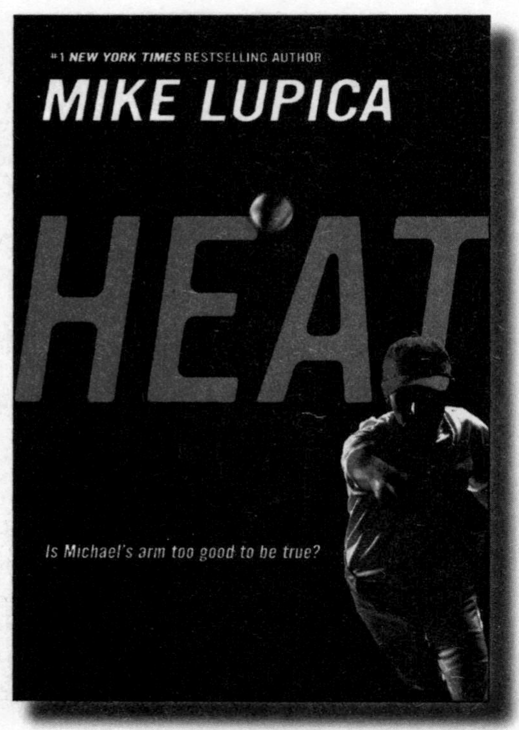

HEAT

Michael has a pitching arm that throws serious heat. But his firepower is nothing compared to the heat he faces in his day-to-day life. Newly orphaned after his father led the family's escape from Cuba, Michael carries on with only his seventeen-year-old brother. But then someone discovers Michael's talent, and his secret world is blown wide-open.

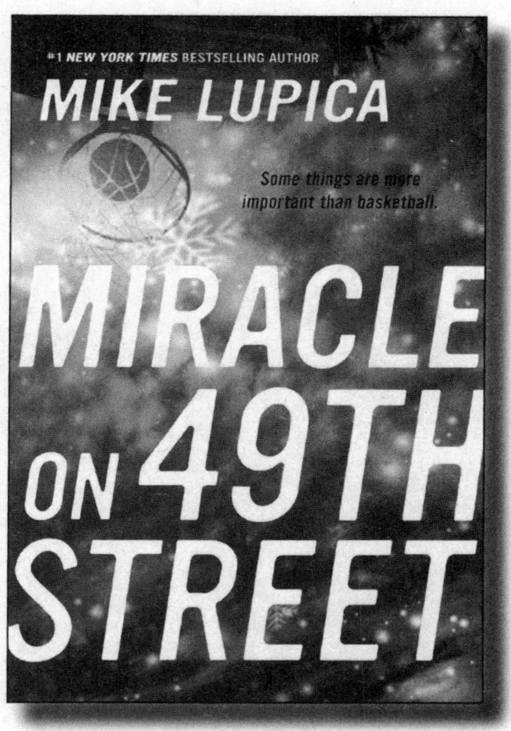

MIRACLE ON 49TH STREET

Josh Cameron is MVP of the championship Boston Celtics. When twelve-year-old Molly arrives in his life, claiming to be his daughter, she catches him off guard. But as Molly gets to know the real Josh, she starts to understand why her mother kept her from him for so long. Josh has room in his heart for only two things: basketball and himself.

SUMMER BALL

Leading your travel team to the national championship may seem like a dream come true, but for Danny, being at the top just means the competition tries that much harder to knock him down. Now Danny's heading to basketball camp for the summer with all the country's best players in attendance. But old rivals and new battles leave Danny wondering if he really does have what it takes.

THE BIG FIELD

Playing shortstop is a way of life for Hutch—which is why having to play second base feels like a demotion. But Hutch is willing to stand aside if it's best for the team, even if it means playing in the shadow of Darryl, the best shortstop prospect since A-Rod. But with the league championship on the line, just how far is Hutch willing to bend to be a good teammate?

MILLION-DOLLAR THROW

Everyone calls Nate Brodie "Brady" because he's a quarterback, just like his idol, Tom Brady, and is almost as good. Now he's won a chance to win a million dollars by throwing one pass through a target at halftime of a pro game. The pressure is more than he can bear, and suddenly the golden boy is having trouble completing a pass . . . but can he make the one that really counts?